# Underworld Takeover

*The follow-up to Underworld Justice*

Written by

Mark Black

*Underworld Takeover*

*Copyright* © Mark Black 2023

The moral right of Mark Black to be identified author of this work has been asserted in accordance with the Copyright, Designs and Patents Act 1988.

All rights reserved.

This is a work of fiction: names, places, characters and incidents are products of the authors imagination, or used fictitiously. Any resemblance to actual events, locations or persons, living or dead, is entirely coincidental.

ISBN 9798865772422

Acknowledgments

Special thanks must be given to the following people who have helped during the creation of Underworld Takeover: Mum, Dad, Caroline Godwin, Clare Middleton, Daniel Westgate, Sara Smith and Helen Wilson. Each of you has played an important part in developing this novel.
I also thank you, the readers, who have followed the Underworld Journey. Stay safe and be happy.

Underworld Climax will be out in 2024.


Also, by Mark Black
Underworld Justice

# Chapter 1

The decade had started poorly for Gary Jones. His only loyal friend, Bob Burns had been taken ill with cancer and met his maker within seven days. The man had fought like a lion until his final breath. Gary had sat with him for the entire time at the Macmillan nursing home. The final three days had been difficult, Bob could barely speak and his breathing was erratic. The rasping sound seemed to stutter in his lungs before release. Life appeared to drain from his body, the beast of man had become an empty, soul less shell. He had become... nothing.

Jones mourned the death of his loyal friend. At the memorial service he had been the only person present, the vicar spoke glowingly of the man having known him for many years. Jones thought it sad that a man's existence came down to two people attending his funeral, and one of those being the vicar.

He had informed the vicar he would pay for everything and would like to dig the grave. The vicar was doubtful, yet Jones convinced him with the knowledge gained from his departed friend it would not be a problem.

The vicar relented and accepted the unusual request once a sizable donation was made to his church. Burns had also informed him where he wished his final resting place to be. He had been the guardian of the grounds for many years. He wanted to ensure the next incumbent of the position be watched over.

After the funeral he ventured to the Kings Head and drank until his liver could take no more, and his legs could barely hold him upright. A caring barmaid asked if he was all right. Jones looked at her and slurred, 'Like shit, more whisky, 3 of them, and a pint of Ben Truman.' He fell out of the pub and stumbled his way to Hornchurch Station, before getting the tube home to Dagenham East. He collapsed on his sofa in a drunken lonely stupor.

In spite of the money gathered he stubbornly refused to leave Dagenham. It was his one and only bolt hole of safety and security. He still enjoyed fine suits, refined dining and the theatre. Yet Dagenham, was Dagenham, a dwelling he loved. Ladies were aghast when they visited his home, they assumed he lived in a palatial place due to his wealth and manners. A night in Dagenham's finest mid-terraced home was not what they expected. Yet Jones did not care, he had been brought up in this working-class paradise. He knew everything, everyone, everywhere. It was his manor, and he was not ready to relinquish his kingdom.

<  >

Johnny Bigtime kissed his wife and ruffled the gelled hair of his children. 'Ave a good day lads, and no fighting unless you think the other kid deserves a dig.' His offspring would never follow in his footsteps, they were privately educated, intelligent, honest and personable. All the traits he did not have, yet they were pussies compared to him. He knew life would be kinder and easier for them, he spoiled them with love, not money. Children from the private school they attended were totally spoiled by their over-the-top parents, and it made them pretentious little cunts. He loathed them. One of the fathers had been surly and confident enough to front him up during a school rugby match. Six slaps later and the parent had a broken nose and split lip. None of the parents fronted Johnny again, in fact, none of them spoke to him. Wanker's.

The school had been good for his boys. Brentwood School was pricey, but it did introduce them to a better class of person. Both his boys had been warned about fighting. He had bollocked them both, yet deep down he was pleased. It showed they had brain and brawn, something which would carry them through life successfully. Both had inherited their darling mother's brains, yet both carried their father's passion. They were good lads.

He opened the front door and bid everyone farewell, before striding purposely to his silver Vanden Plas Rover. He slipped the key into the door and opened it wide before becoming aware of a presence.

'Excuse me, are you Johnny?'

He turned to be faced by two men in Prince of Wales grey checked suits. 'I am he.' It was too late. His last living vision was of a gun being hoisted and fired towards his head, and his last living feeling was the bullet piercing the skin of his middle-aged forehead. Johnny was lifted from his feet and hit the floor with a dull thud. His last vision was of the pale blue sky looking down at him.

Johnny Bigtime, who ran his empire from Romford snooker hall, had been gunned down on the drive of his home in Brentwood. The suspects calmly removed their gloves and deftly placed their weaponry in brown briefcases, before marching towards their blue Ford Cortina, departing the area like two respectable city businessmen. Neither man spoke, they had completed their mission.

<  >

Gary Jones heard reports of two suspects who cold bloodedly walked up to his working friend, before releasing two bullets into his head. Death was instant, although no-one had been arrested, and there had been no witnesses. These men were professional, ghosts.

Rumours swirling around appeared to indicate a new breed of underworld operative who were making significant money through distributing illegal substances. This person was invisible. Gary had a sneaking admiration for the person as they were a little like himself. Yet how could a person remain so inconspicuous? Specifically, in the addiction world, everyone knew the next person in the chain, but in this case the chain was broken.

Gary knew Johnny was dipping his fingers into this lucrative, yet dangerous market. So, Johnny had either reneged on a deal, or was getting too big. Yet Johnny was a person who would do neither, this was the thing troubling him. Johnny was old school, he never let his mouth runaway with information and everything was stored in his brain like a never-ending filing cabinet.

There had also been reports of minor underworld figures missing mysteriously. Whether they were connected no-one knew, yet there had to be a joining of the dots by someone, somewhere, somehow.

What would someone gain by removing everyone violently? This operative had taken a giant step into the

London underworld by removing Johnny. They were making a statement that stood for, 'I'm here, I'm taking over and I'm number one. Be aware.' It was a dangerous game, yet one that received everyone's attention immediately, including Gary Jones, the secret man.

<　　　　　　　>

The newly promoted Batman and Robin of Dagenham's enforcement agency had visited Jones on many occasions. DCI Drake and Superintendent Philips had gained their promotion through breaking the historic child abuse case, yet both were still unhappy about the ex-commissioner and his apparent friendship with Gary Jones. Both sensed each knew more than they were revealing.

The commissioner had retired from the force to enjoy his sizable pension, not that he required it, having been the sole heir of a well-known radio empire. Rumours had grown that he had met a lady and was planning to settle down, something Superintendent Philips had recently done himself with his bride Catherine.

Jack Philips had celebrated his marriage at the Metropolitan Police sports ground located in Chigwell. Everyone attended, celebrating the fact he had finally settled down; it had been a day of lasting memories. His new bride had even persuaded him to leave his home in Dagenham, and move to a superior area. The place selected was Upminster. His life had certainly changed from the previous year. Confirmed bachelor to ever-lasting soul mate.

Gary Jones had brought Philips and Catherine a beautiful petrol lawnmower as a wedding gift. It was unexpected and he did not find out until he had used it. Jones had informed him it was a genuine present. A personal sentence at the bottom of the card made Jack Philips laugh. It read, 'one hundred percent genuine, receipt enclosed!'

Having honeymooned in Majorca, Jack returned to work with a tan for the first time. He arrived wearing fawn-coloured trousers and a lemon short sleeved shirt.

Upon arrival, DCI Drake hollered, 'Blimey, a bruised banana's just walked in.'

The uproar of laughter could be heard from all quarters. Jack stood assessing the characters before him, before taking a bow, 'Ok everyone. I've returned. So hard work begins and good old-fashioned policing carries on.' The retort was said in a jocular yet serious manner. The department understood that playtime was over and work was to resume.

Jack ambled over to his office and sat in the comfort of his well-used chair. It was like welcoming back an old friend. He glanced at the reports and for the next two hours read every one of the informative sheets.

His police antennae remained alert at all times. He knew about the death of Johnny Bigtime. He had known associates, one being Gary Jones, yet he understood Jones was not the problem. Guns were not his style. The shooting was calculated, and lacked compassion. It was cold. He sat in peace evaluating and considering what was going on with the criminal fraternity.

Drugs had changed everything. Youngsters were taking something called Ecstasy. It was considered the happy drug and offered euphoria. The desired effects included altered sensations, increased energy, empathy, as well as pleasure and love towards all. When taken by mouth the effects began in thirty to forty-five minutes and lasted three to six hours! Each one had a picture which indicated its strength. They often had a logo embedded in the tablet's centre. These ranged from FBI, Mickey Mouse or a Dove.

Philips had spoken to someone from Plaistow Police Station who had informed him doormen were controlling drugs in East London nightclubs; and a sting operation was being planned. The drug was also available in Essex clubs; specifically, a prominent club in Chelmsford and another in Southend. He was also informed it was available in a celebrity club situated in Wardour Street and a South London nightclub based in South Norwood. Drugs were everywhere.

Another major night for drugs was a nightclub situated on the A13. Their biggest night of the week was Sunday, gay night. Particular favourites being Ecstasy and Poppers. Poppers were induced by most men as they relaxed muscles, specifically the anus and throat.

Both drugs were widely available from low-life dealers who enjoyed the notoriety of being considered part of the criminal underworld family. They were also sold by a fast-food stall situated outside the venue. Regular buyers would ask for a specific dish not listed on the menu. This was their password. It was spread by word of mouth. The stall holder would then entertain the buyer with their chosen menu.

Jack's concentration was broken by DCI Drake tapping on the glazed door. 'Gov, have you read the files? Anything you want to follow up?'

Jack slowly placed the brown files on his desk before replacing the elastic band. 'Shootings, drugs and iffy people. Not like Majorca, they have a drink out there which is brandy mixed with chocolate called Lumumba. It's right nice Drakey. You can't get Bitter either. They only drink a beer called San Miguel, which is bang average and will never catch on over here.'

DCI Drake studied his friend, he was becoming soft. The old Jack Philips would have stuck to Devon and beer for his holidays. Yet here he was moaning about beer and arriving for work in fawn trousers and a lemon shirt. Retirement was looming, for sure.

'This case, Drakey, smells of a new breed of operative. Someone who will stop at nothing to get their money, and remove the old guard from East London's underworld. If I were Jones, I'd be proper careful. He's now one of the old school. You know where you stand with that lot, but this new breed, they're fucking dangerous, volatile.'

Drake stood facing his superior evaluating the wisdom given, knowing he was right, and feeling a distinct lack of confidence. The man was concerned, and Jack Philips was never concerned.

< >

Gary Jones finished his third slice of toast and marmalade, having already consumed two pots of strong sweet tea. The two paracetamols were beginning to take effect and ease his storming headache. It was like someone banging nails in the middle of his temple. The kind that stopped all traffic in the brain, fuck, it really did ache. His shakes were beginning to ease, yet he still felt like a bag of shit. The pit of his stomach felt like it had been liquidised. His moment of self-pity was broken by a sudden sharp rapping on the door. The noise immediately sent shock waves through his head. Opening the door, he was attacked by bright sun light making him breath in sharply.

'Fuck me Jones, you look like shit. You been on the sauce?'

He opened his eyes and adjusted them to be met with the grinning faces of Philips and Drake, 'As if my day couldn't be any worse. Come in. You're making the street look untidy.'

The three entered the living room and planted themselves on the well-used, yet comfortable chairs.

'Fellas, if you want tea, make your own. I am absolutely fucked. Buried my only faithful friend yesterday.'

Jack Philips assessed the man opposite him. For him to call someone 'friend' they obviously went back. The man was hurting, that was evident for all. He knew he was from the opposing side of the law, but he was a man who understood right and wrong. He knew Jones was not on the law's side, but he never gave anyone a problem, however Jack always had a nagging discomfit about him. There was something bad about him, something they had missed. Yet, he was in with top people, namely the old commissioner, who was reportedly to have dined with Gary Jones at Rules Restaurant on two or three occasions each year, 'Jones, you were friendly with Johnny Bigtime? What do you think of the shooting? Any ideas, thoughts, or guesses? In fact, anything.'

    Gary Jones suddenly felt a wave surround him, and his head pain immediately began to clear. They were concerned about the shooting; worried was more specific. He studied each man, Drake had grown in stature due to his promotion, whereas Philips appeared softer – gentler. He looked a man ready to sail into the sunset, not a man ready for a big and dangerous case, 'Gents, you know I knew Johnny. Yet to release two bullets into his face from close range is something that shocked me. I mean, whoever did that meant business.'

    Jack Philips rubbed his suntanned forehead, privately wishing he were still in Majorca. This was going to be a dangerous case; he could feel it. For someone to end another's life so coldly took a special talent, 'Jones, we may need your help on this case. If I'm being honest, you may know people in these circles, people we may not know, if you know what I mean. In return, I'll turn a blind eye to some of your less than honest activities.'

    Gary Jones leant forward and took a sip from his fourth mug of tea. They were in the shit, big style. He also thought fear was beginning to show. For them to leave him alone meant they had no idea and were prepared to make him their sacrificial lamb. Curiosity was growing within him like a vine. Paying back those who had murdered someone he liked was also enveloping his dangerous side, 'A blind eye?'

'You know what I mean Jones, we'll look the other way whilst you are helping us.'

'So, I gain nothing from this really. You're just using me whilst I aid you during the investigation.'

'Jones, let's be honest. I don't mind you, but you're on the wrong side of the law, so when I say we'll turn a blind eye to your under the counter activities. I mean during this investigation, but after it concludes, our cat and mouse game restarts. Comprende?'

Jones laughed heartily, 'Comprende. You've gone all foreign on us. I'll help you out, for sure, but it needs to be a two-way street. If either of us has info' we share it with the other. I liked Johnny. He had a young family. Whoever did this wants absolute power, and I mean absolute. They also have money, plenty of it.'

Philips immediately jumped on the word *power*, 'What exactly do you mean by power?'

Jones slowly, and theatrically took a sip from his mug of tea, 'Johnny removed, small time underworld operatives missing. Whoever is arranging this is trying to takeover, and the process includes removing anyone in their way, and I mean... anyone!'

There was a stillness in the room as if a sledgehammer had removed all movement. Breathing from all three resembled a quiet wind and realisation was attacking their minds.

Drake broke the endless silence, 'This could be bigger than the last case, Gov, and more dangerous. We're gonna need a room back at the office just for this investigation.'

Philips was in deep thought. He never thought he would work on another case as big as the last, but this could be as big without the famous faces, 'Jones, two-way street then. You want to find out who done your mate, and we need to take everyone down. We share info', and we use your place where the three of us can meet and share updates. Agreed. I'll supply the biscuits, you the tea.'

Gary Jones had a begrudging respect for the two officers. They were calculating, yet used people fairly, 'Ok. What you bringing to this party, Drakey?'

He eyed Jones. He hated being addressed Drakey by anyone from the criminal fraternity. He imagined punching Jones in the Adam's apple causing his airway to collapse. It was only momentary, yet it felt jubilant, 'I'll bring my wit and knowledge.'

Philips knew when two lions were evaluating each other, and this was the time to depart, 'Ok. We'll make a move, Jones. Until our next gathering of knowledge, stay alive and sorry to hear about your friend.'

The door was slammed with ferocity by Drake sending pulses racing through Jones already sore head.

Jones stood and decided he needed to go to bed. Two more aspirin were swiftly swallowed, followed by a large glass of Farmer's Wife pure orange juice. His stomach began to make a gurgling noise like something going down the drain. He slowly made his way upstairs to his bedroom, throwing his clothing on the floor, before falling on his bed. He gently dozed for a couple of hours before being woken by his mind reminding him of Johnny.

# Chapter 2

Love and sorrow went together like twins. Love bounces into a youngster's life like a headstrong puppy, but sorrow quickly clouds all happiness with misery. Loss was more than the heart could take, and Julie Brown was surrounded by a feeling of dark clouds and despair.

She had never known who her father was, and her teenage mother had unceremoniously deposited her with maternal grandparents.

Julie's mother had left home one afternoon having had another blazing row with her parents about her debauched lifestyle. Her final words were, 'Look after, Julie. I'm going out.'

Julie's grandparents never saw their daughter again. There had been supposed sightings with a well-known drug fuelled rock band. Yet, these were never confirmed.

Julie's grandparents never spoke about their daughter, she became a mythical figure to Julie. When questioned about Julie, her grandparents automatically replied, 'Let the past be the past, Julie, and be happy with what you have.'

At family gatherings her mother's name was never mentioned either, although she had overheard two of her uncle's whispering about Julie and what a disappointment she had been. Both men had mentioned drugs and voracious cocksucker in the same sentence as her mother. Julie, during her early age had been unsure what both men had meant, now she understood.

As Julie grew, she thought less of her mother and realised how fortunate she was to have magnificent and loving grandparents. One morning when Julie was thirteen, she felt a weight removed from her shoulders and said to herself, 'I will forget every detail of the ghoul my mother became, and how she broke the hearts of everyone.'

Julie sailed through school, doing particularly well at Biology, Maths and Chemistry. Although the education side had been easy enough, the friendship angle had proven to be more-tricky. Julie had few friends, and tended to align herself with the softer, weaker pupils. She believed they needed a mother figure, and a mother figure who protected her nest she became. Those that were brash and bullish she strayed away from, and if they tried to ruffle her nest, they were informed to remove themselves, by means fair or foul.

Julie's grandparents treated her like their own. Sadly, they had passed away when she was eighteen. Killed in a horrific road accident on the A12.

Rage had enveloped her like an ever-increasing ball of lava. Her life support mechanism had been ripped from her heart. She wondered why the lord had filled her life with so much tragedy. No more. No, fucking more.

Those guilty had not stood trial and were out on bail. They had influential family members in the higher reaches of government and law enforcement, and they had used their influence to remove the boys from all charges. Julie was full of rage and followed the culprit's patterns of movement until she knew them inside out.

The four teenagers' responsible went missing mysteriously three months later.

The plan had been simple. She lured the four young men to the abandoned Petre Chapel, situated in Thorndon Park. Promising sex with them all, at the same time.

Petre Chapel had been tricky to locate due to the dense undergrowth. Yet entrance to the crypt had been simple. The crypt had been guarded by an old black grate that could be comfortably lifted. A person could lower themselves into the entrance, before sliding through windowless opening.

Finding the men had been easy. They were creatures of habit, and frequented the Bitter End public house in Romford, every Friday. Acting suggestive, sexy and easy was all it took. The four males fell for the plan easily, led by their pussy-thirsty cocks.

The hungry young males arrived and broke into the crypt with Julie. She promised a sensual and explosive night of passion they would never forget.

The five of them entered the crypt via the old grate situated behind the church. The area was dark, damp, cold and lifeless.

Situated on centuries old stone blocks lay six skeletons surrounded by thick pieces of dust, remnants of their final places of rest.

Julie removed her clothes and poured five vodkas'. Each laced with Suxamethonium Chloride, 'Are you ready for a night you're never going to forget, boys?' She licked her lips suggestively.

Each of the boys gulped their drinks in one.

Julie stood before the young men, and began dancing suggestively in her black underwear and suspenders, 'What are you waiting for? Don't you all want to fuck me?'

It was the last moment of joy they experienced. The paralysis began to kick in almost immediately. The young men crumbled to the floor like someone had removed the skeletal structure.

Calmly, Julie replaced her clothes and strode over to the individuals. Tossing back her hair, she looked at them one final time, 'You killed the only two people I loved.' Julie covered each with a flammable liquid. Upon leaving she lit four bonfires in the crypt, and left the smoke rising like dancing ghosts. Each boy screaming silently and the smell of burning pork coating the midnight air.

She had been summoned for questioning by the Essex Police to their Brentwood headquarters, yet no charges were made as nothing could be proven - as there were no bodies, anywhere. It was more of a fishing expedition by the police to see if they could lynch anyone.

Again, Julie was alone, but she was tough, calculating and ruthless. Her mind was electric, calculating equations instantly. These involved negative situations which resulted in extreme acts of violence.

Drugs had been her avenue to success. She had started selling insignificant amounts of weed to teenagers, before increasing her stake. She had been careful, venturing into neighbouring towns that did not know her. She would venture into nightclubs selling her mind-altering substances to those that wished to heighten their experience.

One dealer had made the ultimate mistake of non-payment without explanation, and Julie had rules.

I.  If you could not pay, you had to explain why.
II. If the explanation was justified, and the person was genuinely sorry, then they were given seventy-two hours' grace to make payment.
III. If payment was not made, then justice would be served, savagely.

The client in St Albans paid for his foolish mistake. His mother's home was torched in the middle of the night, whilst she was sleeping.

Her reputation began to grow. She had heard her name amongst the underworld was, 'The silent one.'

Constantly moving and changing her looks allowed her to grow, until her name brought fear amongst those peddling drugs. No-one knew who she was. She had become a phantom. A mythical figure which brought fear. Lovers were few and far between, and when she did feel the need for passion, a visit to the local public house sorted that craving.

Only one man had shown her any form of love and respect, Gary Jones. He had been kind and treated her well, yet they had broken up due to his late- night soirees with those he would never reveal. Julie had assumed Gary was a member of the security services, yet there had always been a nagging doubt in the back of her mind. There was something that did not fit. Gary Jones, although honest, was a conundrum, and one she could not fathom.

They had met by chance in Hornchurch town centre. Gary was visiting Fine Fare to purchase provisions for his home. He had been unable to locate Mellow Birds coffee and had asked Julie for help. She had pointed him to the correct area. He thanked Julie by buying her a Texan chocolate bar. She had immediately liked his cheekiness and working-class ethic. After, he had asked her for a drink and that is where their romance began.

Although he was difficult to locate when working, his residence was easy to find. Gary was a Dagenham man through and through and would never leave his home located near The Cross Keys pub. He had the income to move somewhere more opulent, yet his constant argument was, 'Bigger house, means bigger bills and more housework.'

He would not budge. He was a creature of habit. It had infuriated Julie. Eventually, both decided the relationship had run its course. Yet, she felt a nagging feeling inside, it was not what he really wanted. It ate her up inside, and she constantly questioned herself, until one day she decided to forget him, although it was difficult as he had been the only one who had come remotely close to her beautiful grandparents.

Time passed and Julie found wealth was something she enjoyed, and the drug industry returned a handsome profit. It allowed her to experience the finer things of life and she had enjoyed them fully.

To remain anonymous, she did everything herself, from collection, to payment and finally distribution. She trusted no-one. When she collected the merchandise, it was always left in a forest. She would always assess the area prior to deciding on its security. Everything would be considered: escape routes, places to hide weaponry, vantage points and cover. She always paid the money seven days before collection of the merchandise. The seller was informed where to make the drop and the same destination was never used twice.

Only once had the seller, John Mitchell, tried to double cross her. This resulted in his two loyal henchmen having their throats cut. She had followed this by removing their heads and having them delivered to his home addressed to his wife with a typed message, 'Do it again, and you will be receiving your family's heads!'

John Mitchell had taken heed of this message, and never reneged on a deal again, yet Julie had heard through her network that the supposed top-dog was looking for the man who had threatened his family and a handsome reward would be paid for information.

John Mitchell, top dog. She mused at the moniker the small dealers had given him. He was a prick; he had not considered a woman could be the main man. She decided to end his reign and take over his empire.

John Mitchell loved money, spending it, and making it. He was a frequent visitor to local betting establishments and pubs. His gang of runners would relay messages to those he demanded to speak to or meet. Meetings were demanded when he had lost money in the bookmakers.

His routine was extreme. He would visit the same cafe at 10am; enjoy a full English Breakfast with two mugs of tea, select that day's horseracing selections from the Sporting Life and leave at 11.30am. The routine would only deviate to collect money from unsuspecting debtors. He would then visit Coral bookmakers and gamble his money away. Those in the shop understood whether he was winning, or losing due his vulgar attitude blaming everyone; jockey, horse, trainer - but never himself. When he entered a betting shop, many of those in the vicinity swiftly departed.

Women never ventured into betting shops. It was one of life's unwritten rules, yet Julie thought it pompous and antiquated.

Julie's plan was to gain attention by placing a substantial bet on any horse that was favourite. Julie purchased a copy of *The Sun* and noted the day's runners. One horse caught her eye and it had the perfect name, *City Entertainer*. It was running at Worcester in the 3.15pm race. She walked slowly into the shop pretending to be nervous. She slid up to John Mitchell, 'Can you help me, please? I need to place a bet, but have no idea what to do.'

Immediately, she noted the greed in his eye.

'I can help you with that. You got a tip then?'

Julie smiled and whispered, 'I'm not supposed to say anything, but a friend of mine called Mary has a horse running today named City.' She did not need to complete the sentence before Mitchell jumped in with his excitable response.

'Entertainer. I was looking at that myself. Mary... your friend, is her surname Postlethwaite?'

'Yes. Do you know her as well?' Julie was lying beautifully to this neanderthal of a man. She had never met Mary Postlethwaite, or the horse, yet the fool in front of her believed her totally.

'No, but I was just looking at that nag. How much you having on it?'

Julie slowly placed her hand in the black handbag retrieving an envelope. '£500, is that enough?'

Mitchell studied her, 'You're having a monkey on it. Fuck, it must have a chance.'

The betting slip was written with the 10% tax.

Julie left the establishment with her yellow slip having no idea whether *City Entertainer* would run, jump or win. She was happy enough to make informal contact with the narcissist John Mitchell.

A plan began to form in her head. It involved getting close and a little intimate with Mitchell. The thought disgusted her, yet it was something that had to be done. Men were easy, they were led by their cocks, and shallow thoughts.

Gambling, money and pussy were Mitchell's downfall. If the horse won, it would prove to be a remarkable piece of fortune.

<  >

Upon entering Coral bookmaker's, the following day, Julie was met with a booming voice, 'There she is, our little beauty.'

Immediately, four men approached her, each offering their hand. The situation was a little perplexing. Julie understood the implications of this magnificent welcome, *City Entertainer* must have won.

'That bloody 'orse won easy. 11/8. You had a monkey on it. You have £1,187.50 to collect. Nice little profit of £687.50. It's a good nag. I'll follow it. How can I repay you?' He looked at Julie and winked suggestively.

Julie understood that all men enjoyed an easy time, 'Depends how long your tongue is?'

The roar of laughter cascaded around the premises.

Mitchell whispered, 'So you like a bit of tongue then? Today's your lucky day. I own the flat opposite, meet me at the side entrance in five minutes.'

Julie was appalled by the man's arrogance and his over inflated ego. As if she would wish to be attached to him, yet it did allow the possibility of teaching him a lesson. One he would take to the grave, 'Five minutes! I'll wait two, then I'm off.' She left the shop having collected her sizeable windfall, and slowly walked to the entrance, waiting for Mitchell.

He arrived one minute later, and Julie noted from his trousers the erection was fighting for freedom, 'Hope you're feeling hard?' Julie flicked her tongue out and licked her lips.

'Girl with no name. I'm gonna get you in there and fuck you, silly.'

'How splendid. I like a nice rigid cock in me.' Game time was approaching, and her beautifully dangerous game with Mitchell was coming to an end.

As soon the weathered front door was closed, Mitchell dropped his trousers, spun her round, lifted her skirt, and entered her on the stairs leading to the flat.

Julie was on her knees studying the carpet. It was thread bare in places and needed replacing. The neanderthal behind her was grunting and moaning constantly.

Julie had hidden a knife in her bag, which was still situated in front of her. Mitchell was in a world of his own, attempting to fuck her into heaven and fill her full of semen. Slyly, Julie removed the knife from her bag and murmured, 'Stop. I want to taste you.'

The constant pounding against her arse cheeks stopped. She turned around to be greeted with Mitchell's penis standing erect like Tower Bridge opening. Immediately, with a mix of violence, adrenaline and excitement she slashed at the meat textured weapon in front of her.

Mitchell stood frozen. His brain could not compute what had happened. His penis had been removed and blood was pumping out everywhere. Pain was beginning to envelope his body, 'What have you done, you fucking whore?'

'What have I done? An excellent question. The arteries will continue pumping blood from your frightful body until you are like an empty vessel.'

Blood gushed with sickening strength from Mitchell's wound, as if his own heart fought to remove it from the body. Final shouts of anguish were beginning to annoy Julie. She decided only one course of action could end the continuing row.

Mitchell noted the reflection of the knife too late as it travelled towards his neck, gently caressing, and breaking the skin. The red liquid began to attack the walls. His final vision was Julie smiling and mouthing, 'I'm top dog.' His mind finally understood who she was before life left him forever.

She sat in a pool of his blood, which had started to sink into the carpet, and it was now turning dull to a reddish-brown, some of it hidden by the swirling pattern entwined. Violent jets of red decorating the walls were now slowly sliding south. The scenario reminded her of an old horror film. The bloodshed was magnificently macabre.

Julie considered how life had played her. She had been born to love, yet had grown into a monster. Did love conquer all? No. But money and power did.

She now had to dispose of the body and clear all evidence. This aligned itself to only one area, a fire. She rummaged around the Mitchell's pockets for a key. She began to laugh as he resembled a porcelain white cartoon character. Eventually, she located the key in his left-hand pocket.

Next operation was to drag the body to the top of the stairs. Fire would take care of the removal of blood and prints, yet a missing penis would be noted. The fire would strip the body of all flesh, cooking it to cinder.

Pulling the body up the stairs had proven harder than expected. Gravity had been against her, yet after much huffing and puffing Julie got the body on the bed. It resembled a very white puppet without the strings.

Julie pulled a bottle of Teachers whisky from her bag and poured it around the body, before placing the empty bottle on the floor next to the beds left side. She stood and studied herself in the mirror. The reflection indicated someone who had appeared in a slasher movie. She visited the small bathroom and ran a bath, ensuring all evidence of blood was removed from her body. Having done this, she removed a pair of jeans and a blue jumper from her bag and redressed, checking for any small droplets of blood. Julie located a plastic bag in the flat and added her blooded clothing to it before leaving the flat.

Streets during the day were a cacophony of sounds, from cars and lorries to busy people chattering. Night-time allowed life to seek sanctuary by the street lamps, which offered passage to lead life to its final objective. The road, a solid river transporting everything and everyone to everywhere. Yet tonight, it was transporting Julie to the flat to dispose of Jack Mitchell.

Before leaving the flat earlier. Julie had covered much of the flat with flammable liquid. The smell would not be noted unless anyone entered the premises. She had returned home and selected one of her mice that would do the demanding work. Upon returning to the building Julie attached a piece of cloth to the animal's tail. She then lit the end of the cloth before feeding the mouse through the letterbox and walking away.

The flames that consumed demanded everything become ashes, the heat attacking the midnight air as if it were in a monstrous mood. The destruction was a terrible joy. It was as if the fire reflected the arsonist. In the black night, under a bounty of shining stars, emergency vehicle lights danced a brilliant blue to meet the roaring raging red inferno.

Seventy-two minutes later the fire was an empty soul. The black grainy swirls floated towards the endless night time sky to continue their journey. Water was dripping from the skeletal frame of the building as if it were melting.

Fire officers, meticulously manoeuvred their way through the rubble.

'Over here, body!'

Instantly, the situation took on a different meaning when a body was found. Retrieving bodies of people could tear someone apart if it were their first.

The transition from lifeform to corpse was horrific. The soft skin became blackened and crusty if there was any remaining. The teeth gave the appearance of someone screaming, yet smiling. This person had been like any other. They had learned to walk, talk, run, laugh and love, but they were now scorched beyond any recollection, like barbequed meat.

'What do you reckon?'

'There's an ash tray on the floor, and a bottle of whisky beside it. It looks like the poor sod fell asleep when pissed and if he had a fag on the go, then it burnt everything in its path, including him.'

'Call it in.'

# Chapter 3

Ringleader Danny Van der Leer set up a company named Independent Meat Traders Ltd as a front for illicit imports. Drugs were hidden in packets of frozen chicken breasts. The set-up was perfect as the meat was past its sell-by date and the greedy wholesaler was incredibly happy to receive any money for it, let alone the handsome amount he was paid.

The pills had been easy to manoeuvre across the border from Holland, no-one stopped a white van containing frozen chicken.

The journey had taken seven hours, and there had been no inconvenient disruptions to Harwich. Driving along the A127 they were told to look for six yellow traffic cones with a sign that read, 'Good luck WMV'. WMV meant white van man, and this would signal their turning was fifty yards further on. Upon entering the lane, they had to scan for another yellow traffic cone which signalled their final destination and entrance to the meeting point.

The van was parked, and the three men disembarked. Immediately, they were met by five men who patted them down. Once checked, one of the men hollered, 'All clear. They're clean.'

Julie Brown, slowly and confidently approached, 'Van der Leer?' She waited for a response, understanding the man was analysing her. He looked a little confused, as did all men when they first met Julie.

'I was expecting to meet a man, not a chick.'

Julie looked at the man and considered his impertinence, yet decided to give the Dutchman a chance. He was obviously surprised. The look of shock showed in his eyes, and his mouth slowly parted, 'Were you? Interesting, shows I've got the jump on you then?'

The farm was situated five-hundred yards away from prying eyes, and security had been deployed every two-hundred yards in a circular formation, surrounding the delivery. Julie had covered all bases in the event Van der Leer and his cohorts fancied their chances.

Van der Leer studied the woman in front of him. She had dyed her hair, a little of the colouring had attached itself to her left ear. She was abrupt, but not rude. He always went by his inner-feelings and these informed him she was safe, although she was one to keep an eye on. He had a nagging feeling she was ruthless and the feeling would not leave him.

'There's your money, it's all there. No need to count it, I never renege on a deal.' The black briefcase was handed over and accepted.

Van der Leer accepted the briefcase in a slow manner, never removing his eyesight from Julie, 'I trust you, but equally, if it is one-pound light. I shall hunt you down.'

'And if my end is light, you'll be dead before you know it… as will your family.'

Van der Leer thought the last statement tasteless, yet it proved how ruthless and dangerous this new contact could be. He placed his hands into his pockets and removed a mask. Van der Leer threw one to Julie, 'Put it on, the smell will blow your fucking mind, woman.'

Julie understood when someone was being cautious, yet helpful. She wrapped the mask around her face. Instantly, she heard her men raising their voices.

'Fuck me, what the fuck is that shit awful smell.'

The delivery was unloaded into an old, disused, rusty cattle-shed, which was dry and out of the way. The trade took forty-five minutes to complete. The merchandise was removed from the chicken, and placed into boxes. The rotten chicken was unceremoniously thrown into a corner.

Before the buyer leaves, merchandise must be evaluated. Julie understood that it could contain a wide mixture of substances, although what it contained concerned her slightly.

A man and a woman in their early twenties were brought forward. Both looking a little dishevelled. They understood why they were there and what was expected of them.

One of the remaining packs of chicken was selected and opened, which immediately attacked everyone's nose due to the putrid smell. A plastic wrapper was removed from its core which contained one-hundred tablets. These were given to the young couple who immediately ripped open the plastic pouch and devoured a tablet each. The chemicals took thirteen minutes to have an effect. Suddenly, the couple began to laugh and jump up and down excitedly. They then laid on the floor and looked at the sky. Occasionally, one of them murmured, 'Wow.'

Julie looked on in curiosity, 'It works. You can go now.'

Van der Leer and his three men returned to their van; their white overalls tainted with putrid blood. These were immediately removed and placed in a bag with a brick. Once inside the van each looked at the other knowing they had just met the devil. Selling the ecstasy pills had been easy, but this woman could be a problem, particularly as she did not know the drug's ingredients. The formula of LSD, cocaine, heroin, amphetamine and methamphetamine, rat poison, caffeine and dog deworming substances allowed the formula to be enhanced, but not bettered. It also made it significantly more harmful for the person ingesting the drug, particularly as significant amounts of rat poison had been used.

Julie watched the van leave. She walked over to the young couple now experiencing the ultimate pleasure of their high, before depositing one-hundred pounds in their pockets. Neither realised what she had done. Julie gave each one a final look, before leaving them alone.

She paid everyone their agreed amount and left the area. Life had taught her one thing. Everyone had to be paid swiftly. If you did not pay a person, they usually came back to haunt you ten-fold. Julie drove away thinking of the profit she would make and where she would reside next.

<  >

The young man bent over, convulsing. He was struggling to breath. Everyone self-medicates but you can choose good medication or bad. He knew this was bad, unbelievably bad. The pain was taking over. A gentle cough emerged from deep inside; thick blood cascaded covering his chin. His nostrils filled with the rusty smell of blood. He tried to speak, but felt an explosion in his chest. Turning one final time, he looked at the love of his life. There was no movement from her eyes, her chest did not bounce up and down. She had left him. Their life together no more, and their dreams of parenthood a distant thing of reality. He passed out.

<  >

'Come on girl. Where are you? What you doing over there?' Swiftly the old gentleman walked towards his dog, stopping five-feet from it. Two young people lay there. Suddenly, he heard a murmur, 'Did someone say something?' His World War 2 instinct kicked in. He approached and leant down. The girl was gone but the boy had fighting spirit, 'Stay with me son. I'll get help.'

A hand reached out and gently croaked, 'Help me… please.'

The female corpse breathed no more upon the derelict landscape, yet the fire still burned in the male form. The veteran hoped the girl's soul would pass on to pastures new and find peace. He prayed the man's resistance was strong and the lord was batting for him.

<  >

Thirty minutes later police and ambulance were at the scene. The body was removed, and the young man was placed on a stretcher and taken at high speed to Oldchurch Hospital.

Police officers at the scene tried interviewing the man, but all he kept screaming was, 'Get the doves. Stop the doves. Bad. Very bad.'

The area was searched, and it was noted a number of people had recently visited the area. There were tyre marks and many footprints. Yellow balloons were found nearby - although officers took little notice of them. What interested, and sickened everyone was the pile of foetid chicken dumped in the corner of the abandoned shed.

Superintendent Philips and DCI Drake arrived at the scene. Immediately, both knew it was drug related, but what was the connection. They walked by a police constable who was regaling the story to another younger college who had just arrived. Both officers heard the police constable say, 'Dove.'

'Excuse me constable, dove. What is a dove?'

The police constable who had been the giver of the information sprung to life, 'Sir, I may be wrong, but I think the dove could be a link towards ecstasy pills. It is a design on the tablets. Again, you may have to correlate the information, but I heard it mentioned in a local nightclub. There are other names I think as well, although what they are I am unsure.'

Both Drake and Philips acknowledged the officer and thanked him for the extremely useful information.

'Drakey. Drugs. I bloody knew it. They are the nemesis of society. That couple have copped a bad one and it's done them big time. If the police constable is correct and I reckon he is. Then we now have to follow the dove.'

'Gov, we may have to visit some of our local night spots and speak to a few heavies at the door. They've obviously been transported using the rotten chicken as a cover. Clever really. Who'd want to search a van or lorry carrying chicken gone bad.'

Philips considered the news. He understood Catherine would not be elated with the idea. She had suggested he consider retirement, and for the first time in his life he agreed with someone who mentioned it. Married life had mellowed him and Jack realised it. He was worried that those around him may recognise the same symptoms. Yet deep down he knew the end was in sight. He turned to his loyal colleague, 'Drakey, this is gonna be my last case. Don't tell anyone.'

Drake had been expecting the line but not in the middle of a field having surveyed one dead and one nearly dead body. Calmly he turned to Jack, 'There is life outside security Gov. Go and enjoy it with Catherine.'

'Anyway Drakey, less of this bollocks. We need to get ready for club land.'

DCI Drake understood this was his Superintendent's way of saying, 'Conversation over,' without actually saying it.

<  >

Two-hundred thousand ecstasy tablets will create a minefield of money. She would sell them for five-pound each, and the dealers would double their money. It was win-win for all concerned. The tablets had cost her one-pound each. Having seen the couple enjoying them was the final act she needed, before paying Van der Leer with the cash she had hidden away for her biggest and most lucrative deal.

Once home, Julie considered her latest venture and congratulated herself. It had gone smoothly, and through luck had gained a contact in Van der Leer. He was a man she would use again. Trust had been purchased from both sides. He would be feeling the same about her.

She admired her home. It was a lovely old cottage built in the 1700s, yet the one-year lease was up and it was time to move on. Privately, she realised the need to invest in a property, yet her concerns with security never allowed her to find her spiritual resting place.

Julie contacted her regular buyers and informed them what she had. Everyone wanted a piece of the action when they understood what she had. Greed showed when they calculated profit and cost, orders came thick and fast. In no time, everything had been sold. London and Essex were flooded with ecstasy.

Those representing her collected the merchandise and took five per-cent of the deal. Julie realised this kept them all on-side, and meant she never had to meet her clients, ensuring her mystique was kept low-profile. Even those representing her only met her twice, and each time she looked different. This confused matters as the carriers would all describe her differently if the authorities questioned them.

<   >

Van der Leer was glad to be leaving the ferry at Rotterdam. Torching the van in Essex was a necessity, and bringing the second vehicle over had been wise. Each man had showered on the ferry leaving no trace of their activities. Being on home soil was like welcoming your first child into the world. Safety, security, and protection were things to enjoy. The two men were paid handsomely, guaranteeing loyalty and commitment.

They left on foot, knowing their services were not required for up to one-year. The payment of fifty-thousand Guilders allowed them an extremely comfortable life. Both would go back to anonymity and continue building their homes, whilst carrying on with their vocations of carpentry and plumbing. Within their districts they were seen as good, honest, diligent individuals. Pillars of the community.

Van der Leer made the journey to Amsterdam from Rotterdam in his Volvo. It took one hour, and allowed him time to reflect on events of the past twenty-four hours. The woman, Brown, was shrewd, intelligent, yet had a coldness about her but there was something more. He approached his canal house and gently pulled over, sitting in the car for five minutes. This repetitive action was done to survey the area in case his home was being watched, or any unusual activity taking place. However, like any other day in his area, it was calm and peaceful. All his neighbours were respected bankers and diamond merchants. He believed there were a couple of footballers, although he had no interest in the sport.

Van der Leer entered his home. Yet something was wrong, his sculpture of *Venus at the Bath* had been moved, it was facing towards the entrance door. His ears were met with a booming voice.

'Come and join me young man. I've been waiting patiently. Oh, don't do anything silly. There's a good chap.'

Van der Leer stood on the starting step as if it were his last. No sound was made. Upon reaching the top of the stairwell he was again met with the unusual accent.

'Hurry up, Van der Leer. Chop chop. Time waits for no one.'

He entered his living room to be met with a man significantly older than himself. Gaining his poise, he calmly, yet seriously spoke, 'Do not think I am being rude, but what the fuck are you doing in my home?'

'Profanity will get you nowhere young man. Yet, the Queen's English will get you everywhere. Even to a Dutch chap.' He jovially laughed at his gallous humour, 'Sit.' He pointed to an empty chair.

Van der Leer obeyed the command, although inside he was bristling with rage. Yet, curiosity was growing incessantly, 'What do you want? Why are you here? Who the fuck are you? And how the hell did you get in?' He looked deeply into the man's eyes. Unblinking, he awaited an answer.

'You are a jolly impatient man. You need to calm down otherwise you will suffer a mischief.'

Van der Leer considered the advice given. He had no idea what the term 'suffer a mischief' meant. It sounded dangerous.

'You, Van der Leer, are going to help me ensnare a lady named Julie Brown. We, meaning the British government, know about you and your extra activities regarding party drugs, you now belong to us.'

Van der Leer's antennae was activated with *Help* and *British government*, 'I am sorry, man with no name, but I work for no-one, and secondly - certainly not for free.'

The large booming laugh filled the room, 'Leer, may I call you Leer? It appears easier. Anyway, we know about your drug stuffing activities with chickens. What we want is, Julie Brown. She's become a pain in the proverbial. She has upset two members of government. One believes she sold drugs to his son that were bad. The other believes she knows the whereabouts of his son - missing for many years. So, you are going to aid us. Remember, refusal often offends.'

Van der Leer understood he was backed into a corner. He was well and truly fucked. 'What do I get out of this?'

'An excellent question. We will not inform your authorities about your chemical factory which is fronted as a floristry along the coast of The Hague. Does that appear fair? So, Julie Brown. Speak.'

Van der Leer noted a different tone in the man's voice. It had become short and sharp. Game time was over. He was now in business mode, and messing with a government meant one thing. The end, 'Julie Brown. Strange lady. Very decisive and prompt. A lady of few words. The sort who would remove your testicles with a blunt knife using no anaesthetic.'

'Leer. Thank you. I am Perkins, and represent one my government's more covert departments. Everything you have informed me will be checked in depth. What does Brown look like presently? She has a penchant for changing her look.'

Van der Leer finally had an opening. The British government had no idea what she looked like, 'Let me get this right. You come to my country, break into my home, yet have no idea who the woman you are seeking looks like?'

Perkins studied the man. If he were British, he would make a fine operative. He was to the point, and had a razor-sharp mind, 'Leer you are correct. We have only had three sightings, yet every description is different. That is why the finer points will aid us, and in turn we will forget you.'

Perkins removed a Hamlet cigar from his inside pocket and lit it, blowing small plumes of blue smoke clouds into the air. He considered the information he had gained from the man seated opposite him. Van der Leer had told him everything, yet nothing. He obviously did not know her well, yet had been honest to him. He removed the cigar from his mouth, 'How do you contact her?'

'She is a strange one. I've been told to call this number on the 7th of each month.' Van der Leer extended his arm to pass Perkins a tired slip of paper with a London number on it.

Perkins eyed the paper and had no idea what its relevance was, 'Forgive my ignorance, but why is that so strange?'

'Perkins, it is strange as the number belongs to one of your red telephone boxes. She obviously does not have a telephone.'

# Chapter 4

Jimmy Jackson was twenty-one years of age, and a known man. He had the swagger of someone people did not want to lock eyes with, let alone cross. He had been born into crime, a victim of circumstance, yet one he had profiteered from during his early adult life.

He sat pondering life and thought of his mother. He was twelve when she had muttered those immortal words, 'Wanna take a package tonight? It's only a small one you have to deliver.' He knew exactly what was in it, and his mother had told him, 'Never try it.' But he also knew how much it paid and he was hungry. Growing up was not easy for a boy heading over six feet tall. He imagined the two of them gorging on Chinese from their favourite takeaway with profits gained.

Jimmy had rarely attended school, and was known locally as a boy to be careful around. He soon learnt that caution, linked with a calculating, and cold-blooded quality produced results. These attributes had gained him notoriety within the criminal fraternity at an early age, and these techniques had brought him to the attention of Julie Brown.

Since partnering with Brown, profits from drug dealing had spiralled to dizzy heights and he loved the financial rewards.

He also understood why his mother used youngsters to deliver drugs. They were so naive. He would listen to them whining for an hour, after this he usually had enough information to get them to do anything. He would promise them money and security, although this was a myth. Many of his drug runners would become users themselves, or become trusted lieutenants. They would skip school to deliver merchandise, and those that became a little flash with their wages would be given a slap. Jimmy always said, 'Blending in keeps you free. Being flash gets you nicked.' This had allowed Jackson to become the leading supplier in Newham.

    The new batch of ecstasy would show an enormous profit. Messages were sent out to regular buyers. Users were easy to locate. Statistics proved that drug abuse smashed souls like broken glass. Each piece a tragedy or near-death experience. People with addictions never made correct decisions and this is what Jackson played on. His instinct informed him these products would sell quickly to weak minded individuals who liked to hide away in their dens.

    Word quickly spread that Jackson had a new chemical high that would leave the taker feeling euphoric. It was like the January sales, with male and female participants parting with their cash for the substance that offered a one-person party of the mind. Users came from all levels of society; employees from the financial sector, civil servants, blue collar workers and one from the sporting sector. The cross-over in individuals intrigued Jackson, who had never taken any pill, powder or vial. He had promised his mother, and a promise to mother must be adhered.

    Regular users collected their merchandise and swiftly enjoyed the experience. Each considered their drug a toxic lover, and these lovers could drive a person into a frenzy. Occasionally, one could be bad, and these were as addictive as any persuasive drug. Jimmy did not care, cash was king, and he was the king.

<　　　　　　　>

Conor Summerfield always enjoyed life in the fast lane. He relished money, women, alcohol, late nights, and drugs. His family knew of his lifestyle, yet accepted it, hoping he would grow out of this decadent way of life. Having returned home he was eager to try his new substance. Ecstasy was a drug that heightened the senses and he wanted them intensified, maximised, multiplied.

His maisonette contained all essentials required for modern living and had a welcoming feel. Sitting on his soft sofa, which was the place he did his thinking and something he worshipped. Even though it was beautifully designed, the leather had been worn past the point of distress, and there were small scuff marks and looks of tiredness about it. The once bright tan colour had been bleached by the sun that streamed through the window attacking the skin which covered the once beautiful piece of furniture. Yet, it offered supreme comfort and was chic.

The dove emblem was beckoning him, smiling. He threw the pill in his mouth swallowing the tablet like he had not eaten for a week, juices forming in the confines of his mouth, yet it was not a meal he was enjoying. He reached for the can of Pepsi swigging thirstily, with each gulp his Adam's apple bobbed violently, and the fizzy pop flooded his empty stomach aggressively attacking the pill.

The invisible pain attacked the confines of his torso. It felt like a fire starting deep down. He fell to the floor. A loud bang was sent through the room. Crawling across the shag pile carpet made him feel like his limbs were being dragged back by an unseen force. Stumbling towards the telephone, joints screaming, his shaking fingers grabbed the receiver and dialled the three digits that could save his life, 'Help me, please.' He then passed out spluttering red phlegm.

<  >

'We have another one. Same symptoms. Same as the others, ulcers, and perforation of organ walls. Why are they taking this stuff?' Both paramedics eyed one another, before nodding their heads negatively.

Hours later Conor Summerfield awoke from his life saving surgery. He opened his eyes slowly. They felt matted with glue. His insides felt like they had been yanked about.

'You're awake, Mr. Summerfield. How are you feeling?'

Conor considered the question. He felt dreadful, and his insides bruised. He looked at the man standing beside him, knowing he had saved his life. Gravelly he replied, 'Better. Thank you.'

'You are an incredibly lucky man. Whatever you had taken was strong, extraordinarily strong, and almost burnt through your insides. Anyway, you have someone here to see you.'

Conor slowly manoeuvred his head to his left, 'Uncle Gary, what are you doing here?' Conor understood when Uncle Gary was involved it was not a good end for the person dealing with him. The term uncle was a loose term used, a nickname. They were related through Gary's mother, although they rarely saw him.

Gary Jones stood staring at the waste of skin he was related to through blood, 'What happened? Where did you get the drugs? Who sold them? What was it?'

Conor knew bullshitting was pointless. Gary was too sharp; he would see through the lies. The blue eyes were boring into him, waiting for an answer. He understood there was only one way to answer, and that was the truth, 'You want the truth. Pull a seat up and I'll tell you the truth.' Nervously, he began.

Twenty minutes passed before Conor stopped talking. Gary looked at his family member assessing the information gleaned. Everything appeared in place. He leant towards the glass of water and fed the straw into Conor's mouth, realising he would be parched, 'Why did you get involved in this lifestyle. It's full of losers who feed from people like you. These people have money, and keep wanting more and more. You aid their shit for a nothing lifestyle. You are a cunt, always have been. Now, you've ended up in hospital by being a cunt. I'm going to sort this out, and if you ever take drugs, get involved with drugs or get involved in anything iffy. I'll personally open you up with my bare hands and feed your inners to stray cats. Understand?'

Conor sat transfixed. No-one had ever spoken to him in this way. The violent threat was offered in an intense honest manner. The family member stood gazing at him, the outcast of the family, was maniacal – psychotic. He knew it was time to go straight, 'You have my word, but be careful. The man you'll be dealing with, Jimmy

Jackson, is useful, and surrounds himself with an army of dangerous youngsters.'

Gary considered the information, 'How young is young, Conor?'

'Not totally sure, but I'd say the youngest comes from first year seniors.'

'11 or 12-year-old schoolkids? Are you fucking serious?'

'Gary.' It was the first time he had addressed him by his Christian name. 'These kids consider him a father figure. He piles them with gifts and they deliver his gear to people like me.'

Gary listened and studied Conor, looking for signs of weakness and lies, there were none. All he saw before him was a lost, spoilt young man. He was telling the truth.

< >

Steven Jacks wanted to be wealthy, seriously wealthy. He was intelligent, having attended Brentwood private school, which introduced him to wealthy families like his own, although their parents were city high flyers, whereas his father owned a successful scrap metal yard. It had always made him feel a little inferior to his peers, until someone had taken the joke a little too far, which had resulted in the joker receiving a bruised eye and a royal kicking.

Schooling had been easy. Steven had excelled in maths, chemistry and physics. These requisites proved fortuitous as they developed his later life monetary scheme.

Magic mushrooms were Steven Jacks first venture into drug culture. He had read that psilocybin and psilocin were the active compounds in the mushrooms and soon realised to grow these hallucinogenic drugs all you required were sterilised jars, spores and patience. Once he had rectified the art of growing the mushrooms, business began to grow, quickly.

Free spirited, curious individuals took the mushrooms. They caused the participants to experience hallucinations. People claimed to see, hear, feel, taste or smell things that were not real. Users could experience a good trip stating they felt on top of the world, but a bad one could involve paranoia. How the user felt was irrelevant, as long as they paid their five-pound was all he cared about.

He had attracted Julie Brown's attention due to his diligent and quiet method of selling. He was big, but in a small way. Big enough to be known locally, yet small enough so the local police force would remain uninterested. No-one understood where he purchased his product. When Julie Brown had understood his method, she was suitably impressed. This young man was going places, and she needed to keep him on-side. Having gained his trust, Steven Jacks was introduced to Julie Brown's successful enterprise.

Jacks had flourished with his new products. Julie Brown had been manna from heaven. She had fed him gold. He quickly went from being an underground drug operative to number one. He also had the backing of Brown's security; he was now untouchable. No-one could stand in his way. If any person wished to enter the local area selling, they were forced to pass a percentage of their profits to him, otherwise they were moved on, swiftly and unceremoniously. This usually involved a magnificent beating.

Jacks had heard of one man selling on his patch. This man was known as Johnny. Enquiries were made, and he was a local small-time villain who owned a snooker hall.

Jacks decided someone needed to visit John to warn him to stop his activities, yet this was met with a severe beating of his operative.

Steven Jacks decided to meet the man head on. He had learnt Johns liked to collect his sons from the local private school they attended. The very same one he had graced.

The air was cool and the clouds looked menacing and full of rain. The perfect weather for a showdown, 'Excuse me. Are you Mr. Johns?'

Johnny Bigtime turned slowly towards the man addressing him. He obviously had no idea who he was as he had not used his surname, 'I am, who's asking?'

Jacks noted the man was unfazed, and had disrespected him without the need of words. There was more to this man he was confronting and for the first time in his life he felt a nervous grumbling sound in the confines of his stomach, 'We need to talk about your chemical operation in the local area and your need to move on.' He had not followed his non-confrontational script and had gone in like a wild bull. He knew the man facing him had something about him and was considering his options.

Johnny Bigtime laughed at Jacks, 'Are you for real, you silly little cunt? Do you know who I am? Obviously not, you fresh faced prick. I'm the man who will eat you up and shit you down the khazi. Now fuck off before I hurt you.'

Steven Jacks stood open mouthed. No-one spoke to him in that manner. He was number one. His bravado sprung to life, 'How dare you speak to me like that. You are...'

Before finishing his sentence, he tasted iron in his mouth and was admiring the dark clouds. His lip had been split severely. Parents were looking over their shoulders at the commotion, noting a man lying on the floor, guessing the perpetrator was the man waiting for his two sons.

Johnny Bigtime turned and looked down at him, 'Never, ever fuck with me. I'm Johnny Bigtime, and no person fucks with me. Next time. I'll kill you. Now fuck off and play with some toys, cunt face.'

Steven Jacks righted himself, dusted the remnants of mud from his back and trousers, and adhered the pure white handkerchief to his very sore, and now ballooning lip. He had learnt a valuable lesson. He was tough, but not tough enough. He needed help.

Jacks contacted Julie Brown twenty-fours later. He was only allowed to speak to her twice each week, and it had to be a specific time. This all ways puzzled him. The phone rang once and was immediately answered.

'Jacks, speak.'

'Julie, I need the name and number of someone who can remove a subject from my manor. This person is troublesome and is causing me unwanted aggravation.'

Julie listened to the whining from Steven Jacks. Someone had obviously rattled him as he was not a person who asked for help, 'What exactly do you want?'

'I want this man gone, forever. Removed from society.'

The hairs on Julie's arms began to prickle. When violence was activated, it caused problems for everyone, 'Tell me a few more details, please?'

Steven Jacks held the telephone as if he were trying to squeeze the life from it, 'Julie, do not think I am being harsh, but this is one operation I would prefer you were not involved in. This man is trying to squeeze my operation.'

Julie realised Jacks was in deep shit and trying to protect her from it, 'Ok, I do have a number. These men are dangerous, and I mean dangerous. Be careful, and I mean careful. Once you employ them, they won't stop until the job is done.' Julie Brown gave the number to Steven Jacks and disconnected. She did not like this violence as it caused unnecessary attention. She had voiced her opinion, yet it had fallen on deaf ears.

Forty-eight hours later Jacks met the two men recommended by Julie, both former employees of the British army, who were now freelance. Each man wanted twenty-five thousand pounds cash. He had met the men in the Little Chef situated along the A127.

Jacks ordered a coffee, watching the men tuck into a gammon steak, egg and chips like they had never eaten before. He began to speak, but was stopped. A single finger was raised, instructing him to stop. The four minutes was endless. Ultimately, with gleaming plates, both men looked up.

'Man needs to eat. Gotta keep your strength up. Coffee will get you no-where. The job. Tell me about who they are and where there live. That's all. We'll do the rest.'

Both men made Steven Jacks feel uncomfortable. Each had a rugged steeliness about them, yet they were unnerving. Cold. Not likeable would be correct. They were bad, and enjoyed their vocation, killing. He passed the black Adidas holdall that contained money, whilst whispering about the target.

<   >

Gary Jones made discreet enquiries about Jimmy Jackson. For someone so insular, he was certainly well-known, easy to locate. An old drunk in the street had been Jones's fortune cookie.

The old piss-head had been mouthing off about kids on bikes gobbing at him. This was followed with, 'Jimmy Jackson, the jumped-up two-faced cunt.' When Gary had heard the name, he immediately made a detour to the man and enquired if he was all right.

The reply was immediate, 'Suppose you're one of his lot?'

Gary stared at the man, 'Do I seriously look like one their lot?'

'No. You look too poncey. Got any money?'

This was all the information he required, 'Jimmy Jackson, who is he? Sounds a dangerous man?'

'Dangerous. He's a no-good cunt. Just because he owns a few maisonettes and employs kids to dump his gear off. Thinks he's a fucking 'ard man.'

'Where does this Jackson individual live?'

The drunkard rose his head and looked out of his blood shot eyes. His mouth was bone dry and his stomach rumbled, loudly, 'Why you interested in 'im?'

Jones laughed. The drunkard had come to his senses. He also knew what the next question would be.

'You got any dough? I'm a bit brassic.'

'Tell me exactly where I can find Jimmy Jackson and you'll be well rewarded. I'll give you a century now, and other twoer when I see him. Fuck me over and I'll suck your eyeballs out and stamp on them whilst you're watching.'

The drunkard squinted at the man standing opposite him, 'You gotta deal. Got the necessary?'

Jones dug into his pockets and pulled out one-hundred pounds in ten-pound denominations. He counted them slowly, noting the man opposite him lick his dry lips, 'There's the money, Address?'

'He lives in Canning Town, Mona Street, just off the Barking Road.'

< >

Locating Jackson had been easy. There were youngsters in and out his red brick maisonette non-stop. Riding to and from on their new BMX bikes. Diamondback was the favourite mode of transport.

There was a lull in the operation at 5pm. It was obviously time for the riders to ride home for their evening meal. This was the opportunity Gary Jones had been waiting for.

He strode up to the door and pressed the button bell. He was about to ring again when the door was opened by a tall mixed-race man who had not filled out. He was wearing a yellow Fila tracksuit, which made him look like a bruised banana.

Jimmy Jackson stood at the door staring at the man. He had told the last Littlewoods pools collector to stop calling, 'Listen man, I don't wanna do the pool…'

Jimmy was laying on the floor looking up at the ceiling. The rusty taste was entering his mouth. He tried to stand, but was kicked forcefully in the ribs, twice. Jimmy was then grabbed by the zip of his new tracksuit and punched twice in the face. The second removing his front tooth.

'Listen, Jackson, and listen good. If you sell anymore shit again, I will remove your head whilst you are fucking talking. The gear you are knocking out is crap. I'll be watching you, and you're going to tell me where it comes from.'

Jackson understood this man was first division, in the big league. There was something about him. He was different to other people, 'Don't hit me no more man. I'll tell yer. Julie, woman's name is Julie. Don't know anything else about her. She contacted me. Fast mouth, quick thinker, fit, yet ruthless.'

Gary knew Jackson was telling the truth. He had pissed himself and his once pristine yellow tracksuit bottoms were now coloured mustard, 'If anything you tell me is bollocks, yours will be removed with a pair of scissors and then I'll feed them to you. Nod if you understand.'

Jimmy was nodding like an obedient dog, 'Yeah man, no problemo.' He looked at his tracksuit and noted he had pissed himself. The humiliation was complete.

# Chapter 5

Julie Brown entered The Greyhound public house. It had become a popular place for those with red XR3i's to showboat. She approached the bar and ordered a Malibu and pineapple, watching as the bartender purposely placed three glistening cubes of ice in the glass. The ice resembled her heart.

Many conversations were taking place, all parties believing their information was more important than those they were sharing lunch with. The crowd consisted of businessmen, and those wishing to enjoy somewhere quiet to escape.

Julie selected a table in the corner which would allow her to view those entering and leaving the establishment. Before she had a chance to get comfortable, she felt a presence sliding their body in the chair opposite her. The movement silk like.

'Afternoon Julie.' Steven Jacks thought he had trumped her. He felt it had unsettled her. She was a person who expected to be in control, yet this time he believed he had gained the upper-hand.

Julie Brown smiled at the man. He had a smug look on his face. He obviously believed he had usurped her. An amateurish mistake. She had noted him in the bar's mirror as he had sat in the opposing left side snug with his pint of lager, believing he was invisible to all, 'Sit.'

The order surprised Jacks. He had snuck up on Julie, yet she was giving him an order having not looked at him, 'That's rather unwelcoming Julie.'

'Sit down, and shut your fucking mouth you stupid prick.' She glared at Jacks as he sat.

Her eyes had a look of venom. Calculations were spinning around in Jacks mind. He thought he had the upper-hand, yet here he was now being treated like a naughty schoolboy. How did she know he was here? His wandering mind was brought back to task swiftly by Julie Brown's verbal attack.

'I involved you in my enterprise as I thought, no believed, you had nous. I thought you were sharp. Played the game quietly. Yet you've made the biggest fucking mistake I have known anyone make.'

Jacks sat still, rigid. He had no idea what Julie Brown was talking about, although he had a nagging feeling it was about the murder of Johnny Bigtime. 'Come now, Julie. Whatever it is. I am sure I can repair the situation once you inform me what it is.'

Julie could not believe what she was hearing. She leant forward, wrapping her fingers around the edge of the chestnut brown wooden table. Her fingers going white. Fury was beginning to envelop her, 'You murdered Johnny Bigtime, you fucking idiot. Do you know who he was? Did you find out about him?'

Steven Jacks blew out a breath. He now had the reason. He sat back in the red, soft leather chair. Feeling a little more relaxed, he decided to challenge Julie Brown, 'The man had to go. He was selling merchandise on my manor. I cannot allow that. It makes me look weak. I am sure you understand.'

Julie sat amazed. The man's nonchalance was beginning to create a red mist in her mind, 'Understand!

I'll tell you what you need to understand. Johnny Bigtime was connected, and when I mean connected, I mean connected to some of the craziest individuals you'll ever know, and these individuals are friendly with people in the establishment. You are in the shit. Which means I could end up in a giant pool of shit with your sorry arse. You stupid, fucking, private schooled, silly cunt.'

Jacks considered the information. He felt Julie was over-reacting. Who knew of the murder? 'Julie, is there really need for the profanity. No-one knows.'

Julie sat in her chair incredulous. Did the man honestly believe it? 'Excuse me, Mr. Shit for brains, but who did the killing? Were these men paid? Were these men gun for hire individuals? Will these men sell you out for money?' She had hit a home run. The man's poise had changed. He crossed his legs, repeating the action twice and removed a handkerchief from his pocket dabbing his lip. A small bead of sweat was beginning to show on his forehead. It had a reflective sheen to it.

'I am sure the said individuals will not mention a thing, Julie.' Confidence was slowly ebbing away. Jacks realised his vocals had tremored a little, and hoped it had not been noted by Julie Brown. The bombastic attitude he had entered with was quickly diminishing.

Julie sat back in her chair. She looked at her drink and took a slow refreshing sip, knowing she had triumphed. The privately educated schoolboy had no idea how business was arranged by those who wished to remain anonymous. Her fury began to subside, yet the man opposite was beginning to become a hindrance. Julie knew something had to be said, 'Well, I hope for your sake they don't say a word, otherwise you are royally fucked big time and a nice privately educated person will prove popular inside with the lifers!'

<   >

Superintendent Philips and DCI Drake waited for Gary Jones in The George, Wanstead. Both parties desired a rendezvous where neither would be recognised.

Jones entered the public house and immediately saw the serving officers, both sitting with their pints of dark liquid. He strode over confidently, 'Same again chaps.'

Working with Gary Jones still concerned DCI Drake. He found it disconcerting that a member of the criminal fraternity was assisting them with their enquiries and quite possibly participated in some of the activities they were investigating, 'Double Diamond, Jones.'

Gary noted the hostility towards him. It had never changed since they had first been introduced. He understood Drake's reasons. The man was used to trust from those he was working alongside. It dated back to his armed forces career, 'Jack. Same again?'

'Cheers. I'll have the same as Drakey.' Jack Philips watched Gary Jones until he was out of earshot and spoke to his sidekick without moving his head. 'Drakey, I know you don't like him. That's pretty obvious, but he does help us with some tricky situations. Sometimes, and I mean rarely, you need to use people like him.'

DCI Drake mulled over the information. He understood it was useful advice, yet his insides would not allow him to settle. His instinct told him something was amiss with Jones. They were not seeing the full picture. The man was so allusive. He was a phantom, 'Gov, I know you're right, but there's something we're missing with him. I can't put my finger on it, but he's not who you think he is.'

Jack Philips knew he was correct, and also realised one day they would have to arrest him for something, 'Fair point Drakey, but let's enjoy a few pints and try to get him involved with this drug problem.'

Three pints of bitter were placed unceremoniously on the table, each leaving a little pool being absorbed into the yellow DD beer mats. Gary Jones immediately sat on the vacant chair before swallowing half-a-pint of his liquid.

'Blimey Jones, you thirsty? That was like a whale.'

Jones eyed both men, smiling, 'Thirsty work standing at the bar. Anyway, less of my drinking habits. What are you two after?'

This was one thing that Philips liked about Jones. He got straight to the point, 'Drugs.'

Jones looked at Philips, making light of the situation, knowing what was coming, 'What, you want some? Not my thing. Look elsewhere.' He knew it would irritate Drake, who looked suitably unimpressed. His eyes darted towards Jones. The gallows humours not appreciated.

'Don't take the piss, Jones. You know what I mean. We have a problem with people dying having taken a drug that's been doctored. Any ideas?

DCI Drake studied Jones and noted for the first time his weak spot. When uncomfortable he would gently stroke one of his cufflinks. He could not believe he had missed it.

Jones placed his drink on the table and positioned his right hand on the opposing left wrist, caressing the white fabric of his shirt before twiddling with the gold cufflink. 'Drugs. How bad is it?'

Drake now had the evidence required. Jones was playing them. Somehow, he was involved. How deep was anyone's guess, but he was certainly a player in the game. He suddenly felt a deep-rooted ball of quiet anger in his inner region. He knew he had to say something, 'Jones, you know something. If you want a two-way street, then it's about time you stopped fucking with us. You know something. I know you know.'

Jack Philips had witnessed the two gentlemen squaring off before. Yet, he had never seen Drake so brazen. He decided to sit back and allow the sparring session to commence.

Jones had an angry look. He had become stern, and his temple was pulsating. Quietly, yet aggressively he replied, 'Fuck off action man. You know fuck all, which is why you need me.'

Drake knew he had struck a sore point. Jones was rattled, 'You're a cunt, Jones. Let's not fuck about. It's what you are. You say one thing but mean another. You don't want to help us. You want to help yourself. You're in the shit somehow. I've no idea how deep, but you're in the shit. If you want our help, we'll help, but lie once and I'll skin you alive like a fucking pig.'

Philips was shocked by his cohort's ferocity. He had never heard him speak like that; his SAS background had finally shown through. He had waited like a patient animal stalking its prey, before striking.

'Speak to me in that manner again and I'll finish you, Drake. Never, ever threaten me.' The growl was obvious to all those around the table.

Jack Philips thought it resembled Hagler v Hearns, but who was who was anyone's guess, 'Gents, calm down. This will get us no-where. Drake is correct, Jones. If you're not levelling with us, then you are on your own. Is there anything you need to tell us?'

Jones respected Drake as he had arsehole, but he did not like him, whereas he thought Philips a solid person, who he liked. He mulled the situation over, swiftly calculating the odds. He decided to come clean… totally.

Having finished his story, leaving nothing out, Jones sat back and watched the two men digest the situation he had just involved them in.

Drake noted the cufflinks had been untouched during the session, 'Jones, you're telling the truth. For once, you have been straight-up with us.'

Jones looked at the DCI and smiled, 'Action Man, this could be a dirty case and one where we may need to work together.'

Philips was pleased the exploding situation had been defused, 'Ok lovebirds, another?' He stood pointing at the empty glasses.

Drake decided to tackle Jones alone without his superior officer, 'Jones, you're a wrong 'un. I know it, feel it, but he believes in you. Don't fuck it up, as this is his last job. He's calling it a day. Look after him, and I'll look after you, sort of.' Drake placed his hand out for Jones to accept.

Gary Jones was reeling from the fact his nemesis, and occasional friend was retiring to a life in Upminster with Catherine. He reciprocated the hand and shook it honestly and firmly, 'Action Man, that seems a fair deal to all. Let the man leave with his head held high to a new life, and we'll continue the cops and robbers' game, later.'

Both parties laughed. Jack Philips returned with three pints, and bags of peanuts and Golden Wonder crisps. He looked at the two men wondering what he had missed. They had gone from two parties at war, to allies. 'Right, back to business. Jimmy Jackson. Never heard of him. What do you know about him, Jones?'

'Lively lad. Employs youngsters to deliver his gear. The runners are paid well, or hooked on drugs. It's a military operation. If anyone has him over, the consequences are huge for that person. Comes out of Newham, but moves addresses. That is about it.'

<  >

The fresh-faced new recruit approached Jimmy Jackson, 'Jimmy, I got some news you may want to hear.'

Jimmy pretended to be uninterested, but internally he was like an electric current, 'Oh yeah, what's that newbie?' The young lad began to stutter with nerves. This pleased Jimmy, it showed they were intimidated by him.

'Well, Jim-Jim-Jimmy. There is a man in hospital who took drugs and he is not well. I think his name is Conor. He nearly died.'

Jimmy Jackson was now alert. He knew this could spell problems, and he also realised he was lucky to be the receiver of this news, 'How'd you get the news newbie.'

'I was on the fifteen bus and heard two women talking. Think they were nurses. That's about it Jimmy. Is it ok?'

Jimmy stood up and walked towards the thirteen-year-old boy who flinched and took a step back, 'Calm down newbie, there you go, take twenty pounds and get yourself something for the info.' Good lad.'

Jimmy stood calculating the information. He was still sore from the kicking he had received from the middle-aged man. Whoever he was must have form, and if not, must be known. Secondly, Conor in hospital. That meant a visit to Newham General Hospital.

<   >

'Hello Conor. How are you? Brought you some grapes.'

Conor knew Jimmy Jackson was not here for a friendly visit. He wanted something and this worried him. He noted a bump above Jackson's left eye. It looked like an egg. When he pulled a seat up, he did so carefully, 'You all right Jimmy? You're walking a bit slow, not brisk like you usually do.'

'Yeah. I need to speak to you about that.'

Conor understood this was not a friendly visit. Jimmy's reasons were fact finding. He obviously wanted something and this something had to do with the shoeing he had received, Conor also realised, Uncle Gary had been busy, remarkably busy.

Gary Jones decided to visit Conor and give him update.

As Jones wandered around, he considered the hospital and its purity towards the patient, their humanity and what any hospital endeavoured to uphold. There was a clinical openness, yet nothing sparkled. The fading smell of disinfectant had crept into the walls throughout the years. People were being wheeled about on trolleys or wheelchairs like it was a narrow motorway.

As he slowly walked along the corridors of the hospital, he caught glimpse of a man in white tracksuit. The individual had a languid look about him. It was Jimmy Jackson. The icy cold exterior that protected the lava flowing beneath began to thaw. His mind began to formulate a plan, yet he kept returning to the same place. Stay out of sight, but still be aware. He did not want Jackson realising he was related to Conor. One thing he did know. Jackson's time on this earth was ending.

He sat quietly, unfolding his *Daily Mirror*. Turning to the back pages he noted Arsenal Football Club had made a young player their new captain. He fleetingly thought of Malcolm Mason, and Shaftsbury. Times had changed, but was football ready to accept another gay player? He turned to page 3, and admired a young lady named Kathy Lloyd. A beautiful little thing. He wondered what she was like in real life. Physically, she was perfect. Unlike this situation with Jimmy Jackson. This man was stupid, an absolute prick. He needed to be educated in the art of respect.

Jones sat alone, waiting for Jackson to leave. Finally, he watched the man bowl out of the hospital. He walked directly passed Gary and did not note him. He was so wrapped up in his own world. He was a walking dead man.

Jones entered the ward where Conor was stationed. Eight beds, on each side, all full. The ward was a unit in an institution. An area where illness or injury needed to be fixed in the world's never-ending assembly line. It was a place to recuperate and not a bed. Bed means warmth, comfort, safety and privacy. Yet with Jimmy Jackson visiting you, it was not that.

Conor had seen his family member approaching. Today was a difficult day for visitors. He lay still, wishing this day would end. He had already been threatened by East London's biggest thug, yet now Gary was approaching. Which was worse, he had no idea.

'Morning Conor. I see you've been left provisions.' Gary nodded in the direction of the grapes, which had been half eaten.

'You saw him leave didn't you Gal'? He was here fifteen minutes and he kept on babbling on about a man who beat him up. Know anything about that?'

Jones was wrestling with his conscience. Should he be up front with the man lying in bed. Conor looked weak. He was not like him; he now understood the complexities of life. He also knew he had to remove Jimmy Jackson, otherwise Conor would receive continuous visits until he had no fight left in him, 'Listen son, I am sorting it. You made me a promise, and one I expect you to keep, forever. Are you, all right? Does that man intimidate you? If so, don't. He is nothing.'

Conor's mind was buzzing like a hive. No-one nice had visited him. The only people to arrive had threatened him indirectly. One out of love and the other out of fear, although the family member worried him more. He slowly lifted his head towards Gary, 'I'll be all right. Just ensure Jimmy doesn't bother me.' Regarding the promise. Don't worry. I'm on the straight and narrow from now.'

Gary looked at the man and knew no bullshit was coming from his mouth. Conor had got mixed up in a game that had turned dangerous for all those participating, specifically Jimmy fucking Jackson. A man who fed on the weakness of others. Gary knew a man's weakness was his strength, just as every curse was a blessing. Yet he knew Jackson's weakness was money and over-confidence, and these were the areas to exploit.

# Chapter 6

'Perkins, remember you work for us. You may be a member of the British government, in a secretive manner, but we aid the lifestyle you so enjoy. So, start spilling the beans. Your information has become, how can I say, shit lately.'

Perkins sat in the luxurious Howard and Sons Gainsborough carver armchair. He had been summoned to the meeting by the Grimes family. They had made their fortune through money laundering, security and drug culture. He was surrounded by art and antiques valued at seven-hundred and fifty thousand pounds, and each member employed by the household was immaculately turned out in designer black suits. They resembled a group of pallbearers.

Perkins, although seriously educated and devious, due to his vocation, felt a little intimidated by the Grimes family. To the man on the street, they were faceless, yet to those who knew them they were ruthless, totally.

The family had made enquiries about Perkins when he had been involved in ending one of their lucrative enterprises in Amsterdam. He had been seen by members of Hollands underworld operatives *Penose* meeting with officials from their countries General Intelligence and Security Service. Having made discrete enquiries, they had discovered the man was shrewd, sly and professional. Yet hid a dark secret. Perkins enjoyed visiting the casino, with a penchant for playing blackjack.

Perkins frequented one specific casino situated in the West End. They offered good credit, and it was something he had taken advantage of many times. His credit limit had been lifted to one-hundred thousand pounds and he had been rewarded by the club many times with gifts offered. These usually included scantily clad young ladies who were broad minded. Unbeknown to Perkins, his favoured casino was owned by the Grimes family who had slowly, but surely, been feeding his habit. The family knew he would hit a losing streak and would dangle a large financial carrot, which he would not refuse. Eventually, Perkins struck that incredible losing streak, which resulted in the club allowing him a limit increase to two-hundred and fifty thousand pounds.

Sitting in the chair, Perkins assessed his situation. How foolish he had been. Getting caught was bad enough, but being a lap dog for London's biggest, and most dangerous crime family unforgivable. He thought about the initial meeting, and how they had hooked him like a fish.

He had been sat down in a dark boardroom, facing three men, all dressed in black suits, white-shirts, and red ties. The ties gave the impression their tongues were hanging out like expectant dogs. No-one uttered a word. The head of the family, Joseph Grimes, stood and placed a VHS video in the player, which showed Perkins having sex with two women. No problem. The problem arose when he was informed both were fourteen-years of age.

Both Grimes brothers bore their eyes into him. Before Joseph Grimes followed it with, 'Remember, you owe two-hundred and fifty thousand pounds.'

Perkins remembered the feeling. Not only had he been caught having under-age sex. He was also in a depth of debt. He had a feeling there would be a quid pro quo conversation about to take place, and he had been correct.

Perkins was brought back to the moment.

'Perkins, you all right? You looked miles away.' Joseph Grimes stood up from the chair, and his eyes never left Perkins, 'Ok, first things first, your debt now stands at one-hundred thousand pounds, well done. Now, do you want to lose the remaining debt, and receive the only copy of the possible award-winning VHS tape?' Grimes looked at Perkins, who although professional, looked a little defeated.

'What do I have to do, and do I have your word that is the only copy of the tape?'

'Regarding the tape. Yes, it is the only copy, and one I'll be disappointed to lose.' Grimes could see the relief falling from Perkins. He asked about it all the time. Grimes, although a criminal, played by the rules, and a gentlemen's agreement was sacrosanct, 'Perkins, we want a lady called Julie Brown brought to heel. She is a ghost. All we know is she's from London or Essex, sells plenty of drugs, and is becoming a pain in the rear end. You tell us where she lives, and we'll do the rest.'

Perkins understood. 'Do the rest,' meant end her life and feed the remains to the award-winning pigs the family kept, 'So, this is my last job for you?'

'It is. Your account will then be zero pounds, and you will be the owner of an award-winning VHS film.' His mouth opened showing perfectly white straight teeth and a deep chuckle emanated from the depths of his insides, 'Should you ever wish to star in a film, allow us first refusal. Your cock certainly works, specifically with female spring chickens.' Grimes let out a deep throaty laugh, 'When that young girl sat on your face and the other rode your cock you resembled a horse with two jockeys.' Again, Grimes stifled a guffaw.

Although Perkins felt relief knowing his problem was ending, he still felt sickened knowing he had been played, and only employment by those he fought to bring down had aided his spiralling situation. Julie Brown had to be found.

<  >

Van der Leer had been the opening Perkins required. Calling in favours from people he had networked with throughout his service had allowed him to locate the dutchman. Breaking into his apartment had been easy, gaining trust from Van der Leer had been even easier. Yet Julie Brown was a cunning fox. She played hide-and-seek with those who collaborated with her, meaning no-one got to know her or her habits. She could prove to be a tricky customer to locate and bring down. Foxes were greedy, curious and wild creatures, yet man always defeated them, and Perkins understood he would have to lay a trap for this lady of invisibility. Locating her was the initial problem, and a problem he could do without. How could a person remain unknown by everyone? Someone, must know her, yet this vixen had remained invisible.

Julie Brown took the invisibility cloak to a professional level. She participated in day-to-day life as an observer without anyone saying a thing to her or knowing who she was. She was obviously an outsider and that was an advantage. She was seen, yet unseen by everyone during their hectic lives. Clever, jolly clever.

< >

Carefully, Julie approached the red telephone box. She was constantly concerned someone would be watching her. Once inside, she applied her gloves and cleaned the receiver ensuring no marks were left from her body and guaranteeing the phone was clean. She dialled the number, waiting for the reply.

'What?' An angry, abrupt, and unwelcoming reply came from the other end.

'Jimmy, you need to relax. You'll give yourself an ulcer.'

Jimmy Jackson listened to the self-righteous bollocks being preached to him. The fucking skank had aided him in receiving a visit from the old bill, and a severe kicking from an old fella. Who did Julie Brown think she was? He was volcanic. The inner-fire could take no more, 'Relax, you fucking whore cunt. Fucking relax. I'll fucking relax you. Once I fucking kill you and fuck your dead body.'

Julie held the receiver considering the barrage of abuse she had just received, 'Could you not be a little more-polite Jimmy, and tell me what has happened.'

'The filf has been round, and I've been done over by some old guy who knocked three of me teef out, and broke me wrist. Fucking man was mad. He didn't say a word. He just kept whacking me. And at the end he fucked orf.'

Julie considered the news and assumed Jimmy had tucked someone up for a few quid, knowing the nature of the beast. It would have to be someone mad enough to take on and beat Jackson. He was one fucking hard man. Julie decided to tackle Jimmy head-on. She needed to know why he thought it was her that had turned him over, 'Jimmy, unless you calm down, I won't speak to you and both of us will get nowhere with the situation. Now, tell me exactly what the police and the old man said.'

Jimmy listened, knowing he was going to rip her apart like a fucking rag-doll, 'That gear you supplied me is shit.' Spittle spewed from his mouth like angry droplets of lava, 'Two people are in hospital because of it. I don't know what you put in it, but it's bringing everyone down. There's a proper shake down happening and once it's over I'll find you and shake your bones until they rattle like a dead snake's final breath.'

Julie listened intently. Jimmy was erupting, near explosion. She also knew he would eat her alive. There was only thing she could do... find Van der Leer, and swiftly, 'Ok Jimmy, message received. Give me a few days to find out what has happened, then I'll pass on any information I have. Remember one thing, I've never fucked anyone over, and the people who did - got burned alive, in their own crypt.'

Jimmy listened. The ending intrigued him. What did she mean by burned alive in a crypt? He realised she had passed him information inadvertently. It was the first mistake he had known her make, 'You got seven days, girl.'

The phone went dead. Julie was still holding the receiver. For the first time in her life, she felt nervous energy pumping through her body. It was a mixture of excitement and worry. A heady brew for revenge.

<   >

Jack Philips and DCI Drake strode up to the home, but six paces away from the shiny, black Georgian double doors both officers became aware of a presence. Immediately, three large aggressive men made themselves known.

'Go away, no-one is in.'

Jack Philips spun around and stared at the head goon, 'Excellent, it speaks. Tell Grimesy, Jack Philips is here, and if I'm not admitted in ten seconds I'll return with an army of officers.'

The security guard stared deep into Jack Philips soul, before turning and striding towards the entrance. At the last moment he looked back at DCI Drake.

Jack Philips noted it. The other security personnel had missed it. It was like two warriors staring off.

Both officers were led into the inner sanctum of the Grimes empire. Joseph, head of the family was present, as was brother Luke. The younger brother asked the officers if they would like a drink and pointed to a place to sit,

'How can we help you two crime fighting officers, today?'

Drake was studying the younger brother. Physically, he was not as strong as his brother Joseph, yet had a bounce to him which was almost dainty. He assumed he had studied martial arts, due to slim muscular stance that shone through occasionally. He was a little flamboyant, possibly gay. He also noted a video on the Thomas Hope mahogany desk. On the label it read, 'Perkins.'

Joseph Grimes decided to enter conversational arena, 'What do you two want? We've done nothing wrong.' His gleaming smile lighting up the room.

Drake entered the forum first, 'There has been an influx of drugs. These drugs are really bad. Making people ill, as in admitted to hospital ill. Know anything?'

Grimes immediately liked DCI Drake. He was not a pussy, got down to things, and did not waste time, 'To answer your question. No, although I am aware of bad gear going about. Word gets about when things are hot. And when people end in hospital, rats scurry from their lair looking for the supplier. Know what I mean chaps. No offence.'

Drake could see Luke Grimes in the reflection of the mirror looking uneasy. He immediately spun around, making Jack Philips startle, 'You're quiet. Cat got your tongue. You a nervous person? You haven't stopped rubbing your hands together. Something you want to share with us. You're the weak one, aren't you? The one this lot worry about.'

The immediacy made Luke Grimes jump like a scolded cat. His vocals unravelled and his answer wobbled, 'No, course I don't.' The policeman's eyes were drilling into him making him feel uncomfortable.

Joseph Grimes looked at his younger effeminate brother knowing he was up to no good and it could bring them all down, 'Gentlemen, gentlemen, come now. I am happy to help you. I don't want anything going tits up on this manor. I love Chigwell. It's my home and you are my guests. Look, we have nothing to do with this. I swear on my mother's heart.'

Jack Philips knew Joseph Grimes was being up front. He was an old-style villain, like Gary Jones, their word was their bond, and they all loved their mums. What was it with villains and their mums?

Both officers stood and left the meeting.

Upon entering their car Drake turned to his superior officer, 'Luke, he's the weak one. He's up to something and I'm not sure Joseph knows what it is.'

Philips started the car and drove for thirty seconds down Chigwell High Road before replying, 'Think you're right. Joseph Grimes had a quizzical look about him. You did make me laugh when you verbally assaulted Luke, he jumped like he'd been plugged in.'

< >

Drake entered The In-and-Out Military bar in Piccadilly. It was pie night, and he attended this occasion monthly. It had become a routine pleasure he looked forward to. Upon entering the opulent surroundings, he made his way to the well-stocked bar ordering a vodka and tonic. The surroundings still amazed him. Everything stood to attention like a well-ordered platoon. He immediately became aware of a presence standing to his right.

Drake immediately knew the entity. He had been stationed at the front of the Grimes home. He had all the hallmarks of military. He was smart, up-right and proud. This also meant he was loyal and honest. Drake considered how a man from the military gained employment with London's largest crime syndicate?'

He spoke in a gruff northern accent, picked up his drink, and strode to a table situated in the far corner.

Perkins, entered the club and parked himself at the bar, acknowledging the Grimes employee with a dutiful nod. The bartender recognised him and immediately made polite conversation.

'Evening sir, how's protection of our nation today? Located any security risks?'

Perkins was comfortable with the conversation, 'Nothing happening, Barlow. All's quiet in Century House.'

'Excellent news, sir. Hopefully, it stays that way.'

Perkins about turned and made his way towards the employee of the Grimes family.

Drake noted the entire conversation. This was becoming another puzzle. The pieces were not where they should be. Why would an M.I.5 officer be drinking with an employee of the Grimes family? Curiosity bested Drake and he asked the bartender who the man was.

It was custom not to reveal anyone's identity, yet money always jogged a person's memory. Drake surreptitiously slid a ten-pound note under the parachute regiment coaster, which was swiftly collected by the bartender.

The bartender polished the bar, and magically removed the financial gift. His eyes darted about like a hungry falcon, ensuring no-one was watching or listening.

When confident there were no prying eyes he quietly whispered, 'Perkins, M.I.5. The other was in the SBS.' He then turned and strode towards the other end of the bar.

# Chapter 7

DCI Drake entered the station and surveyed it. It was built back in God-knows-when, although it was a time when buildings were erected properly, although asbestos was prevalent somewhere. The walls were as thick as a medieval castle, and the windows as menacing. They looked like giant tired eyes surveying those approaching. Entering the office, he approached the area which Jack Philips liked to command from. His superior had been granted an office, yet rarely used it. Jack Philips thought he was a man of the people. 'Gov, all right to talk?'

Immediately, DCI Drake was given the attention he desired, 'Park a chair up. What have you got for me?' Jack Philips was wily, and knew when his DCI wished to speak to him in confidence, he would always approach like a sly fox.

'Gov, strange thing happened last night. The security guard based outside the Grimes family home dined with a member of the security services, named Perkins. They were obviously friends, yet it was a strange situation. Both obviously served time in the military.'

Philips did not wish to pry which establishment it was, but curiosity would eat away at him if he did not enquire, 'Where was this Drakey? One of your military haunts.'

Drake smiled, he knew when his superior officer was keen to know information as he would indirectly ask, without actually asking the question, The In and Out, gov. It's a military place, genuinely nice. Popped in there last night to have one of the club pies of the week, always liked them. It's a magnificent place. Built in 1679 for the Earl of Kent. The club houses an impressive range of grand rooms that emit history, beautiful paintings, sparkling chandeliers, sweeping staircases, and spectacular fireplaces. It's a place to think.'

Philips looked at his number two and laughed, 'Blimey Drakey, you on commission?'

Drake smiled. He knew his superior would not understand unless he was able to view the opulence, 'Anyway, gov, what do you think? It's certainly an odd turn of events. Why would those two be meeting unless they had an agenda?

'Perkins, Perkins. I know that name from somewhere.' Jack Philips was allowing his fingers to dance to an unheard tune. Deep thinking mode was taking place. 'I know. He approached me a few years back about joining the secretive world of MI5. He was a sort of enquiries man. Tried to see if you wanted to aid your country in the fight against the ruskies. Smart man, full head of hair.'

'He has no hair now, gov, but he's still dapper looking. During the night I woke because I knew the name Perkins from somewhere and it came to me. There was a video cassette on the desk of the Grimes family. The label read 'Perkins.'

Jack's head shot up, 'Yes, you are correct. I remember it. So, the Grimes family employs Perkins?'

'Could be, gov. We need to pull him for an unofficial chat, and I feel an army briefing coming to mind. Somewhere quiet. I'll sort it, and do it.'

Jack looked at his colleague, friend, and knew he still had some craziness in him from his time in the forces. Occasionally, the inner demons surfaced and they were dangerous, extremely dangerous. Specifically, for the receiver. The only time he had fully seen him lose control was with Harry Huge, the fallen pop-star, 'We'll do this by the book, Drakey. It's the correct way, and you have a long future ahead of you, son. But what about the bloke he was dining with? I remember the goon from outside the Grimes house. Big fella, very upright. Any chance you may be able to make discreet enquiries about him from your club?'

The conversation was interrupted by a loud ring from the telephone.

'Jack Philips, speaking.'

There was a slight pause, before a well-spoken male began to speak. 'Philips, you may, or may not remember me, but my name is Perkins.'

Jack looked swiftly at Drakey, silently mouthing, 'Perkins, line 2'.

'Perkins you say. Don't think I'm being rude, but which department do you work for?' Jack was hoping the delay would allow him thinking time, and antagonise the caller.

Perkins felt a little insulted. He hoped Jack Philips would remember him from their previous meetings. Jack Philips was exactly what the security services required. He was honest, dedicated and loved his country. Yet sadly, the man loved crime fighting and Dagenham more. He tried a different angle, 'Come come, Philips. You remember. Perkins. I tried to recruit you for a position within Her Majesty's security service.'

Jack smiled. Downplaying Perkins affected his ego. He was man who enjoyed being recognised, not in an over-the-top manner, yet he liked people acknowledging, remembering and using him. How ironic, he was now being used by the Grimes family.

'Sorry Perkins, please forgive me. I do recall you, although it was some time ago.'

There was a chortle from the end of the line, 'You could say that, Philips. Anyway, I'm not calling to offer you a position. Piece of advice really.'

Immediately, Philips internal antennae kicked into life, 'Advice? How can you aid us, Perkins?'

Perkins sat in his office feeling a sense of triumph. He always understood when he had hooked a fish and this time it was a big fish. He remembered Jack Philips; he was sharp, very sharp. He also knew he would not be hooked that easily unless some honesty was thrown into the conversation, 'The Grimes family participate in the drug trade,' which he already knew Philips realised. The news that followed would help him, 'A lady by the name of Julie Brown is a significant accomplice of theirs. A major person, shall we say.'

'Julie Brown, never heard of her. You're selling us a load of rubbish, Perkins. We already know about drugs, and regarding Julie Brown, she's a minnow. Never heard of her, she's of no relevance.'

'Sorry, I forgot some information. Jimmy Jackson is linked with Julie Brown.'

Jackpot. The sound of nothing told him everything. He had given them something, 'I have your attention now, Philips. Do I not?'

Jack sat in his chair. He looked at Drakey, who moved his finger around informing his superior to keep Perkins talking, 'We know of Jackson, but again, small fry compared to the Grimes family. To be honest Perkins, your information is bland. Don't think I'm being a bit off.'

Perkins had a feeling of exasperation. Did this man know everything? He made one final gambit, 'Julie Brown has no telephone, and uses the telephone boxes to run her empire, she is an enigma. She is also a main player in the recent spate of hospital death and injuries involving drugs.' He heard a sudden intake of breath. Total jackpot. Home run.

'Ok Perkins, you now have my ear.'

Perkins relaxed into his padded chair. He could feel his muscles unwind. They mirrored his anxiety. He let out a slow controlled breath and attempted to loosen his body movements. Since childhood he had been told nerves were good, they kept a man sane and protected his values. His nerves, although steel-like, had recently corroded slightly.

< >

Jimmy Jackson was not an early riser. Locally, it was known not to disturb him until mid-day, at least. He was awoken by the bell ringing. He turned and his digital clock read 07.00. Immediately, he was fuming. Even the milkman did not knock before 11am. He rubbed his eyes and slowly walked downstairs, trying to become alert.

Reaching the door, he opened it.

Instantly, the door was smashed wide open with incredible force knocking Jackson to the floor. An immediate kick to his testicles forced him to scream out. He tried to look, yet tears were cascading from his eyes.

'You were told. So, you don't listen. And for not listening, you are now going to die. You went to one of my family and threatened him.'

Jimmy slowly looked up, and raspingly cried, 'You're related to Conor, the no-good cunt.'

These were the last words Jackson said on earth. His last vision was sunlight bouncing from a glint of metal. The axe fell upon his head with ferocious speed, splitting it in two, like a coconut. The sound resembled a sharpened blade slicing through a piece of wet wood.

Gary Jones looked upon the body. There were blood splatters on his trousers and shoes. He went to the door and opened his holdall, removing another set of clothes, trousers, shoes, shirt and socks. He knew he had until mid-day to dispose of the clothing. The fire grate had not been used for some time, now was the time to use it. The clothes were deposited, fire lighter fuel added and the match flicked. Straightaway, the flames grew in ferocity, hungrily attacking the clothing. The fire assaulted the clothes savagely, fifty minutes later the grate was full of ashes.

Jones stood and admired his handy man work. Jimmy Jackson had the look of a jester's smile with his head in two pieces. Beautifully horrific.

<  >

Word swiftly spread concerning Jimmy Jackson's demise. Exact details concerning the death were kept secret, although rumour reached fever pitch concerning his downfall and theories were put forward by all who wished to be heard, yet no-one had witnessed the murder.

Jack Philips and DCI Drake attended the scene. Both were shocked by the sheer strength the murderer had used to chop a man's skull in half like an apple.

Philips turned towards his colleague and whispered, 'I have a horrible feeling about the person who did this.'

Drake replied quietly, 'I agree. Our friend in Dagenham could be involved. It has his M.O. Justice with a lack of feeling.'

Philips stood looking at the congealing blood. He hoped it was not Jones, but an inert feeling was jingling inside and it was something he always went by, 'Drakey, fancy a pint? There's a pub down the road, Ordnance Arms. Just me and you.'

Drake loved working with this man. Problems were discussed away from the office in a local pub. Today's venue in Barking Road. Drake being a boxing fan wanted to visit the Royal Oak, famous for its stable of fighters trained by Terry Lawless. He had attended the Kaylor v Christie fight at Wembley, which had been explosive, and being an enthusiast of the art, he hoped to see one of the fighters, 'Gov, can we go to the Royal Oak?'

Philips smiled, 'No problem, Drakey. Course we can.' He understood the reasoning behind the request.

Both offices strode up the road channelling their thoughts, studying the local landscape. Shops included Woolworths, Murkoff and John Bennetts and the beautiful red brick library which encased a sweeping staircase and was a beacon amongst the dour grey London landscape.

Both officers stomped towards the bar, ordering two pints of Courage Bitter before nesting down away from the bar by the window.

Jack Philips felt his arm being grabbed.

'Did you see who that was? Charlie Magri. He's a warrior. Flyweight. He's one of the British boxers who fills Wembley.'

Jack Philips smiled. His DCI was obviously a man who enjoyed touching the coat tails of the famous. He did not understand that a boxer's fame was built on sand, and they were only one defeat away from poverty, yet they were civil to those outside their sport, and to those inside their chosen arena.

'Gov, someone once said to me, 'You can't learn how to take a hit if you don't get in the ring. Boxers are like army personnel. Bombs are coming your way, yet it's how you manoeuvre away from them.'

Jack placed his glass on the table, and considered the words. 'Drakey, that was almost Shakespearean, I'll remember that quote. Anyway, less of this boxing romance, back to work. What you said about Jones. It's made me feel uncomfortable. I always go by my gut feeling. These feelings are short term guests, but these feel like unwanted long-term guests.'

'Gov, it's Jones. I know it. He is bad, but only to bad people. He's becoming a bit of a superhero character. He's ridding us of shit bags, but in a violent manner and he shows no shame. He's a psycho. He's cold and uncaring. Anyone in his way gets offed. Psychopaths are unable to feel emotion and are selfish. They dehumanize their victims. Does that remind you of anyone?'

Jack Philips lifted the half-full glass to his lips. Consuming the rest of the dark malty liquid. Carefully, he placed the glass on the Skol lager beer mat, 'I know, but he's the sprat that catches the mackerel. And the mackerel is supplying the drugs.'

<　　　　　　　>

Gary Jones returned home and placed his new set of clothes worn into the washing machine. He understood minor mistakes could be a man's downfall. He then ventured upstairs and pulled the cord to the shower before hopping into the bath, hoping the warm water would wash away all his sins. Jones found it meditative and boosted his senses. Showers were his mood elevator. He would stand as the hot spray attacked his skin. This was his peace and thinking time. Alas, peace time was disturbed by an urgent rapping at the door.

Jones answered the door with his hair dripping and his dressing gown tightened around his still wet body, 'Hello chaps. Come in, stick the kettle on and I'll be with you.'

Philips stood looking at the man in front of him, although he was in his forties, he still looked good. Any woman would want a piece of him, 'No problem, Jones. We'll get a brew on the go.'

Gary Jones realised the two men always arrived at his home when they required, or had information. His sixth sense also told him to box carefully, today. His private moment was broken by the shrill of the kettle.

Jones arrived in the living room, noting Drake was sitting in the armchair that gave him a view of everyone walking past. It was also the place where Jones would reside. Drake had sat there out of devilment.

Jack Philips understood what Drake had done, but also realised it would not ruffle the feathers of Jones. He was too wise to be snared by a basic trick like that, 'There's your tea.' Philips pointed to the coffee table situated in the middle of the room. Philips did not want to play the waiting game, 'Jones, we found Jimmy Jackson today. His head was split in half like a fucking pumpkin. Totally in half.'

Gary Jones blew the top of the tea before taking a sip. The five seconds had given him time to think. He decided to go in with force, 'So what, man was a fucking cunt. It's a result, and whoever did it I will shake their hand with gratitude.'

Philips and Drake had expected a response from Jones, but neither expected this rant. It had wrong footed them both.

Drake decided to jump in, 'Jones, whoever did this is a psycho. I also think it's the same person who poured battery fluid into Michael Dawson's head a few years back.'

Gary Jones stood and walked towards the window. He turned and faced both officers, 'Dawson deserved what he got, and again, whoever did it, did the world a good thing. He was another cunt.'

Philips noted how Jones had used unpleasant profanity when describing both men, 'What interests me Jones, is that you knew both, particularly Dawson. Ok, I know that's in the past, but Jackson is very much the present, and you are the only person to cross both their paths, and… you did not like either.'

Jones stood reliving the moment he poured the fluid into Dawson's head. It had been grizzly, even for his stomach, but it had been beautiful as well. He then recalled the feeling of watching the axe slice Jackson's head in half. The axe had felt like an extension of his arm. What had interested him was Jackson's eyes. They appeared to still move for a couple of seconds, 'Gents, I have welcomed you into my home, yet you have entered and accused me of two barbaric murders. I thought we were working together?'

Both officers looked at the other.

Philips was first to respond, 'Ok Jones, we'll leave it there. We do need to find out about the drugs. All we have are the names Julie and Perkins, and the Grimes security man.

Upon leaving, Jack Philips thought he would try to activate Gary Jones interest, 'Jones, before we leave, you can help us… all.'

Jones curiosity was peeked, 'How's that?' He felt being inquisitive could be discouraged, yet when his curiosity tap was turned on to figuring out a puzzle, then he knew had to find entire solution.

'Perkins, M.I.5. We can't follow him or get to close, whereas you can. We need to know what he is involved with, and how he became involved with the Grimes family. You have a certain skillset for that job. Being a man of the people.'

Jones smiled at the last comment. He felt, no knew, that Jack Philips was indirectly warning him to tread carefully. He also felt it was a signal to say, 'We are watching you.'

Drake decided to enter the affray of conversation, 'Just follow the man, and see if you can glean what the slippery fucker is up to.'

Jones paced around the room, knowing both men were watching him. This was like being a spy. He wanted to smile. Lifting his mug, he took a deep satisfying swig of his sweet tea. The sugar making him grate his teeth. He lifted his head slowly, 'Yeah, I'll do it. In fact, I quite fancy doing it. I'll speak to him. I may be able to remove some information from him.'

Philips did not like the word remove being used. It had ominous connotations. He looked at Jones, 'No violence. This bloke is a big fish from the security empire that manages our nation, tread carefully. He is slippery, like a bag of eels.'

# Chapter 8

Van der Leer was in an explosive mood. Perkins had summoned him to London, and no-one spoke to him in that manner. Self-control was an expression his brain did not understand, and his lack of control was boiling up. He was struggling to cool it, and if it exploded the recipient would be scared mentally and physically for life.

Perkins was becoming a pain in the arse. Since breaking in to his home, he had become a tyrant. Now he was demanding Van der Leer travel to London, and what fucked him off mightily was he had no choice but to go.

He booked the tickets from Amsterdam Schiphol to Gatwick airport. The flight was due to take one hour fifteen minutes. Like all forms of air travel the plane was cool, yet comfortable and there was a breeze dancing amongst the legs of those seated on the orange seats. Van der Leer thought that sitting in the aeroplane resembled waiting in the cinema for the main attraction. The little trays of food became elevated in their interest.

The flight gave Van der Leer time to think. He realised he had to put Perkins straight and he could not keep ordering him about. If Perkins chose not to listen then the only remaining option was to remove him, permanently.

He departed Gatwick, jumping into one of the very traditional London black cabs. The curvaceous beetle-like shell gave them an iconic look, and the black leather seats offered affordable luxury. The drivers offered opinions, and facts gained from their many years of serving the streets of the capital.

The fifty-minute journey brought him to the centre of London, and Rules restaurant. He entered and was immediately greeted by the cheerful maître d' who asked if he had a reservation.

Van der Leer explained and pointed towards Perkins, who waved in an encouraging manner.

'Dear boy, thank you for arriving so promptly.'

Van der Leer felt his anger beginning to envelop his body, 'Do not, and I mean DO NOT call me boy again, otherwise I will ram that fucking knife in your eyeball.'

Perkins was a little shocked by the unexpected and expletive outburst. He also realised the condescending greeting had not been embraced by his guest, 'Please accept my apologies. I was only welcoming you, although I do believe your unwelcome eruption was a little over the top. Do you not think?'

Most people would be unnerved at the furious, yet quietly spoken threat offered by Van der Leer, yet Perkins had not flinched. This confused Van der Leer. Did the man have no nerves? He was confused because he needed to gain the upper-hand, yet Perkins had remained perfectly calm, and this mystified Van der Leer.

'Please sit, Van der Leer, people will think you have piles. I ordered you a Black Velvet. A devilishly fine concoction.'

Van der Leer knew he was being played like a chess board, and he was being out-manoeuvred comfortably. He obeyed the request and took a sip from the dark liquid served in a pewter jug. It did not look particularly appetizing, yet sweetness from the champagne worked beautifully with the velvet-like texture from the stout. He smiled, 'Perkins, you are a cunt, yet one who has introduced me to a fine drink.'

Perkins felt his inner being relax. His muscles expanded and he felt a mountain of anxiety remove itself from his body. It was like an invisible shield leaving his body, 'Van der Leer. Julie Brown. I need Julie Brown found and I need her found swiftly, as in super quick.'

Van der Leer lifted the pewter to his lips. The metallic taste added to the wonderful liquid that coated his palate. He now understood why Perkins needed him. The man was in the shit and someone was applying pressure. It would not be his government department. It had to be someone from a less desirable background… underworld. This also meant Perkins had done something wrong, really wrong. It had to be money or sex. It was not drugs; he was too pompous. He had money, which leant itself to sex. If it was sex, it was either gay or under age. He was not gay. Bingo! Someone was applying pressure because of underage sex. So, Perkins was a nonce. He liked the younger girls. A smile spread across his face. Van der Leer was not a gambler, but he suddenly felt like a game of chance could be welcome, 'Someone applying pressure. What is it, young girls?'

Perkins sudden jerking movement answered everything Van der Leer needed to know.

Beads of sweat began to form on Perkins's forehead. They were like miniature pools ready to run south.

'What are you talking about Leer?' The answer was said with a slight stutter, and the sign of someone a little agitated. Perkins also forgot to use the man's full surname and was annoyed with himself. He now knew Van der Leer had the edge over him.

&lt;         &gt;

Two tables along sat Gary Jones with Charles Johns, the ex-commissioner of the Metropolitan Police. Both gentlemen were ploughing through their Steak and Kidney pudding, a speciality of Rules.

Charles Johns placed his cutlery down and whispered, 'That's an unusual coupling, Gary. The man seated against the wall is employed by the security services, goes by the name Perkins, bit of a busy body. What is strange is the man who has just entered is a well-known dealer of drugs called Leer, Van der Leer. Why would they be meeting in this fine establishment? That was one to ponder. Interesting.'

Gary continued devouring his magnificent meal. It was his turn to pay this time, although he never did mind. He really enjoyed the company of the man he was dining alongside. Yet, when the names Perkins and Van der Leer were mentioned, his memory banks began to kick in. He heard the phrase 'young girls.' He noted that Perkins looked nervous, and the Leer man was delighting in the fact. He assumed the drugs man had been ordered to meet Perkins, and was expecting a shakedown, yet being a wily fox had found information about Perkins which had turned the tables in his favour. He decided to ignite the conversation with his guest, 'Don't let your pud' go cold, Charles. I'm sure their lover's quarrel will sort itself out.'

Charles looked at the man's plate. It was empty, like it had been washed. He began to attack his meal once more, but he had a nagging feeling about the unusual coupling. Although he had retired from the force, he still felt a yearning towards law and order.

During the meal, Charles Johns had listened intently to the conversation taking place. The meeting was like a tennis match, both operatives had tried to outfox their opponent, yet both made elementary errors. A basic error was showing emotion through their facial gestures. Both had made them, although Van der Leer had ignited his opponents. The look of surprise was obvious when he mentioned *young girls*.

Charles understood the man he was dining with had also listened to every word. Gary Jones was unique. He was fierce, respectful, honest, dishonest, intelligent and vengeful. He was intrigued why Jones would pretend to be unimpressed with the coupling, yet was incredibly interested in the meeting, more so than himself.

<   >

Perkins knew he would have to regain his composure, and swiftly. His hands had become a little clammy, and he felt like his insides were being twisted by an invisible force, 'Van der Leer, shall we start again?'

Van der Leer supressed laughter; game, set and match. The man facing him was crumbling, and quickly.

This meeting had gone cyclical, to his advantage, 'How old were they Perkins? 12,13?'

Perkins screwed his face and stared into the man's eyes giving him a piercing look, 'Fuck you Van der Leer. You need me, badly. You see the man two tables away. He's the ex-commissioner of Metropolitan Police. If I call him over you will be arrested tout-suite. And as regards to the other thing, you have no evidence.'

Van der Leer sat motionless. He had no idea whether the other man was the ex-commissioner, yet he did know he had no evidence to back up his strong theories, 'Ok, let's call it a score draw. What do you want?'

'Julie Brown, and I want Julie Brown dead.'

<  >

Hearing the name Julie Brown made Jones stop mid-flow. It was like slow motion. He had not heard that name for a while. She had been the one who had nearly ensnared him. There was a difference in age, which was why they had ended their affair. Yet here he was, listening to a conversation naming her as a person to be murdered. What had she got herself into?

Charles John had been talking when Jones had suddenly become vacant. What interested him was the two words, *Julie Brown*. Charles, although tact, also realised sometimes you needed to go head on. He whispered, 'Gary, what's the story? Who is Julie Brown? You obviously know her.'

Jones sat still for a couple of seconds, collecting his thoughts, 'I did. She was the one I nearly settled down with. She is about 10 years younger than me, which is why it did not go any further. Interestingly, I never really understood what she did for a living. Mind you, she felt the same about me. But for someone to want to kill her, that's another thing.'

Charles Johns knew Jones was fighting demons, having entertained the same problems himself. To learn that a person you had feelings for was in serious trouble was a bridge too far for Jones. He also knew if someone did harm this lady, then their life would be over shortly after. He initiated the conversation, 'Maybe the two of you were never meant to settle down. Too many secrets, so to speak. Your life would have taken a totally different path had you done so, similar to me.'

Jones listened with interest to the wise words offered by his dining companion. He knew he was correct, but the fact someone wished to end Julie's life was not right. Having considered the advice he replied honestly, 'Charles, you are right as usual. Yet, the fact someone wants to end her existence, and the bloke that wishes to do is sitting approximately six feet from me is agging me. Fuck knows what she's got involved with.'

Johns placed his cutlery against the rim of his plate. A delicate ching was heard. Staring squarely at Jones he mulled it over whether to be blunt. He decided he would. Leaning closer he whispered, 'Drugs, it has to be drugs she's got herself involved with, and you know it deep down. How the other man is involved is intriguing as it is odd? That is the interesting question. The Dutch chap I believe was a supplier. He was one of those that the police or Interpol could never quite snare. The dealers and middle men always get caught, yet the suppliers rarely do. I would suggest he is a supplier, and an incredibly careful one.'

< >

Van der Leer felt an icy cold presence trickle through his body. His mind was in overdrive. Did Perkins just say he wanted Julie Brown dead? Did he honestly believe he would give her up that easily? 'Perkins, are you losing control of your senses? What makes you think I'm going to do that?'

Perkins was again feeling the strain of this situation, 'I need Julie Brown, and I need her quickly. Someone wants to speak to her and when I mean they wish to speak to her, I mean they want her now!' The man could feel the anxiety in his chest beginning to takeover. His body was feeling brittle as if it might snap in to small pieces.

Van der Leer sat motionless. Perkins was crumbling, totally. He could not look him in the eye, his posture shifted constantly and his vocal tone had changed, confidence was ebbing away. Van der Leer could hear Perkins's speech in a unique way, not for the spoken words, but for what they told him about the man's current emotions and perspective. He was shit scared.

< >

Julie Brown sat in her home. She had heard people were being rushed to hospital. The merchandise supplied by

Van der Leer was contaminated. She also guessed he had been cutting the drugs with cheap shit to double or treble the quantity. Her money was on rat poison or laundry detergent. She also understood she was in the shit big time. All the dealers she supplied would now have people looking for her. There would be a bounty placed on her head. Fear was natural and there to keep you alive. But this something she had never encountered. She was always in control. Now she would understand and learn her strength.

Being unsafe is a form of risk, and risk is needed for development. However, there are levels of risk, and that was the encounter Julie was ready for. Risk reward decisions were tough, but Julie considered it part of her empire and this empire was ready for a change of direction.

She sat on the wooden chair in her kitchen pondering her next move. It had to be a move that was correct. One thing she did know, Van der Leer was a dead man walking. He had tucked her up big time, and no-one ripped her off. Her reputation being ripped apart had really annoyed her. Reputation took an eternity to build, but a day to collapse. She would plan something beautifully bad for him.

Wallowing in self-pity got you nowhere. Mistakes had been made, so people needed fronting. Julie felt an aura of strength encapsulate her. Dealers would be first and Jimmy Jackson would be her first port of call.

Julie visited the local telephone box situated near Ongar station. Slowly, she dialled the number, the bell rang continuously, yet no-one answered. For the average person this would not be a problem, but Jimmy Jackson was not the average person, he lived for his communication device to the outside world, specifically, the drug one. Julie immediately became a little nervous, things were not in place like a jigsaw. The pieces were scattered. Everything was strewn haphazardly, drugs, Van der Leer, Jackson. There were too many variables, yet they had to be connected. Linking the pieces together would take action, and a devious mind so extreme that the recipients would be shocked by the swift response.

There was no other alternative other than to visit Jimmy Jackson. She ordered a mini-cab and waited for its arrival. Waiting made her nervous. Finally, the saloon arrived. The driver had received its destination, the Canning Town.

The journey took thirty minutes, and although the driver tried to make conversation with Julie Brown, he eventually gave up.

She looked out the window, surmising every different scenario. Eventually, the mini-cab pulled over on the corner twenty yards from the pub. She paid the five-pound fare, and strode towards the area known to many as Jackson manor.

Mona Street was like any other in the area. Julie thought they all blended in. She knew where Jimmy resided and became aware of a police presence in Jimmy's area. She slyly studied Jimmy's place and noted the yellow and black tape stuck across the door.

A group of boys were playing near-by. Casually, Julie walked towards them, 'Excuse me lads, what's the area like around here. I'm thinking of buying a place nearby.'

The tallest boy who was about 12 years of age eyed her suspiciously, 'You serious? This is bandit country. Bloke in that house got killed.'

Jackpot. Julie had the information she required. She had to compose herself and looked shocked, 'No, how awful, poor man. Hope it wasn't tragic?'

'Darling. Tragic. Jimmy had an axe shoved through his head. His head was split in half.'

Julie sat on the wall feigning surprise.

The oldest boy walked up to her and whispered gently, 'Listen love, you look real-good. Don't live around here. You won't last five minutes.'

'Thank you for your words of wisdom young man. You have saved me a lot of money. Please take this as a sign of my gratitude.' She passed a five-pound note to the boy.

'You don't have to do that miss.'

Julie liked the boy. He had integrity, 'I insist. In fact, there's another £5 for your friends.'

Julie removed herself from the wall and began to walk back to the Barking Road wondering who had ended Jimmy Jackson's existence on earth. They had done her an amazing favour without realising it. She stood hoping a black cab would avail itself to take her home.

# Chapter 9

Van der Leer returned home. His meeting with Perkins had resulted in a major win. He had learnt many things about the man and it had given him an edge. He sat in his favourite chair sipping a glass of jenever, although slightly neutral in taste, it had a faint aroma of juniper and malt wine which made Van der Leer feel relaxed.

Van der Leer was startled by a shrill from the telephone. Placing his drink on the table he lifted the receiver to his ear, 'Hello.'

Julie Brown was frothing at the mouth. Hearing Van der Leer's voice was like a trigger to her already dynamite temper, 'Van der Leer?'

Van der Leer already understood who was calling, 'Good evening, Julie.'

If Julie could get her hands down the receiver and strangle the man she would, 'Van der Leer, you are a dead man. You have tucked me up, big time. The gear you sold was cut with whatever shit you added. You have upset the wrong person you stupid ignorant Dutch cunt.'

The phone-call was immediately ended. Van der Leer was left holding the receiver. Calculations were swimming around his head. No-one had ever spoken to him in that manner. He had underestimated Julie Brown; she was a dangerous adversary. Extremely dangerous.

Van der Leer was considering the message from Julie Brown when he was once again startled by the telephone ringing. He was annoyed as his relaxing selfish evening had become an annoying working one, 'Yes!'

Van der Leer placed the phone back on its cradle. His floristry on The Hague coast had been torched. He had lost everything. Once again, his focus was broken by the telephone ringing, 'What?'

'Van der Leer. The Hague coastline is beautiful place, particularly when it's lit up. I'm still going to end your life.' The call disconnected.

Van der Leer sat in disbelief. Julie Brown had been the architect of the fire. He had been ready and aware that revenge may be swift and calculating, yet he had never expected war of this magnitude. He could feel fear rising in his body wanting to escape. It sat there angry.

Drug trafficking and floristry had been his life. Van der Leer had been involved in the illicit trade, cultivation, manufacture, distribution and sale of mind-altering substances. Floristry had given him a fine lifestyle, but not the one he craved, yet drugs had introduced him to the lifestyle of a high-roller.

He considered the life he had led, but now it had ended. This deal had cost him everything, it was to be his final payday. Anger was being taken over by a feeling of retribution. He began to shake; adrenaline was jumping around his body. He knew what he had to do, finish her. It would benefit both he and Perkins.

There was a straightforward way, the roots of Aconitum Napellus. 3-6mg would do it. Being a florist, he would be able to source it. The plant material would cause fatal cardiac poisoning. He would then turn her body into compost for the worms to feast upon.

Perkins would be the bait. The man was desperate to succeed. He was obviously being leant on by someone who had something over him. Sex was his guess, although he did not care. Crushing Julie Brown was all he cared about. He had returned home briefly, although he realised there was only one plan, returning to London, swiftly.

Van der Leer grabbed the receiver, which was now hot. Pressing the digits, he dialled Perkins. The call was answered with a well-spoken typical middle English inflection.

'Hello, Perkins here. How may I assist you?'

'Perkins, it is me. Van der Leer. Julie Brown. You want her. I'll give you her, but I want to finish her.'

Perkins smiled. Inwardly he felt jubilant. He had already been informed of a colossal fire on the Hague coastline. The owner of the area under fire was the man calling. Bingo, 'Van der Leer, we only met last night. Julie Brown. What is wrong?'

Van der Leer noted a sense of confidence in Perkins's voice. Did he know what had happened? He was in no mood to be antagonised with flippant chit-chat, 'Do you know what has happened?'

Perkins's mood was beginning to shine like the sun. The vibe emanating from his being was breaking free, 'Happened? Sorry, you are speaking in riddles, dear man.'

'That bitch burned my hanger. It contained all my flowers, and product.'

Perkins wanted to belly laugh aloud. Product. Why did the man say product? 'Julie Brown, are you sure?'

Van der Leer could feel anger bouncing around his body, 'Sure, am I sure? She telephoned and told me. That bitch is going to be terminated, and you and I are going to be the people who finish her.'

No more Grimes family ordering him about. He would have his life back. Perkins only worry was the video. He hoped Joseph Grimes was a man of his word and would pass the X-rated and career ending tape to him, as agreed, 'Van der Leer, I do believe we need to meet to discuss your problem.' He then replaced the receiver.

Van der Leer sat still, holding the telephone. Did Perkins say he wanted to discuss the problem? Discussion, was not what he wanted. Retribution was required. Tomorrow, he would return to London.

< >

Perkins felt a sense of jubilation. From feeling like a great boulder was heading towards him, he now felt it was a rock. The relief was immense. Van der Leer now had a reason to locate and remove Julie Brown.

Perkins was still digesting the information, but understood he needed to keep the Grimes family out of the loop. He had read documents about the family. They believed they were untouchable, yet the security services were well aware of their activities, all of them. They were known for their violent repercussions for those who went against them. This was the reason he needed to keep Van der Leer's involvement out of reach. If they realised someone else could aid their mission to locate Brown, then his involvement, and life, would prematurely end.

Van der Leers involvement had thrown up two problems. He was another part in the jigsaw, and secondly, one of them would not survive the adventure. The Julie Brown angle had thrown everything up in the air. She was a major part of the puzzle, yet she was also someone who was extremely guarded and considered secrecy part of her life. Moreover, she was ruthless, as Van der Leer had found out.

Sitting in his Chesterfield leather armchair, sipping his Jameson, he thought of Julie Brown. She must be known to someone, somewhere.

His mind then wandered to the previous evening. He was sure someone had been following him, yet when he took a small detour, he noted nothing. He had spent too long in the service and his mind was wandering. Yet, there was something. He could not place it, but there was something.

<  >

Gary Jones admired the area where Perkins lived. Princes Gate in Knightsbridge was a beautiful place. The solid red brick buildings spoke of age, class and opulence.

Locating Perkins had been easy, he had trailed the man after the previous evening's meal. Surprisingly, for an overweight gentleman, he moved gracefully and quickly, walking the two miles from Covent Garden to Knightsbridge without missing a skip in twenty-five minutes.

He learnt from his friend, the ex-commissioner of the Metropolitan Police - Charles Johns, that the man he was visiting was a well-established member of the security services. Yet, it was surprising how he had not realised he was being followed.

Jones considered his options and decided the best method was to present himself at the man's door. His mother had once said, 'Never make a decision so far away from sunset, yet so far from dawn.' Yet sometimes a man had to go head on.

Perkins took a sip from his glass, before being startled by a rapping sound at his door. He took a look at the grandfather clock, it read 10.17pm. He considered who would visit him during the evening, it could only be a fellow colleague. Standing, he slowly walked to the door. His moccasins leaving no sound on tiled floor. He slid the handle and opened the heavy weight deep oak door.

'Perkins. We need to talk. Julie Brown.'

Perkins studied the man. He was clean cut, dressed in a navy-blue formal suit, red tie with sparkling clean black shoes. His hands were hanging by his sides, meaning no weapon. He had a London accent, although not aggressive in tone. He opened the door, 'Please enter, Mr. Whoever you are. Looks like we may need to talk.' He strode into the flat with purpose. The man had confidence, and was used to opulent surroundings. He had experienced the softer sections of life.

Gary Jones admired the interior of the flat. It spoke of wealth, class and old money. Everything had its place, and in its place was everything. The flat was perfect, plain, relaxing, simple and inviting. If anything, James Bond had taste. The man had welcomed him gracefully, although he would be a sly dog.

'May I ask who you are and how you would like me to address you?'

'Jones, Gary. Shall we forget the pleasantries and get down to business.'

Perkins was a little surprised by the authoritarian and brisk manner in which Jones wished to get down to business He needed to break the man's rhythm and gain control, although, his opponent was formidable, that was obvious, 'Whisky?'

Gary wanted to laugh aloud. The man was confused and unsure what to do. He was trying to break-up his flow. Gary had him on the ropes already, so decided to press on with the friendly attack, 'No, thank you. Have one yourself. I'm more of a let's get down to business sort of man.'

Perkins strode to his decanter and refilled his glass. The Jameson refuelling him, the warming sensation travelling towards his inner core. He turned abruptly, deciding to lock-horns with his adversary, 'Gary, may I call you Gary?' He did not stop for a reply and decided to go head on, 'Julie Brown. A lady most of London's elitist underworld want, and someone from Amsterdam also. Have I gained your interest?'

Gary sat perfectly still, digesting the information. He had not heard Julie's name for a long time, yet he had heard it a number of times inside twenty-four hours. What was she involved in? 'You have my attention fully. Please proceed Mr. Perkins.'

'Julie Brown supplied drugs, which were contaminated, to a number of people. One of which was seriously unwell and related to a member of parliament. She also torched a man's hanger, although that may have been retribution. The man, Van der Leer, wants to end her life. To say he is annoyed is the understatement of the year.'

Gary sat their perplexed. Confusion was like a mist that needed clearing from a person's mind, and the mist was slowly dissipating, but not quick enough. Yet, he could not get his head around Julie Brown being involved in drugs, villains and arson. Where had she gone wrong? 'Perkins, we are talking about Julie Brown from Essex?'

Perkins did not show surprise, yet it was the first piece of information he had gained about Julie Brown. She came from Essex, 'It must be the same one Gary. May I ask you something personal?'

Gary knew what the man was going to ask, so decided to pre-empt the question, 'I knew her in a previous life. Many moons back. She was not involved in anything dodgy.'

Perkins decided his counterpart was telling the truth. The response was too swift, too heartfelt, 'You obviously still have a place in your heart for her, that is obvious to any man, but, but… she is involved with some difficult people who want her removed. As we are talking frank to each other. It is better we lay all our cards on the table. This is not the sort of way I play the game, yet I am in a tight situation myself.'

Gary's head shot up sharply, 'How much shit are you in? And if I find you're playing me I'll cut your balls off, mince them and feed them to you.'

Perkins swallowed deeply, hoping Gary Jones had not witnessed it. He now had the Grimes family, Van der Leer and Gary Jones involved in the hunt for Julie Brown game, yet he thought the man he was conversing with was the most dangerous. He was quiet, unruffled, sharp and icy cold, 'I am in a tricky situation. I would be telling an untruth if I said anything else. But you and I could, should you choose, sort this situation out, and I will be in your debt.'

Gary Jones sat rigid. Ideas and specifics were spinning around. To have a member of the security services in your debt could be useful beyond means. Along with the ex-commissioner, he would have some immensely powerful allies. A boy from Dagenham East, he began to smile.

'Are you feeling all right, Gary? You are smiling. Why?'

'Perkins, I am from Dagenham, born and bred. Yet, people from the establishment always seem to ask me for help. You couldn't make it up.'

Perkins chuckled, 'You are correct Gary. Very few people from your neck of the woods has allegiances like you do, although, that does speak highly of your integrity.'

'Less of the back-slapping, Perkins. I need to know everything and I mean everything. If we join forces, we can bring everything to its knees. So, you are aware. I work with Philips and Drake from the local nick. Two good solid blokes. They will help us. Their involvement is sacrosanct.

Perkins felt relief enveloping his body like a giant coat. Since meeting the Grimes family his life had imploded, yet now he felt change was on the way. He also felt the man sitting opposite, although rough around the edges, was up-front, honest and a man to get things done. He was also not a revealer of secrets, a silent assassin. He took a warming sip of his Jameson and began to unravel himself of his burden to the man he had known only twenty minutes.

Jones calculated all the information passed and decided the man was on the level and playing with a straight bat. Composing himself he spoke swiftly to Perkins, 'You are in the shit, although I feel you're keeping something from me and if I find it is key to the operation, I won't be best pleased, understand.'

Perkins licked his lips. The taste of whisky had gently coated them, 'Everyone has secrets. Anyone who has no secrets has no life. You can trust me.'

Jones stared into the man's eyes. They were wistful, soul less and tired, 'I never trust anyone. Whatever anyone tells me I half immediately, and half again. Then I feel the truth is honest. I believe fifty per-cent of what you have told me is bollocks, or is missing significant pieces of information. People tell the truth, but generally remove one or two pieces of information because they can be negative to their story.'

Perkins felt a little trapped like he was surrounded. He knew this man was different. His eyes were like those of a Great White shark. He also felt a little relieved. Hopefully, the Grimes problem could finally be removed.

# Chapter 10

Jones sat pondering the Julie Brown problem. Stirring his steaming mug of tea, he looked at it hoping the tea leaves at the bottom would solve the conundrum. She was public enemy number one and a target had been placed firmly on her head. Everyone wanted her: Perkins, Van der Leer, the Grimes family, and minor drug handlers. She was in deep shit and had upset everyone. Her whereabouts was unknown and the fact she used a public telephone box made the situation a little more complex, although Gary realised straightaway, she was renting a place to live, which was very shrewd on her behalf.

When they had been together, he had never understood what her vocation was, although she had thought the same as him. The time they spent together had been good. It was the nearest he had felt to love, yet the selfish section he controlled did not want to escalate the emotion. He had not thought of her for some time, yet now he could not escape the name. It was like destiny was dragging them together, nevertheless, he knew it had all the hallmarks of a tragedy. Shakespeare would have entwined their lives and dismissed it. were destined to never end together.

His concentration was broken by the clang of the toaster and the smell of overcooked toast. Removing the toast pinched his skin with its heat. He coated it with lashings of butter, before a thick bed of course marmalade was flopped on and spread with undignified skill. The coated toast was a good morning condensed into a sweet bite. Each mouthful held a bursting memory. His mother had loved thick cut marmalade. She used to make marmalade tarts. Gary smiled; they were best thing he had ever eaten. Every mouthful was a bountiful of flavour. When she had passed away the secret formula of the tarts had gone with her.

He engulfed the last segment of his toast, before swallowing the remnants of the now lukewarm tea. He peered into the mug, hoping to find an answer to the problem.

Opening *The Daily Mirror,* he noted on page seven the Grimes brothers with members from the latest boy band. The younger brother had a radiant smile standing with them, whereas Joseph Grimes maintained the moody grimace he always had. They were at the opening of a new nightclub and restaurant they had invested in.

An idea began to form regarding the club and their home. He knew where they lived and their lifestyle, having heard about them through the underworld network. Jones also knew they did not know him, which made his idea that little more promising, easier, and exciting.

His concentration was broken by a banging on the door. Jones rose his head and stared at the window, it needed cleaning.

Slowly, he paced to the door and opened it to be welcomed by Philips and Drake, 'Come in gentlemen.' He left the door open and walked towards the kitchen.

Drake looked at Philips and raised his eyelids. There was something troubling East London's secret underworld ghost. He never walked away from his front door allowing the guest to walk in freely.

Both officers walked in and immediately noted the acrid smell of burnt toast. Their senses burst by the shrill of the kettle.

Piping hot mugs of tea were offered to each man and a packet of Rich Tea unceremoniously left on the table. The packet was split at the half-way point allowing biscuits to tumble forward.

Gary sat in his chair and took a reassuring sip of his sweet tea, 'Help yourselves.'

Philips leant over and removed two biscuits from the blue packet, 'You, all right? You appear a bit distracted. Something on your mind?'

'Fella's, the problem is the Grimes family. Think they're pulling the strings. They've got something on all those involved. I spoke to Perkins last night. Don't ask how I found out about him. He'll help us, fully, and something else, an old flame of mine is involved, heavily. Plus, a drug supplier from the Hague, named Van der Leer. It's all murky. You now know all the contestants in the game.'

Philips sat still. His biscuit in his left hand. The sudden crunch broke the silence. Philips began to speak, allowing dried minute crumbs to fly from his mouth, 'I was hoping my final case would be a simple one, yet every time you're involved Jones, it gets bigger by the day.'

'Hell, Jones. You learn more information inside twelve hours than we do in twelve days. You're in the wrong job.' Drake hated saying it, but realised Jones was a man for information, how he got the information he did not wish to know, but had a horrible feeling pain would be an ingredient, 'Joking aside. This has big players involved.

We need to tread carefully, or go in all guns blazing. Thoughts.'

Philips knew decisions should come with logic and understanding. Deep thinking allowed better choices and less mistakes, and wisdom was handed from one generation to the next. If a person was wise, they learnt to distinguish right from wrong. This decision needed to be correct. His mind calculated all scenarios and deduced their outcome, 'One at a time, but the Grimes last, although we'll have to make sure each person does not inform the next in the chain.'

Jones sat still. Philips was sharp and wise. The local nick would miss him when he left, and he would miss the job. Yet the time was right to go. He would leave on top, 'I agree. Slow and steady, with the occasional livener to jog proceedings along.'

Both officers raised their eyes sharply.

Drake was first to react, 'When you say livener. What exactly do you mean?'

Philips interrupted knowing how quickly this could escalate negatively, 'Right, decision made. Slow and steady. Not sure about the livener part, although we will cross that bridge if needed.'

'Who's first under attack?

Jones raised his head, bringing the mug to his lips slurping from the rim, 'Why don't we hit the younger brother from the Grimes family. He's weak and breakable.'

Jack Philips interjected, 'I think you mean pliable, not breakable.'

Drake jumped in to the conversation, 'That's a good shout. He's the nervous type we could pressure info' from. You're right Jones. Hit him first, and hit him hard. Fucking hard as well.' He looked at Jones and smiled, 'Fucking hard.'

Philips noted the look between the two men. The pit of his stomach spun like a washing machine. They were going to form an allegiance. This could prove dangerous for all those stood in their way.

<    >

Luke Grimes loved the quiet Tuesday nights over the park. It had an air of mystique and menace, with a hint of the unknown.

He drove to the area leaving his car in Pilgrims Lane. Before leaving his vehicle, he finished listening to 'Smalltown Boy.' The song resonated so much about his life, and always left him in an upbeat mood. He loved the lyric 'But you never cried to them, just to your soul.' It summed up his life and the way he felt. No-one had ever understood how he had felt. He had always been in the shadow of Joseph, although his brother had tried to save him from the occasional night times sleeps with his paedophile father.

The ten-minute walk allowed him to psyche himself up for the evenings forthcoming entertainment. The main cruising area was located near Jack Straws Castle and close to the Pergola and Hill Garden. The area was busier during dusk there was a greater diversity of gay guys availing themself, mature men, younger ones, joggers etc… definitely worth checking out for any red-blooded hot gay male seeking quick fast love. The mix was an endless bounty of cock, especially in summer, even though the cruising area remained busy all year long. Luke thought the Heath was a special place to combine a nice walk during the day, and a cruise during night.

<				>

Gary Jones had logged Luke Grimes routine of depravity. Grimes was a creature of habit. Sunday nights he attended The White Swan in Limehouse, Monday nights he visited The Hippodrome, Tuesdays were spent in Brompton's, Wednesday and Thursday he ventured to the greenery of Hampstead. Friday and Saturday, he gave his arse time to recuperate.

Luke Grimes was not like his older brother Joseph. Luke was flamboyant, excitable and very gay. He enjoyed nights of excess, which usually involved snorting vast quantities of cocaine, vodka and cock. He also became very loud, buying everyone bottles of Moet and Chandon, specifically those he thought would be joyful receivers of his ever-ready cock. Luke Grimes was incredibly popular when experiencing such acts of extreme generosity and flamboyancy.

Gary Jones considered Luke Grimes. By the look and appearance of his smile, he could tell he was a loving soul, yet one born into the wrong family. He would be a constant threat to Joseph Grimes and one which would ultimately bring down their family institution bred on violence and negativity. The boy was a softy, yet one who had to be removed to start the ball rolling and to grab the attention of Joseph Grimes.

Luke Grimes made his way through the tall trees and long yellowing grass. Upon the forest floor lie trees of yesteryear, where naked bodies had rolled and entwined. The seasons had been harsh, stripping away the bark and outer layers, yet rendering them all the more beautiful, like the sexual encounters witnessed by life itself. Birdsong arrived in sporadic bursts, the silence and singing working together as well as any unrehearsed chorus. The occasional moans of ecstasy entwined with their evening chorus.

The site of men vanishing into bushes turned the stomach of Gary Jones. Walking past one he saw another being ejaculated over by three others, which resembled pearls raining. It was disgusting, yet he had to locate Grimes, and quickly.

'Over here, big man.'

Jones swiftly spun to his left to be met by the man he was seeking.

'I'm all yours if you like what you see?' Immediately Luke Grimes dropped his jeans exposing a large erect penis.

Gary Jones assessed the situation swiftly, knowing he would have to allow his trousers and boxer shorts to hit the floor, 'I'm feeling hard, and your backside looks ready for taking.'

Luke Grimes liked this man. He was smart, forthright, and ready for action. His desire and excitement teased and encouraged his erection further – could it be that this man could take him to somewhere he has never experienced? 'Where do you want me?'

'Somewhere no-one sees us. I'm a private person, very private.'

'A secretive man. How exciting. Let's go a little deeper.' He winked at Jones and walked further into the undergrowth.

Jones placed his black leather gloves on, and silently followed Grimes into the dense undergrowth.

Grimes lay his jacket on the floor and got on his knees. Something made him turn around, 'Why are you wearing gloves?'

Jones was on his knees behind Grimes replying, 'So I don't get any dirt on my hands and under my nails. Don't want my wife finding out.'

Grimes noted the man's lack of erection. 'You'll need that to stand up as well and are you using lube, or are you going in dry? I prefer lube.'

Jones sprang into action and placed his hands around the throat of Grimes and began to squeeze with all his might. The soft flesh embedding into the man's windpipe. Squeezing hard would stop blood supply going to the brain, or air reaching the lungs. Jones knew Grimes would lose consciousness and stop breathing in seven to fourteen seconds and would be dead in three minutes. In a quiet tone Jones muttered, 'Relax, it'll make it easier. Don't make me hurt you more than I need to.'

The eyes of Luke Grimes began to bulge. Rasping with his final breath he cried through a bruised throat, 'Can't breathe.' His last thought was, 'So I look back upon my life' a lyric from The Pet Shop Boys. He tried to smile, thinking it was an apt ending for the sad life he had lived.

The final words Grimes existence heard were, 'Rest in peace.' The body went floppy and dropped to the floor.

Eighteen-feet away, two men were pleasuring another orally. All three heard the commotion from the couple obviously taking each other aggressively. Neither understanding murder was taking place.

Jones stood, replaced his clothing, and made his way from the brush. Acknowledging no-one, ensuring his focus remained north.

Gary Jones reached the bus stop situated in Hampstead High Street. The walk took ten minutes.

In the distance he noted the welcoming sight of the crimson chariot and its chauffer.

Jumping on the number fourteen Routemaster to Central London. He paid the 80p fee and sat wondering when the body would be found and the message it would send to Joseph Grimes.

<   >

'Buddy, you, all right? You wanna get dressed. Joggers and walkers will be around in a few hours.'

There was something about the man laying down. It was not right. There was no movement. Gingerly, his conscious got the better of him. Approaching slowly, he whispered again, 'Mate, you ok? Come on say something.'

He stood above the non-breathing male, knowing it was a body, 'Fuck! Fuck!' Strength had left his body, he cried out, 'Is there anyone around? Please. There's a body here.' The lifeless body constricting movement from the watching leaves and brambles. Below, the corpse looked like a well-trodden blanket.

He heard a commotion coming towards him. He looked up to be met with the gazing stares of two uniformed police officers.

'What's happened here then?'

He looked at the two officers in disbelief, immediately pointing at the body, 'That man is dead.'

Slowly, the officers stepped towards the corpse. One slowly bent towards the body and touched the cold pure white naked skin. The body had lost the spark so needed by the soul, 'Dead people are like meat when they've passed on. Call it in.'

'Can I have a unit attend Hampstead Heath referring a suspicious death, IC1 male found naked in West Heath.' The officer turned; the witness had vanished into thin air. 'Fuck. The witness has fled.'

The experienced officer turned slowly facing the inexperienced police constable. Looking at his young colleague he knew he had made a newcomer mistake that could haunt his future, 'You dumb fuck. Ok. Story is we were on patrol and came across the body by chance. Do not, and I mean DO NOT mention the witness. That'll open a can of worms that will result in disciplinary action for both of us.'

The officers made a search of the area. The usual items were found; used condoms, poppers, amyl nitrate and pots of lubricant. One couple were ensnared engaging in anal activities. When arrested the giver of the passion was complaining about his sore knees and how the council was responsible.

# Chapter 11

Joseph Grimes received news within two hours. He had been woken by one of his protection detail.

When the aid relayed the news to him it took four or five seconds for it to register. Did he say Luke, his younger brother was dead? How could that happen? They had dined together before Luke had left for the evening.

Immediately, he jumped from his bed and made his way to the office. Twenty minutes later to had learnt everything there was to know. Luke had been strangled in Hampstead Heath, in the gay cruising area. This made it difficult, was it a gay sex game gone wrong? Who was the participant? Was it a rival gang? Was it someone with a grudge? This could be explosive and a fucking unwanted problem. Someone was going to pay, and pay big.

He sat privately thinking about his baby brother. He had been different from birth. He had never been one to enjoy sport and confrontation. Luke had been happy indoors listening to music, dancing and singing. Gentle tears began to glide down his face. Joseph Grimes knew crying was natural, as it encouraged a person to remember forgotten memories. The grief arrived in waves. At first it was random moments, yet in time, good memories began to flood in and allowed for waves of smiles and happiness. Yet the tears suddenly stopped like a tap being turned off. Vengeance would be paid in full and justice would be dealt with maximum force. The perpetrator would be found and skinned alive, literally.

News travelled swiftly concerning the death of Luke Grimes. Theories were discussed and dissected. Feeling amongst the underworld family was one of shock and surprise. Anyone who touched a member of the Grimes family faced immediate retribution in a shocking and violent manner. Gossip throughout the underworld was one of curiosity. The main question everyone was asking was, 'Who would do it?'

Those involved in illegal practice knew the Grimes family, or had been involved with them realised Joseph Grimes was the head of the family, and a man not to be crossed, whereas his younger brother Luke was a person who presented nothing. He only offered problems to his older brother.

Everyone knew the younger brother was gay, yet no-one would dare discuss it aloud. Someone had made the mistake in calling Luke Grimes a 'fucking poof' in the presence of Joseph. This person was never seen again, although word had got out that he had been boiled alive, and the flesh which had fallen away from his dead body had been fed to Joseph Grimes prized black Iberian pigs who usually fed on a diet of acorns, yet Joseph had not fed them for three days, so when the soft-boiled meat was fed to them it was manor from heaven.

Joseph Grimes contacted everyone he knew seeking information. Frustratingly, there was no news. Whoever had murdered his brother was either incredibly lucky or very professional. His security personnel were sent out to shake a few trees to see what information they could glean, yet again – nothing. Joseph Grimes head of security gently tapped on the door and entered the inner-sanctum where Joseph Grimes ruled his empire. Although he was military trained, he always felt like he was visiting his headmaster.

Grimes studied the man coming in. He guessed there was no news. The man was walking slowly, his nerves were showing. His inner madness was building, 'Well?'

'Sir, we have spoken to loads of people who may have, or have crossed paths with Luke, yet no-one knows anything.'

Joseph Grimes inner rage exploded, 'It's twelve fucking hours since my brother's murder, and you're telling me there is not one piece of fucking news. Absolutely nothing. Someone somewhere must have seen something. The area is full of shit-stabbers. Find 'em, and do what you have to, but do not, and I warn you. Do not come back without any news. Now fuck off you useless fat cunt and earn the 'undred grand I pay you.'

<　　　　　　　>

The gentle chatter of the typewriter could be heard throughout the department. Reports were being readied for filing. A police constable walked into the department with a memo and immediately moved towards Jack Philips.

'Sir, I've been asked to pass this to you.' He about turned and returned to where he had come from.

Philips read the note and called for Drake to enter the office, 'Shut the door, Drakey.'

His cohort moved the chair a little and sat opposite his superior, 'What's up, gov?'

'Just received news that Luke Grimes has been murdered in Hampstead Heath,' Jack Philips saw his colleague blow out his cheeks and look towards the ceiling.

'You already know what I'm thinking, gov.'

Jack Philips did not wish to mimic Drake's feelings to his face. This murder had the hallmarks of Gary Jones gaining Joseph Grimes attention without being noticed himself, 'Luke Grimes and Jimmy Jackson, both players in the game… removed. That leaves Julie Brown, Perkins and the dutchman. If I were the three of them, I'd tread carefully. Someone is removing pieces from the board. If, and I say if it were Jones, he'd have been super careful. Jones is nocturnal. He's a creature of the night. This would play into his strengths. No one recognises someone who blends into the scenery.'

'Gov, are you saying Jones bats for the other side?'

'No. What I'm saying is he may have studied these people. Noted where they spent time together, where they went. People are creatures of habit, and that is where we will find something. See if Luke Grimes had a habit, a routine he followed. If he did, then he would leave a trail of breadcrumbs for us to follow.'

The calm nature of Jack Philips allowed those around him to bring their suggestions forward, making him approachable to all ideas.

Drake's mind was spinning with thoughts and calculations. His superior officer had produced the same scenario that he had considered. It did not matter whether the person investigated was friend or foe. What mattered was how judgement was made. Clues to social class, life style and group associations. Being logical needed to dominate their process. They needed to walk in the footsteps of Luke Grimes to understand the life of Luke Grimes. 'Ok, I'm on it.'

Cautiously, Drake was speaking to the man on the telephone, listening intently when information was given. He replaced the receiver considering the news he had been given. Luke Grimes was a constant visitor to Chariots Health Club and Spa in Shoreditch. He thought of Luke Grimes. He was slim, yet toned, but there was something else he could not put his finger on. There was something missing. Luke Grimes had a death wish, but why. He manoeuvred his way towards Jack Philips and whispered in his ear, 'Fancy a bit of lunch in London, gov?'

Jack Philips immediately stopped typing, grabbed his jacket, and stood, 'I'm most certainly do my friend.'

During the journey to Fenchurch Street station Drake filled Jack Philips in with the information he had found.

Jack Philips had heard it all. He knew there were places for gay men, but a health spa in the middle of the city of London, 'Are you sure about this Drakey? A gay spa in broad daylight. Really?'

'I spoke to someone at the club. He was a regular, and I mean a regular. It's not seedy, if you're broadminded. It has showers and a swimming pool, but it also has a thing called dark rooms where men go for sex, lots of sex.' Drake realised Jack Philips was shocked. Words had stuttered and stopped, stopped because his mind had entered a new direction, one he had never anticipated.

'I just want to confirm we are going to Chariots. The place where all this depravity happens? Drakey, I should've retired.' He stifled a small laugh.

Approaching the establishment in Commercial Road both men noted how congested the area was. The transport was the arteries, the blood that carried everything the body needed to survive.

Walking through the door both officers were met with a stale smell mixed with a heady brew of chlorine.

The assistant immediately offered a gleaming white welcoming smile, 'Afternoon gentlemen I assume you require a cubicle, or just a swim?' He raised an eyebrow, mocking them.

'I'm DCI Drake, and beside me Superintendent Philips. Tell us about Luke Grimes.'

The assistant became a little nervous. He had heard about the demise of Luke Grimes. He had already been visited by two employees of the family, and told them everything, yet now he had the opposing end of the law asking the very same questions. He decided to tell them everything about Luke Grimes, at least both parties could fight over the scraps.

Both officers listened intently, neither interrupting.

Jack Philips was the first to speak up, although he felt uncomfortable asking what he was going to ask, 'Whilst we are here, you may as well show as around. This way we will know first-hand what it is like.'

The assistant grimaced. The Grimes employees has asked the same thing, and it ended with one of the men becoming a little angry due to his religious background, 'Are you sure? You may witness things you do not like?'

Philips stood his ground, 'Get on with it, young man.'

The tour lasted 10 minutes, and had made both men feel incredibly uncomfortable. They had witnessed a man servicing another anally in one room, and in another a staff member cleaning a blue vinyl covered floor that smelt a little of excretion, yet looked bloody as well, with four men sitting in each corner facing one another.

They thanked the assistant and left the establishment swiftly.

'Drakey, I'm broadminded, but fuck me. That took seediness to a professional level. Let's wander to the Apple and Pears in Liverpool Street and have a beer. After that, I need it.'

Fifteen minutes later both officers were sitting at a dark solid wood circular table used in the public house, which faced platform eighteen. They both took large reassuring gulps from their pint of John Bull bitter. Looking into the beer both were transfixed, their minds elsewhere. Drake swallowed the beer in two gulps, 'Another?' He did not wait for a reply.

Jack Philips pondered Luke Grimes and his lifestyle of excess. The murder had the hallmarks of Gary Jones, yet he felt Jones would not visit an area frequented by gay after dark. The murder was meticulous and would send warning signals to Joseph Grimes. His security detail would be doubled. It would be impregnable.

'There you go and a little short to go with it.'

Jack Philips took the whisky and swallowed it swiftly. Replacing the glass on the table gently. He took the pint glass and took a huge gulp. Licking his lips removing the excess, 'Drakey, I have no idea who's involved in this one. The only thing that is going to happen is it'll get Joseph Grimes attention totally. That man will be frothing at the mouth to seek justice.'

'To do this the person must be slightly psychotic and incredibly sure of themself. It has to be Jones. He's cleaning everything up and he's the type who would take pleasure in removing the Grimes family. He'd see it as a game.'

Both looked at the other wondering what the other was thinking. Their quiet time was ended abruptly.

'I hear you two are looking into the murder of my brother. Make sure you leave no stone unturned. If anyone refuses to speak to you tell me and they will.'

Both officers looked up to be greeted by Joseph Grimes, who was pulling over a chair to sit with them. A glass of pure orange juice was passed to him with two cubes of ice and a dash of lime.

'What are you doing here Grimesey?' Jack Philips knew Joseph Grimes did not enjoy his name be used in pet name form.

'You visited Chariots. I did as well. Fucking shit hole. What goes on in there makes your fucking hair curl. Can't believe my brother went there to get his kicks. I knew he was poof. Knew when we were young. He was different, not like me. I always had to look after him.'

'Grimesey, did it bother you. Luke not being straight?'

'Listen, he could fuck who he wanted, as long as it didn't fuck with the business, yet he was up to something with someone. I think that something was drugs. It was this shit batch of drugs being hoisted about that is putting people in hospital. Now I want you to find out who did him. If you need money just say.'

Jack Philips took another sip of his beer, 'I have to be honest with you, off the record, we have no idea who murdered your brother, and that's all I can say.'

Joseph Grimes studied both officers, specifically Jack Philips, 'I believe you. It's early days. But it's a race. If I find out who did my brother first then they will suffer.' He engulfed his drink, stood, and left both officers to their own devices.

Jack Philips surveyed his drink before swallowing it like a man who had not seen water for a week. With each gulp his Adam's apple bobbed violently and the fluid vanished from the glass. Gently, he placed the pint glass on the beer mat and looked at his colleague, 'Drakey, I've a bad feeling that a good ole fashioned shoot out is imminent.'

# Chapter 12

Julie Brown had to contact Van der Leer, yet, having his building firebombed had proven to be a mistake. She had acted without considering alternative actions and the possible repercussions. She had acted swiftly, too swiftly. There was only one thing to do, contact the man.

Her lack of self-control was taking control. The repressing anger needed careful thought, yet it was boiling up like a steaming kettle, and it needed to be cooled? How a person dealt with anger is crucial. It is the steam in a pressure cooker, you have to find a way to let it out in a safe secure manner. It can be through physical activity or by finding inner peace. She could find neither. She realised some things had to be met head on.

Julie made her way to the red telephone box and dialled the number, waiting for the telephone to connect. Finally, it was answered.

'Hallo?'

Julie loved the extended *a* used in the Dutch greeting. She swiftly shoved a number of five-pence coins into the slot, 'Good evening, Van der Leer. We need to meet.'

Van der Leer gripped the receiver with such force he thought it may splinter. Never had he experienced such rage. It was flooding him like a tidal wave of anger.

'Are you there, Van der Leer?'

'You are a fucking dead woman walking. You fucking whore of a jackal. I am going to obliterate you.' He then crashed the receiver on the cradle.

Julie stood in silence, knowing she had upset the mad dutchman. She was running out of friends. These drugs had fucked everything and everyone was after her. Luke Grimes, the silly cunt, had been distributing behind his psychotic brothers back to all his poofy mates, thinking he was going to take over the Grimes empire. He had sold the drugs supplied by Van der Leer to people in clubland, specifically the poofs he was fucking, and hanging around with. Whereas, she had sold to dealers, about a dozen individuals. It was a complete mess, fucking carnage. It had started to go wrong with Steven Jacks, the silly private schooled prick who had removed Johnny Bigtime. Since that moment, everything had fallen apart. She realised she had to tidy this mess up, although knowing it would leave herself wide open for recriminations. Yet, Van der Leer had played with the drugs. So, he must have expected some form of revenge payment.

<  >

The shrill of the telephone broke the concentration of Perkins. Immediately, he grabbed the receiver, 'Good afternoon, Perkins present.' His ears were attacked by a guttural barrage of Dutch phonetics.

'It's me.'

Perkins felt in a playful mood, 'Excellent. Then how can I help you, Mr. Me?'

Van der Leer stopped. Did this imbecile on the telephone believe there was someone conversing with him named Mr. Me? 'Are you sure you wish to play with me, Perkins?'

Perkins now understood Van der Leer had a problem, 'Is that you Danny my boy? You sound different.'

Van der Leer imagined reaching down the telephone and squeezing Perkins's neck until the veins exploded due to the pressure applied, 'You know it is me. Julie Brown. She needs to go, and I mean forever.'

Perkins sighed extending his bottom lip, redirecting the air-flow to towards his receding hairline. Van der Leer was fast becoming an inconvenience to all and sundry, 'Danny, the Julie Brown situation from what I can gather is all of your own making. From what I know, please correct me if I am incorrect. You amended the DNA of the substances you were supplying to Julie Brown. You are in the shit because of your own fucking greed.' The final sentence felt euphoric. Speaking to Van der Leer in that manner made the situation feel electric.

Van der Leer was shocked by the mouthful of profanity passed his way by Perkins. He had never heard him use any form of guttural language. He was also concerned where Perkins had received his information regarding the drugs. He decided to play dumb and ignore the retort made, 'Drugs? What are you talking about? I've.'

Perkins knew he had Van der Leer against the ropes, and decided to charge in for the knockout, 'You've what? Never been involved in drugs. You fucking liar. I know what you do, where you sell and to whom you sell. Do not insult my intelligence, and the way intelligence is gathered. Do you honestly think I do not know everything about you? You were born in 1950 to a young mother and placed in foster care with Mr and Mrs Jansen, who resided in De Pijp. Mr and Mrs Jansen adopted you and you were educated at Barlaeus Gymnasium. Mr and Mrs Jansen mysteriously went missing in 1970, yet were found in the canal with their throats slashed and heavy weights tied to their ankles. How is that for starters?'

Van der Leer sat stunned. It took a second or two for it to fully enter his brain. He felt his emotions take an instant beating. The situation was turning into a nightmare. How had Perkins located the information? He immediately began to think of his parents and how he had watched their bodies sink. His emotions finally turned to rage, 'Shut the fuck up. Shut the fuck up, now.'

Perkins felt a sense of jubilation, touché, 'There is more Van der Leer, lots more. Should I continue?' He allowed the final word to trail off knowing Van der Leer had suffered a knock down blow.

Van der Leer wanted to speak into the telephone, yet was unable to find any words to communicate. He had safe guarded and hidden the past away in the deep recess of his mind, yet the verbal attack he had just suffered proved he was far from healed. The years of torment had finally come home to roost. He knew Perkins would be expecting a reply. He gathered himself, 'Really.'

Perkins had perfected the art of self-control. It was one of the things employments within the services taught you. Psychologically, he had beaten the man to a pulp. Having beaten the man, he now wanted him gone forever, 'Julie Brown. You want Julie Brown. I can give you Julie Brown. But you will need to come to London and stay in the same hotel you always do.'

Van der Leer was astounded. This man knew everything about him. Finally, he knew Perkins was as big as adversary as Joseph Grimes. He also knew he was fucked, or as the Dutch said, 'Ik ben flink geneukt.'

Perkins disconnected the call and began to dial a new number. The phone began to ring, and on the third sound it was answered with deep estuarine accent. The accent was certainly working class, 'Jones, Perkins here.'

Gary Jones was immediately alert. He and Perkins had agreed contact was only needed should they be in trouble or if there was crucial news. Jones understood that breaking news leant itself to truth and reason, yet can offer a form of psychological damage should the recipient be unlucky, 'I can only assume this is not a social call.'

Perkins smiled. This man had a dull sense of humour that he quite enjoyed. He was a tad downbeat, yet ensconced a positive vibe, 'How droll, Jones. Anyway, shall we meet? Kensington Palace is beautiful place. There are benches surrounding the lake. It is a safe place to go. No chance of walls having ears.'

Jones smiled at the man's quip. Perkins was so old school he was almost medieval, 'Perkins, that sounds nice. I haven't been there. When, and what time?'

Perkins cleared his airwaves, 'Shall we say 11am tomorrow? Before the minions run for their lunch.'

Jones considered the sentence spoken by Perkins. He made lunch sound working class, 'Minions, don't take the piss, Perkins. These people do an honest day's labour for an honest day's pay. They are not fucking minions.'

Perkins assessed the retort from Jones. He was obviously a lefty, and one who would bat for the working-class section of society. Interestingly, he enjoyed dining at fine restaurants and clothed by suits made in Savile Row. A severe conflict of interest was swimming in the waters of Jones, 'Righteo, see you tomorrow, Jones. Toodle pip.'

Jones considered the telephone call. Perkins obviously had information or wanted something. What was it with people in prominent positions? They have all the trappings from society, but they lacked savvy. These people were not street smart. Something was seriously wrong. Working class people were savvy, but those of the upper echelons had brains. It was a proper mish-mash of society, but somehow it worked. Sitting down he pondered whether to tell the dynamic duo, but after careful consideration he decided to keep things quiet until the meeting.

<   >

The wrought benches facing Kensington Palace offered a wonderful view of a most stunning piece of architecture. Originally, it had been known as Nottingham House and the original inhabitants had been William III and Mary II. Over the years the building and gardens had been extended to create an opulent outlook. The swans graced the Round Pond like floating kings and queens and the Queen Victoria statue maintained a watchful eye on proceedings taking place from all forms of life.

Perkins perched on the bench with his polystyrene cup of coffee. He assessed the aroma and decided the shop he purchased it from used a mass-produced formula and not the fresh ground variety. Morning coffee was a ritual every person should enjoy. Its routine was both refreshing and comforting. It allowed the individual a time of reflection without the chaotic scenes that followed them throughout their hectic lives. These moments of rare peace allowed clarity of the mind. Perkins suddenly knew his inner peace was broken. A shadow loomed over him.

'Good morning, Perkins. You are right, that is a most impressive place. Can't believe I've never been here. What a smashing view.'

'Jones, take a pew. We need to talk about Danny Van der Leer. He's proving to be an inconvenience. He also is interested in your old acquaintance… Julie Brown.' Perkins raised an eyebrow and gave Jones a knowing look.

Gary Jones sat upright on the bench, and wondered how many people before himself had sat admiring the resplendent residence. Perkins had selected a fine venue for their impromptu meeting. He now needed to get down to business, 'So, what's up, Perkins?'

'Van der Leer, is what's up. He is becoming a rather tiresome pawn in our game, and I believe your old acquaintance, Brown, has ruffled his feathers, somewhat.'

'Julie, what has she done?'

'It appears your old girlfriend had Van der Leer's drug factory firebombed, and to say he is unhappy would be an understatement.' Perkins realised he had struck a hammer blow. Jones's silence told a multitude of musings.

Jones was dumbstruck. Words stopped flowing like a dry river. They stopped because Perkins had shown him a path, he never anticipated Julie would walk down. Regaining his composure, he turned towards Perkins.

Before Jones could mutter anything, Perkins chastised him, 'Look ahead dear boy. We're not supposed to be meeting. Don't want anyone knowing this meeting was planned, do we?'

Jones felt like he was back at school in Dagenham, not that it had benefited him. He had been cleverer than those employed, yet the authorities always liked to belittle the local minnows and that feeling had followed Jones into his adult life. When he felt he was being belittled he only knew one method of retaliation and that usually resulted in the person receiving a few smacks of Jones's wisdom, 'Don't be so condescending, Perkins. Just tell us and get off what's on your chest.'

'Sorry, old chap. It's the way we privately educated individuals speak. Anyway, I have an idea, of sorts.'

For the next five minutes Perkins laid down the formula of a plan he had set in motion. Gary listened intently, again understanding he was being used as the scapegoat should it go wrong.

Gary quietly murmured, 'Alea iacta est.'

Perkins was astounded. How did a boy from Dagenham understand Latin? He decided to reply in Latin to see if Jones did actually understand him, 'Carpe diem.'

Jones wanted to smile. Perkins was evaluating his Latin. Instead, he decided to reply in English, 'We do need to seize the day, Perkins.' He then stood and decided to wander around Kensington Palace gardens.

Perkins sat watching the man stride away with purpose. He sipped the final drops of his now tepid coffee. Jones was an intriguing chap. Had they schooled together he felt they may have been friends. There was something nasty, yet decent about him. He was a mixture of all things. Yet the Latin thing had surprised him. When had he taught himself? There was not much the man could not do. He would make a perfect recruit to the security agency. He was also a fast walker. The man was out of sight and now a blur on the horizon.

Perkins stood, slowly moving his eyes, surveying the area ensuring there was no-one present who should not be.

# Chapter 13

Van der Leer based himself in the Grosvenor Hotel. The Superior Rooms were beautifully furnished and opulent in comfort. The hotel held all the amenities he required. The Bourbon Bar and restaurant were highly regarded, and the pianist played from 2pm. If Van der Leer could die in a place, then The Grosvenor would be his choice.

His mind journey was broken by the lifeline of his world ringing, 'Van der Leer, meet me at the old warehouse in Tobacco Dock. There's a good fellow. Nice and prompt, 7am.'

Van der Leer was in the process of replying when the caller disconnected. He stood still transfixed. What was with this population and their abrupt rude behaviour?

He knew the warehouse, although it was an odd choice. Why did they not meet in this beautiful place? They could have pre- dinner drinks before enjoying one of the splendid meals. Due to the timing, he would miss the lavish breakfast. One thing the British prepared beautifully was the traditional breakfast, and now he would miss it. Who held a meeting at 7am? Only the English would do that!

The old docklands warehouse was a shadow of its previous life. The building had once been the hive of activity with workers buzzing about their business, yet now it stood lifeless, an empty soul. The metal door was hanging like a dead man from the noose and the rafters creaked like an old man's bones. The groaning noise sounded like the roof was fighting to fall in and join the party. Windows no longer welcomed light, just damp wet misery from the sheeting chilly rain and the wind penetrated the dull surroundings adding to its desolate death like misery.

Van der Leer trod carefully, knowing any false move could result in a catastrophe. There were a number exits, should he require them. He noted paint peeling from the soft wood that was now like an overworked sponge. It was a desperate place and a strange choice to meet. He still could not comprehend why Perkins had chosen such a place at such a ridiculous time.

Due to its architectural significance, the building was granted a Grade One listing in 1979, protecting it from demolition. Why? The place was a shit hole and needed to be demolished. It was wet, dark and inhospitable. The only lifeform taking residence would be illness spreading rats.

Gary Jones watched Van der Leer enter with the upmost trepidation. The man was out of his comfort zone, and it showed. He looked nervous, like a furtive fox. His head constantly moving, surveying the area, obviously evaluating the landscape. Jones understood the face of a coward is the back of their head when they run, yet Van der Leer had agreed the meeting, in spite of the location. This proved he had an inner-steeliness. This intrigued Jones. Van der Leer was a man of two faces.

Perkins stood from a safe distance watching the on-going proceedings. It was like two lions circling before battle commenced, although he knew there would be only one victor, he also knew who his money would be wagered on.

Jones removed himself from the gloom, its protective cover shrouding him like a mystery. His approaching footsteps leaving a wet slapping sound on the miserable sodden concrete floor. The sound offered confidence and purpose.

Van der Leer heard the footsteps and came to halt. They resembled the sound clogs from his homeland made. There was a crunch of gravel, not the kind of continuous noise you would hear from a moving car, but the sharp short crunch of a footstep, 'Where is Perkins and who are you?'

Jones listened carefully to the accent that told of distant shores, a slower mundane life and a sense of home longed by many – yet realised by few. The man's business suit was beautifully crisp and navy blue, with a pale line running through. The white-collar shirt had a metal bar ensuring the tie hung straight. The man was impeccably dressed, 'He couldn't make it, and he doesn't send his apologies. Perkins said you were a festering pit of filth praying on the weak and innocent.' Jones noted Van der Leer's eye twitch. He was annoyed at the comment.

Perkins blanched in the shadows. He had said no such thing.

The comment rattled Van der Leer. It was a term Perkins would use. He probably used it with his old boy's network back when speaking about those less fortunate than himself. Rage was beginning to envelop him. He thought of gouging a silver spoon in Perkins's throat and watching him choke on his own miserable words.

Jones realised that Van der Leer was daydreaming. This gave him the opportunity to strike the first blow.

Swiftly and accurately, he leapt at the man striking him perfectly on the side of his head with the cosh, which had been hidden in his waistband. The resounding thump and crack reverberated throughout the warehouse.

Van der Leer looked at Jones through misty eyes before plummeting to the floor.

Perkins looked on in astonishment. He had witnessed countless forms of retribution, but never one so swift, violent and uncaring. He held an unerring respect for Jones, although he realised, he was a beast. Ready to harm anyone standing in his way. In the distance he heard a lorry approaching and quickly slunk back into the shadows.

The lorry driver had been directed to drop a quantity of three hundred and forty-three cubed feet of concrete into the hole outside the warehouse. He eyed it and thought it looked like a bomb crater. Releasing the lever, he watched the concrete enter the hole. The job would take just under one-hour to fill. He did not care as he had been paid a grand to do the job. Easy money. The concrete would take forty-eight hours to dry, and after seven days it would be at seventy per-cent strength. It was thirteen times the size of the hot tub he and his wife shared at home. A salacious smile spread across his face thinking about his young wife's sexy body and her tits bouncing on the bubbles that attacked her like hungry bears.

Gary Jones watched the lorry leave the area and removed himself from his look out. He called out to Perkins knowing he was in the vicinity. Thirty seconds later the man appeared.

'Jones, why have you filled up that hole? Odd thing to do if you don't mind me saying.'

Jones stood looking incredulous. Not a muscle on his face moved, 'This mess is yours Perkins, and I'm once again tidying up a member of the establishments mess. Now come here. You have a job to do.'

Perkins look of astonishment would have not looked out of place in a slapstick comedy, 'A job. I don't do jobs.'

Jones turned angrily and spoke ferociously towards Perkins, 'Well now you fucking are! Move.'

An entrance that had once been an office was their destination. Upon entering it looked bleak and uneventful until Perkins noted in the corner something trussed up with thick tape. He eyes became accustomed to the dark and he took a shoot sharp breath, 'Van der Leer?'

A set of aggressive growls could be heard from the thing that resembled a trussed-up Christmas Turkey.

'Why have you done that to him? And where is the man's attire, he'll catch his death?'

Jones swivelled slowly and walked towards Perkins. Perkins felt his nerves begin to jangle. He remembered this man was one to be wary of, very wary.

'Unless you want to end up like him, I would seriously reign your tone in, Perkins. Regards to his clothes, we don't want any fibres or anything else in the concrete. It'll take longer to decompose.'

Perkins's head shot up like a bolt of lightning, 'Did you say decompose, In what?' His voice trailed off. He now understood the reasoning behind the concrete.

'Perkins, get the platform trolley and I'll put our passenger on there.'

Perkins was about to mouth, 'Why?' but stopped mid-flow.

Jones looked down at Van der Leer, who still maintained an indignant look, 'Van der Leer, you and I are not so different. Our main difference is greed, and it's the thing that has done you. Now you are going on a life journey… an end-of-life journey.' Jones smiled at his gallows humour, 'Ok Perkins, push the trolley.'

Realisation suddenly dawned on Perkins. It was he who was going to end Van der Leers life. He placed his hand on the cold metal handle and began to push following behind a strident Jones. Upon reaching the hole Jones turned towards the victim, 'Van der Leer, this is where you and I depart. Perkins now has the honour of making your departure a more permanent exodus.'

Fright began to show on Van der Leer's face and tears began to stream down his naked skin.

Perkins felt sorrow for the man. The last visions of life would have been of a repugnant warehouse, Gary Jones, and a swimming pool of concrete.

Jones stood watching the nervous looking Perkins. He did not want to follow through to end this dangerous road. He would need a little cajoling.

'Perkins, tip him. You need to end this thing once and for all. You've done worse.' Before Jones could say another word, he heard a dull splash, and slowly watched the live body sink in the thick grey treacle substance.

Van der Leer could not move. He was very slowly sinking. He made one final gasp of air. Panic, fear, and more panic began to set in. He had been able to hold his breath for fifty-seven seconds when he had been younger. It now needed to be longer. His final picture of life was of two men watching him sink. Density was dragging him to the bottom. Suddenly, he stopped. The shock opened his mouth unexpectantly. The cavity was filled with a thick gritty flow of sludge that trickled slowly down his oesophagus. He knew he was going to die, but the calcium hydroxide would promote his death. The final memories Van der Leer had been of his flowers and who would tend them.

Perkins and Jones stood side by side watching the non-moving grey substance. Jones moved towards the warehouse and returned with two long pieces of wood, placing them over the drying cement. He then walked back inside and dragged a large piece of corroded metal fencing out towards the hole. He then lay it across the wood planks safeguarding the area. He knew Perkins was watching, 'Safeguards anyone falling in the hole, something we don't want, and in 48 hours it will be solid.'

Perkins for the first time thought the man beside him was psychotic. He was too cold. An absolute ice-man. He showed no feeling. Did Jones have no soul? 'Jones, we have just buried a living man in concrete. Yet you have shown no emotion. You are not happy, sad, angry, elated, concerned. You are a person, at least show some feeling. Even a little remorse.'

Jones considered the statement made by Perkins. 'Perkins, my father was a cunt, an absolute cunt. I murdered him in front of my mother, who I loved dearly. I lack feeling. End of conversation. We'll leave the area now and I'll pop back in two days' time to ensure everything is all right.'

Perkins considered the response and understood that his Van der Leer problem had been eradicated, yet another could be looming with the psychopath he had just buried a man in concrete alongside. Gary Jones was a dangerous entity, and any person who crossed him would be wise to move continents, yet Perkins thought they would still be located. Jones was the quiet type who did not cause controversy or stand out. The sort of chap who would stand in the corner and no-one would notice, yet would notice all. A most dangerous specimen. He was a perfect fit for the security services.

Both men walked away, neither considering the solidifying body now encased in concrete forever.

Jones broke the silence, 'Never return to this place, Perkins, and remember, you were the one who dropped him the concrete, not me. Try to stiff me, and you'll go the same way, in less salubrious surroundings.'

Perkins knew he had been trumped by Jones. He was a man who thought two or three steps ahead of most individuals. Jones was obviously a man of his word, yet Perkins realised he could not be beholden to a man connected with those associated with illegal practices. Something needed to be done and swiftly, yet carefully.

# Chapter 14

Tiny knew what he had witnessed at Hampstead Heath. He dare not say anything to Joseph Grimes as he was on the war path looking for anyone with information. Rumours were circulating that he had already beaten four gay men to death. Tiny knew he had to tell his boss about his lifestyle, although he was concerned about the outcome. He had been struggling to sleep. The effects of P.T.S.D igniting the ghost of that night. Insomnia was a cruel illness. The body kept replaying the actions of that night. It was like the mental recording was a predator slowing eating away at his soul.

Joseph Grimes knew his number one man was fighting a demon, and he guessed he was a poof. Tiny never had a bird, and was always down the gym. He had seen him comparing biceps with another man at the local gym and at that moment he knew. There had been a special smile shared by both parties. He had been waiting for his main man and friend to come clean about his lifestyle, 'Tiny, you all right? Lately you've looked like a bag of shit. Something to tell me?' He raised his eyebrows. The differential smile wanted answers. Joseph Grimes was beginning to calm down, yet there was a nervousness still floating around his being. He was expecting a reply, yet not the one he was due to receive.

Tiny eyed his employer looking for signs that he was about to explode. There appeared to be no ticks around the eye, and no movement from the fingers, as if they were playing an invisible piano. He decided to tell

Joseph Grimes, yet a nagging feeling in the pit of stomach informed him it could be a bad manoeuvre, 'Boss, I need to tell you something, and it's personal.'

Joseph Grimes pretended to be uninterested, yet inwardly he was ready to tell his main man he already knew, yet the dramatic effect had to be played out, 'What is it, Tiny? Spit it out man. We've a busy day.'

Tiny swallowed. His strength was beginning to leave him. Nerves were making the top of left thigh shake a little. He decided to disclose information straightaway, 'Boss, I'm not into women.' As soon as he said he knew it sounded pathetic.

Grimes nodded, 'So you're a shirt lifter? Do you honestly think I didn't know? It was obvious. Is that it? If so, let's get down to work.' Grimes was about to turn when he was stopped.

'There's more, Boss. Something so big. It's been keeping me awake.'

Curiosity and instinct made him face his employee. The friendship was broken when it came to business, 'What else?' Grimes had deep rooted feeling the information he was about to be party to would be bad, unbelievably bad.

'Luke.' Tiny's mouth suddenly dried.

Joseph's inner body became alert like an electric current had been powered into him, 'Luke. Did you say, Luke? What do you know, Tiny?'

Tiny felt his inner temperature core was increasing, and he felt beads of sweat forming on the back of neck, 'The night that.' He was stammering his words and he knew it. He also noted his boss playing the imaginary piano.

Joseph felt his annoyance levels begin to rise like a roaring fire, 'Speak up, man.'

Tiny understood that nerves were markers for success and bravery, and anxiousness was supposed to be short term, yet this had a long term and career defining end. He could sense it, 'I was in Hampstead the night Luke was there. I was within twenty feet of him. I heard Luke say something about the man's erection. I knew his voice. I also heard a gagging noise. Luke was murdered by someone who had been trailing him and someone who is straight.'

Joseph Grimes stood perplexed, stunned, and shocked. Shock indicated a change in the game. His mind was reeling, unable to process the information. He imagined the scenario on the heath. The situation was being played in his mind. His inner madness kicked in. He grabbed a coffee mug from his desk and whipped around striking it upon the bald head of Tiny. Repeating the action before Tony had time to recover. The jagged edge of the mug was sharp enough to cut flesh like it offered no resistance. It was like a hot knife through butter.

Tiny held his hand over the deep gash, but no matter how much pressure he applied the blood still spurted between his fingers and leaked, dropping onto the floor. The blood was determined to find an exit. Inwardly, Tiny was screaming silently.

Joseph Grimes looked at the man. His head resembled an exploded tomato. He laughed, 'Clean yourself up, and get yourself to the surgeon, and if you ever, ever lie to me, or withhold information again. I'll dice your head like a fucking potato. Oh, and I know about you and the M.I.5 man, Perkins. I know about your service background together.' He then began to laugh. Tiny looked like a toffee apple.

Tiny lifted his head. His face coated in the red sticky warm substance. The only words he could muster were, 'Thank you, boss.'

Grimes hated himself for what he had done, but word would go around and it would be good for fear, and removing four queers from the earth would contribute to that. Drowning them had been interesting. One of the unwilling participants had lasted ninety seconds submerged. It had impressed him that a man had that capacity for survival. When the men had been thrust into the water the bubbles had been fast and active, yet when they were running out of air the bubbles were small and sporadic. Grimes smiled; it was like a school science experiment. It had also proven beneficial to his farm. The pigs loved raw human meat. Fuck the acorns.

<  >

Tiny approached the house in Green Lane, Dagenham. It was a typical red brick solid terraced building, erected just after World War 2. The house had not been maintained, and the front garden housed lush long green grass, which had not seen a lawn-mower for a considerable length of time. What attracted Tiny's attention was the old sofa that had been unceremoniously dumped in the front garden. It had been there so long it resembled something that had taken root. Carefully, he walked along the short path before stopping at the solid wood door. It was coloured green, yet the paint work was tired, and peeling like a person's orange and the sun had bleached the paint work giving it a sickly colour of vomit.

Tiny rapped on the rusty knocker. The door was opened by a man who resembled a ghost. He was porcelain white and had not seen the sun for a considerable period of time. He wore a black suit, which looked a little ragged, and his white shirt had a creamy look to it. Tiny studied the man's features closely. He looked sad, almost beaten. His mouth had long seen a smile. Yet, there was an inner-strength to him. This man was a survivor.

By trade he had been a veterinary surgeon. Yet, his veterinarian license had been revoked due to his liking for opioid consumption. An addiction which cost him his marriage, money, and friends.

'Tiny?'

'Surgeon, that's me. You can see my problem.'

The surgeon looked at the wound. It was a fresh deep laceration, 'Don't just stand there, come in. I don't want a man with half his head hanging off to be noted by the locals. Go in the kitchen, and sit on the white plastic chair. Don't go anywhere else and don't touch anything.'

Tiny could not believe the change. This man had gone from a ghost like figure to a surgeon in under twenty seconds. He had also become authoritative. Someone in charge usually made the correct decisions. Tiny had no complaints with the situation. He strode ahead and entered the kitchen. It was out of context with the rest of the home. It resembled an operating theatre. It was pure white and smelt of disinfectant. There was a selection of razor-sharp knives in a cupboard, and packets of sutures.

The surgeon returned wearing a pair of latex gloves. He cleaned the area surrounding the wound, and picked up a pair of tweezers, before gently lifting something from the gash, 'Whatever hit you was coloured black.' He selected a needle and thread the suture, before pushing the spike through the skin at a 90-degree angle, about 10-millimetres to the right of the wound. He was careful enough to twist his hand clockwise so the needle began to emerge on the opposing side of the wound. The minor procedure took ten minutes. He inspected his work, 'You're done, three-hundred and fifty pounds please, cash, no cheques.'

Tiny rose from his place, opened his wallet, and placed thirty-five ten pounds notes on the white unit. He looked towards the man, whose facial features had still not changed, 'Thanks for the work. It's appreciated.'

The surgeon nodded, 'If you play football, don't head the ball, and if your head hurts take paracetamol. Goodbye.'

The surgeon's abrupt manner was off-putting, yet he had completed the job. One thing Tiny was aware of, his tenure with Grimes was ending. He was going to consult with Perkins. He was trustworthy and an ex-military man. His advice would be succinct and concise.

<  >

Tiny agreed to meet Perkins in the Prospect of Whitby located in Wapping. The Prospect of Whitby was London's oldest riverside pub dating back to 1520, with magnificent views of the river Thames. The pub had originally been frequented by those involved in life on the river and sea, it was also a notorious haunt for smugglers, thieves and pirates. Other notable customers had been Charles Dickens, Samuel Pepys, Judge Jeffries and artists Whistler and Turner. In recent times the pub had been popular with major A list stars and royalty including Kirk Douglas, Paul Newman, Glenn Ford, Rod Steiger, Princess Margaret and Prince Rainier. A heady brew of the rich and powerful. Yet here he was waiting for Perkins to discuss the removal of Grimes.

Occasionally, Tiny would gently caress the top of his head, which was still very sore. The plaster, although skin coloured, stood out like a Belisha beacon. He wrapped his hand around the pint of I.P.A and took a long satisfying swig. He placed the glass on the table noting another had been settled and Perkins pulling a chair out to sit opposite him. The scraping noise from the chair reverberating through his head.

Perkins had noted the vast plaster on Tiny's head, which obviously hid a pretty dreadful wound, 'Tiny, you look like a man who's been to war, again.'

Throwing two paracetamols in his mouth, Tiny lifted the glass and took a large gulp swallowing the tablets, 'Perkins, Grimes is an absolute cunt,' the words were said with venom and heard by those in close proximity, 'and he deserves to die a fucking painful death.'

A couple heads swivelled at the word death.

Perkins was shocked by the ferocity of Tiny's outburst. The vein in his head appeared to be moving. Tiny resembled a man who could explode at any moment, 'Tiny, come now. Losing your focus, loses the battle. You need to calm down and think straight, as if you were in the trenches. I assume, you are the recipient of that from Grimes?' He nodded towards the blemish on Tiny's head.

Tiny's large hand immediately reached for the wound and stroked it. Violence was enveloping him, 'Yes, that little no good cunt did it. Whacked me with a mug, twice. Sliced the top of my head. Skin on my head was flapping about like two slices of corned beef.'

Perkins laughed, spilling a mouthful of beer on the table. Tiny himself smiled. The ice had been broken between both men.

Tiny replaced his glass on the red and black Trumans beer mat and slowly ran his finger around the top of the glass. He then gently tapped on the dark solid wooden table before lifting his head, 'Seriously, we need to remove Grimes. He is a menace. I want to leave his disgusting and depraved life. He drowned a number of innocent gay men whilst trying to locate Luke's murderer. He gave me this as I was in Hampstead when it happened.'

The pint of Perkins glass rested on his lips as if he were frozen. No drink flowed into his mouth. It took an effort to remove the glass. He did not know whether to consume a vast quantity or place the glass on the table. He was in a state of shock.

Tiny noted the quandary in Perkins actions and decided to put him out of his misery, 'I'm gay, and I was in the vicinity the night Luke's life was ended,' he felt an inner relief saying it. Perkins was the first he had told, 'Grimes is planning to end your life, and the life of the two police officers. He believes you are a snake who will talk to save your skin.'

Perkins was shocked by the information. Grimes had said he was a man of his word, yet the man facing him told him differently. He considered the information and decided there was only one option to prove his worth.

# Chapter 15

Berners Roding had been a strange choice, even for Joseph Grimes, yet an abandoned church gave it the terrifying feel he obviously craved. Julie could not decide if it was madness or genius. Yet, it did indicate Grimes had a vivid imagination for the dramatic. She understood time was running out, and that concerned her.

Joseph Grimes had found her through Steven Jacks. After a severe beating he had willingly given her up thinking it would save his sorrowful skin, wrong.

The man had been marched towards the altar which linked to Grimes and his vision for the dramatics.

The altar had a deep-seated meaning for Grimes. As a youngster, a vicar had taken a particular interest in him. The man had abused him anally for five painful years. Grimes himself had been the sacrifice. This had ended when Grimes became a man. He had returned to the church and abducted the employee of God, before returning to his farm. He proceeded to slice the man's Achilles and left him in the pigsty with his very hungry and aggressive porkers. It had taken five minutes for the screams of pain to begin and the pigs to gorge on the fresh juicy religious human flesh.

Yet this time, Jacks was the sacrifice.

Jacks was told to get on his knees and pray eternal forgiveness. He began to weep, and his nerves were shaking like old bones in the wind.

Grimes lifted his arm holding the nail gun and rested it against the man's head. Coldly and without motion he spoke, 'If you play with the big boys - you die like the big boys.'

Tears were cascading down his face, 'My girlfriends having our first child next week.'

Grimes laughed hysterically, 'I'll pass your best onto her, as you won't see her or the baby. In fact, I might eat your baby.'

The button was released. The ninety pounds per square inch tool punched a nail into his 7mm thick skull, leaving only the nail's head protruding. Jacks had a sudden look of surprise. His eyes blinked, and he hit the floor with a resounding thump.

Julie had been forced to watch the event; such was the devilment in Grimes. Insanity was a curse bestowed upon him, and he revelled in it. She had watched the surprise on one of his security personnel, even they looked appalled by the scene.

Grimes turned, a look of fury on his face, 'Now truss her up to the cross. Fun time begins.'

For the first time in her life Julie was frightened. She felt her underwear begin to dampen. She now knew how Steven Jacks had felt. A sense of dread was flying through her body. It was like a flag of fear. Never had she been in a situation or position like this. Now she understood how the four teenagers she had murdered in Thorndon Chapel felt.

One of the security officers growled at her, 'Stop wriggling like a worm, you bitch.'

A hard slap was administered to her face. She felt the warmth of it, and imagined it was reddening. Strong tape was being wrapped around her ankles, linking them together. Dread was now running throughout her body and her dream like state was broken.

'Pick her up and dump her on the cross.' The command was said with a complete lack of feeling.

Julia wanted to scream, but the Gaffa tape was stopping all forms of communication. She was unceremoniously hoisted like a rag doll and dropped onto the cold, smooth wooden surface. Suddenly, she felt her arms being yanked out. She tried to resist, but she was not strong enough.

'Don't resist, Julie. Your death will be religious. After all, you are keen on death in a church. Don't look so surprised, Jimmy Jackson thought it odd and told me. You did those boys years back, didn't you? I had you checked, thoroughly. Those boys killed your grandparents, so you did them. I don't give a fuck, but you're proper guilty.'

She heard a hearty laugh and understood the significance.

'Hold her arm against the wood.'

She then felt a searing pain shoot through her palm. It was like a bolt of lightning striking her. Tears were flowing. She thought of her grandparents and knew she was going to see them again, soon. Her other arm was grabbed. This time she offered no resistance.

The thud sound echoed throughout the deserted church. Julie's other palm had been nailed. Her mouth was dry, and she began to feel tired.

'Force her mouth, Tiny.'

Julie felt her chin being pulled vigorously and fingers shoved up her nose, making her yelp. Through her closing eyes she saw Joseph Grimes about to put powder in her mouth. She realised this was her final chance of redemption.

'Now, Julie. You're going to receive a dose of your own medicine.' Again, a maniacal laugh emerged from the bowels of Joseph Grimes. He began to poor the powder in her mouth, but made a mistake. He allowed his index finger to enter her mouth.

Julie was exhausted, yet found the strength to bite down on the grisly finger, ploughing her teeth through it until her they met again. She then swallowed hard, ensuring the remnants entered the deep dark confines of her stomach.

An agonising howl was heard by everyone in the church. Grimes was jumping up and down, 'That fucking bitch, that fucking cunt bit my finger off.'

Those based in the room all smiled inwardly. It was what he deserved, yet no-one would admit it.

Joseph lurched towards the nail gun and fired it ten times in the direction of Julie Brown. The accuracy of the nails was random. Hitting her in various parts of her body. One thing it did complete was the end of Julie's term of life.

Joseph Grimes casually placed the nail gun on the floor. He turned towards his security personnel who were a little shocked by the sudden outburst. He slowly walked around the body admiring the cross, the nails, the powder falling from the mouth and the overrule effect of the crucifixion and smiled. Turning towards his employees he happily remarked, 'That is art. I almost feel choked. I'm gonna call it *Death after Life*. It has a mythical feel about it. If I could take it home and place it in a preserving substance, I would. It's beautiful, absolutely stunning.'

Tiny assessed his employer and remembered how he had attacked him with the ashtray, leaving him with thirty-nine deep stitches. He knew Joseph Grimes was dangerous, but now realised he had entered into a dark arena of no return. His venture into the dark place meant life meant nothing to any unfortunate soul who crossed his path.

Joseph Grimes was hypnotised by the scene in front of him. The effect was mesmerising him. He could not be drawn away from trickles of blood trying to escape from the puncture wounds left by the nails. His brain kicked in and he turned to those awaiting his orders, 'Get the cross up, and ensure it is facing the church entrance.'

Tiny was the first to respond, 'Anything else, boss?'

Grimes looked at the man. He knew he should not have attacked him, yet it had shocked everyone in his employment, and since then everything had been stepped up 10%, 'It's ok, Tiny. I'll sort it all from here. I believe a few people we know may be interested in this beautiful piece of art. I'm sure the two police officers will be interested, along with that fucking slime ball Perkins and the other bloke Gary Jones. Once it's erected, tell everyone to fuck off home.'

Julie heard every word. The name Gary Jones shocked her and gave her renewed hope, although she was clinging on for life… just.

< >

Jack Philips returned to his office to find an envelope with his name left on his desk. He slid the letter opener in the corner and carefully opened it. He read the contents, 'Church, Berners Roding. Urgent.' He sat back in his chair wondering where Berners Roding was. Standing, he walked over to the map on the wall and searched for the area, finally locating it near to Epping. He had a bad feeling about this in the pit of his stomach. Something was not right, 'Drakey, assistance.'

DCI Drake briskly walked in, 'Alright, gov?'

Jack nodded at the letter on the table.

Drake leant forward and studied the writing. It was basic, yet detailed a message, 'Are we going then, sir? It pretty apparent that an urgent visit is needed.'

Jack looked at his heir apparent and knew a visit was needed to Berners Roding, yet something was worrying him. The person who had sent him the message knew him, yet he did not know them. There was a feeling in his inner regions that said, 'Do not go,' but another in his heart said, 'Hurry, go now.' Jack Philips understood he had to find the courage to do what was right. He knew he had to make a choice that was right, the one he believed in, and one a serving officer would make, 'Drakey, get yourself ready, we're on our way to Berners Roding, and I've a feeling it's not going to be a bed of roses.'

The forty-five-minute journey to Berners Roding gave Jack Philips thinking time. Silence during the journey was so brittle it could snap. Neither man spoke, what was there to say? Jack had a feeling of anxiety in his chest. He knew it was there to protect him. It sat there like a guardian angel.

Drakes glanced at his superior officer during the journey. It was unusual for Jack not to discuss theories and ideas, instead both sat knee deep in silence. Fear is natural and there to keep you alive, but there was a change in Jack. He had mellowed, and it worried Drake. When security personnel lost their edge, it was bad for the troop, yet the one who had lost his edge in this case was the superior officer. The man was planning retirement with Catherine. What he did not require was a dangerous case which could explode at any moment and Drake had a feeling this was going to be a case that could detonate at any time.

Berners Roding was not overly populated. It was home to 481 residents. The village was a close-knit family, small enough for everyone to know one another. The homes were much loved and well maintained and surrounded by lush green land.

Both officers arrived at the church and viewed the building that once been the centre of community. Now, it looked ready to be pulled down. The mysterious looking church lay just off a public footpath which ran through its graveyard towards the churches entrance. Both officers stood transfixed. The silence was finally broken.

'The difference between a gloomy church and a sanctuary of the soul is the sense of love felt by the individual. It's the inner peace felt by those entering the worshipful place.'

Jack Philips turned slowly and looked at his deputy, 'Fuck me, Drakey, where did that come from? That's pretty prophetic. Bet you went to Sunday school.'

'I most certainly did, gov. When I see an old ruin like this it makes me feel melancholy. Don't know why. I was the same when I served.'

'Hope you're not going soft? Come on. In we go.'

The damp long grass was attacking their footwear, darkening the shoe leather. Both noted how the graves and gravestones needed urgent repair, they resembled rotten broken teeth. Finally, reaching the churches entrance they were met by an old dark solid wood door that needed urgent attention. Twisting the handle, the door opened easily. A high pitch squill omitted from the old metal joints. A stale smell gate crashed both officers nose holes.

Gently, Drakey pushed the door open. Both officers tiptoed in being careful not to disturb anything. Two paces further and both were met with a sight they would never remove from their minds.

In front of them hanging from a cross was a woman. The gruesome outlook made both want to remove their breakfast, yet both were transfixed. She had been crucified. Her clothes had been removed. The only clothing remaining were her black lace knickers and bra. They approached gingerly. Neither removing their eyesight from the hanging master piece.

'She's alive. Her toe just moved. Drakey, go to one of the neighbouring houses and commandeer their telephone. If they give you any problems, do whatever you have to. Get everyone here as soon as possible.'

Drakey did not need another syllable. He was gone, like a flash.

Jack Philips was standing looking up at the hanging figure. She had been beaten up, the blue and yellow marks revealed that. Blood was running down her leg like little rivers, some congealing, others enjoying the ride, 'Julie. It is Julie Brown, isn't it? If you can hear me move your toe.' Jack looked at her feet, praying for movement.

Julie Brown, heard the command, and with all her remaining strength attempted to move her toes. She then passed out.

Jack saw the toes on her right foot move slowly. He had no idea how she was still alive. Each foot had been nailed, along with a nail through each palm. He stared at the lady, knowing she was something special. She obviously had an inner will he had never experienced in anyone. Tears began to form in his eyes, wiping them away he composed himself, 'Julie, stay with me. Help is on its way. Fight, do not let it beat you. Come on. Fucking fight, girl.'

The inner being in Julie restarted like an invisible force. She had to fight death. The pain had gone, to be replaced by despair. In her present state she welcomed death, but she had more to offer life. Confusion was enveloping her. What was that noise? She could hear a voice. They wanted her to fight. Fight, in her current predicament. If she could laugh, she would, but exhaustion was creeping towards her like a silent being. It wanted her to join deaths army.

<   >

Julie Brown was blue lighted in the ambulance to Oldchurch Hospital, and immediately rushed to the Trauma Unit. Doctors arrived from all areas to aid her. The wounds witnessed by the miracle workers shocked even their life-saving brains.

In her subconscious Julie heard someone shout, 'Come on Julie, survival takes courage, you are worth it. When you survive your life starts again. You will understand the power it took to survive, and how it made a giant of you. You will then walk with giants. So, start surviving, come on, Julie.' It was the final thing she remembered.

Julie was placed into an induced coma to allow her body to heal, having suffered a trauma few had experienced in their profession. Those nursing prayed her stay was short, allowing her a restful sleep enabling her brain, body and soul to rest and heal.

Her dreamlike state forced ideas of retribution. They swam through Julie's mind, continuously paddling backwards and forwards. The four-day coma would give her time to plan. Her mind continuously told her, 'You are strong. You are brave and a survivor.' Thoughts of crucifixion interrupted her positive pattern of thought and made her heart race. The red light on the life support machine began to jump about like a bouncing ball.

<  >

Gary Jones, sat still like a statue in the blue plastic chair, legs crossed, fingers intertwined over one knee. He leant forward and kissed the porcelain white cheek of the lady he had once adored.

During the lengthy process Gary had read about the machinery aiding Julie's recovery. The term *life support* referred to any combination of machines and medication keeping a person's body alive when their organs could stop working. It also gave doctors the ability to perform complicated surgeries and could prolong life for people who were recovering from traumatic injuries. Julie fell into the latter category. Traumatic being an understatement. Life support could also become a necessity for some people to stay alive.

Gary felt hollow inside. He had only experienced this feeling once before when his mother had passed away. He pondered how life had treated him. All his friends had died, his mother had been ravaged by cancer, and now Julie Brown – his one chance at redemption had been treated like a religious artefact by a seriously insane person. Dying could be fast or slow, painless or painful, yet you were still dead. Where you went, nobody knew. He remembered his mother saying, 'Birthing gives new life, and your body at the end generates life.' The words were prophetic. He smiled, a tear slowly descending down his face. His mother had been a great lady and one he still missed.

He bowed his head and lovingly examined Julie. Tubes emanated from all areas of her body. Some replacing fluids, other removing unwanted substances. The bandages showed an act of loving care, reassurance and competence. The red marks on the palms of her hands made the bandage look like the Japanese flag. It was truly horrific spectacle. Her feet were bandaged in the same manner, little pink blotches of blood were still trying to escape. The constant beep from the life support machine informed everyone that Julie Brown was still alive, just, and fighting for survival.

A radio was placed next to her bed, its volume kept low. The subtle sounds of George Michael singing 'A Different Corner' floated through the air. Gary considered how ironic the song was. Had he not bumped into Julie, then he would never have experienced her excitable lifestyle and criminal links. He still could not comprehend how she had entered the criminal fraternity. She always appeared so frail and innocent.

Julie moved her hand, grabbing Gary's.

Immediately, he called the night nurse.

Julie began to murmur. All they could hear was 'Nana, where's grandad?'

Gary understood the significance of these vital words. It showed her mind was functioning. Julie's grandparents had been killed in a road accident when she had been a teenager. Strangely, the men involved in the atrocity had gone missing and were never seen again.

As soon as the words ended beeps began emanating from the machine keeping her alive.

Gary Jones stood amazed. She had given up. Julie wanted to see her grandparents again.

Doctors rushed towards her bed.

Gary heard one doctor call out, 'Electroencephalogram, shows no sign.' He realised the life-ending words, even if he did not know their terms specifically. He knew enough for it to mean brain-death.

Swiftly, the nurses surrounded Julie's bed with curtains to give her privacy, for the final time.

Gary pushed through everyone standing before him and leant over Julie, kissing her softly on the lips, before whispering, 'Second to no-one, my love.' Julie grabbing his hand had been her final valour of strength and he had been the recipient of it. He then wept like an angel knowing she had loved him and he would never love again. His body a tidal wave of sadness.

# Chapter 16

Jack Philips sat in the office. Closing his eyes, he felt his brain stutter for a moment, his mind replaying the events he had witnessed. He had barely spoken since looking up at the hanging victim. He was still processing the enormity of what he had seen. Retirement was looming and he knew this was not a case to end your career on. It was big, too big. All those involved were big players and utterly ruthless.

Drake sat in his chair with his feet on the old wooden desk. He momentarily closed his eyes and his mind wandered. Every murder is the end of a story, but in this case, Julie Brown had survived, and her story would reach a conclusion, good or bad, it would reach an end. He hoped it would be good, although he was not convinced. This drama had plenty of twists and turns still to play out. Criminals acted for greed and selfishness. They damaged society, community, family, in fact - everything they touched. Criminals were a pariah on society. They offered nothing positive for life, and Joseph Grimes was an extremely negative man. He had to be stopped.

Drake's eyelids snapped open; he knew what had to be done. Standing, he walked purposely towards the office of Jack Philips. During the five second walk he noted his boss looked to be resting his eyelids. He rapped on the door and walked in before being formally welcomed.

Jack Philips was immediately alert. Years on the job has taught him to be sharp straightaway. He looked up, his eyes clearing in micro seconds, 'Drakey, you look like a dog who has located a big bone.'

'Gov, to bring down Grimes we need to bring down those who work for him and the man to start with is his head of security, Tiny. They'll corrupt themselves like a rotten apple.'

'Go on, Drakey.'

'If we can break them from the core, then the maggots will turn on one another, or they'll run for cover, leaving Grimes alone and vulnerable.'

Philips leant back in his chair and placed his hands behind his head looking at the ceiling that had become musty white due to the cigarette smoke continuously attacking it. He felt a chill in his blood. The coldness bringing him back to reality. He considered the idea put before him. It had positives and negatives everywhere, but it was an idea.

Drake had Philip's attention. The idea had grabbed his boss. When Jack Philips went quiet, he was pondering the success of an operation.

Jack Philips tilted forward looking at his colleague, 'The idea sounds plausible. It means we'll need proper safety nets as something always goes tits up somewhere along the line. Why Tiny?'

'Tiny knows Perkins. I reckon it's through the services. He has no allegiance towards Grimes apart from financial gain. So, he can be turned. We can use Perkins to speak to him. Also, I heard it was Grimes that smashed Tiny's head.'

'Why did he smash his head in? Bit extreme, even for Grimes.'

'No idea, but knowing Grimes it was to show control and put fear amongst those working for him. I also heard it was a bad cut. Whacked him with an ashtray.'

'Then Tiny is the object of our investigation. Hopefully, we can glean some information from him, and then we attack Grimes, and bring him down finally.'

Both men were considering the information, before their concentration was broken by a sharp rap on the glass window.

Philips waved the police constable in knowing it must be important, 'What?'

'Sir, been told to give you this information straightaway. Someone called Julie Brown died. That's it, sir.'

Both men stared at the other knowing the fall-out from Gary Jones could prove nuclear.

< >

He had been played like a pawn in a violent game of chess. How did Grimes always stay one step ahead of the game? The man was either a receiver of visions, or someone was feeding him information.

Tiny's mind could not explain how Joseph Grimes had known he was going to be in the White Swan. Vaguely, he remembered leaving the pub in Commercial Road – alone, and the next thing he remembered was being trussed up so his arms and legs were tightly and roughly bound with rope to prevent him from moving or escaping.

Tiny considered his Royal Marines career and its motto, 'Per Mare, Per Terram.' How ironic that neither linked to the situation he was in.

The canal was filling fast and there was little or no chance of breaking free from the hinged handcuffs. Having been handcuffed to the penultimate run at the bottom of the ladder had meant bending over at a ninety-degree challenging angle. It also gave him a noticeably unobstructed vision of the water rising in the lock. The pound lock on the canal gate had been opened and the area was filling with unwavering speed.

'Tiny, I thought men of the military were loyal, not snakes?'

Tiny lifted his head, although the angle impacted on his spine, sending a sharp jolt, 'I was always loyal, yet you've lost it since your fucking brother got done. He was a cunt anyway. No one liked that festering piece of dog wank. He was a fucking fairy. He was the sort of boy all us gays fucked for something to do. When I meet him in the afterlife, I'm gonna slice his throat slowly and enjoy the experience.'

Joseph Grimes was ready to explode, 'Don't speak about Luke like that you fucking traitor.'

Tiny smiled, home run. He had hit a nerve, 'No one likes you either. Everyone knows you're shit scared of me. You don't even realise what's going on around you, and how you're being played. Fucking idiot.' Tiny understood this would scramble the mind of Grimes.

Joseph Grimes considered the information. His inner being was in melt down, 'You fucking liar. You don't know anything.'

Tiny was smiling, broadly. He knew what he was going to do, but he also understood that Grimes was suffering an internal panic, 'Don't I.'

The rage in Grimes finally exploded, 'Tell me, fucking tell me you no good cunt.'

A glow began to form inside Tiny. He had Grimes in a corner. One final act would send him over the edge. He began to laugh, and laugh aloud. He hoped Grimes did not realise it was false laughter.

'Stop laughing, stop it now you no good cunt!' He felt he was ready to explode like a missile. His mind was a mine field. The laughing continued and Grimes was now in meltdown. His mind began to remember his father laughing at him when he had been a youngster, bullying him. Shoving him in the dark coal bunker during the cold nights when it had been snowing. Fighting his father off when he had tried to slide into bed next to him. Cries from Luke when his father had become intimate with him and the never-ending gaggle of laughter from his father as he penetrated Luke continuously. He knew he could not take it any longer. Removing the pistol from his waistband he aimed it at Tiny.

Tiny noted a dull glint from the metallic object. Inwardly, he smiled, although it was pained. He realised his life was near its end, yet he was pleased he would not drown. He would not fail his unit. Receiving a bullet was an honourable way to leave life. He had entered this world with nothing, but strength, loyalty and nous. He had served his nation with honour and was now ready to accept his last mission.

'Tiny, I always liked you. You were different from the rest, but you're a traitor, a fucking dirty no good treacherous traitor. Any last words?'

Tiny considered the request, and thought of something that would play on the mind of Joseph Grimes forever, 'I do, thank you,' he paused for breath and blurted, 'I know Perkins is the mole and I fucked your brother Luke. He yelped like a fucking weak girl.'

The snap and crack sound from the pistol were the last heard by the recipient. His body flopped forward. The water from the canal was now knee deep. In 45-minutes it would cover the corpse removing all the evidence.

Joseph Grimes stood looking down at the pathetic body. The single circular wound to the head looked peaceful and the death had been like taking medicine for a headache. Grimes thought he should feel regret, but felt nothing. Did this mean he was emotionless, like an empty vessel.

The old tramp sat in the shadows watching the man hoping he could not hear his breathing. Surrounded by the previous week's empty bottles. He dare not move in case the clinking sound gave his hide out away. Studying the man, he tried to capture key areas of his face with his photographic memory, or what was left of it. He already remembered the fallen man. They had served together in the Falklands. His name was Tim and they had both been decorated for bravery. How had he ended in this way? The man had charged an Argentinian machine gun nest single handily. Yet, here he was, the receiver of a bullet to the head. It was the wrong way to end for a man so brave. The man in the black suit with the weasel like chin would be shopped to the police. Tim deserved it. Tim deserved better. There was an oddity to the man. He was missing a section of his index finger.

Grimes slowly looked around, ensuring he had not been seen. If he had, the recipient would be the receiver of another bullet. Confident there was no other lifeform present he left the area. He looked at the sagging body of Tiny and mouthed, 'Traitor.' He then excessively growled in his throat producing a mouthful of phlegm and removed if from his mouth onto the bodies head. He then waked away and left the area.

<　　　　　　>

The body was removed from the water and the forensic pathologist slowly walked around the corpse before deciding to spout his information, 'Decomposition proceeded more slowly in the water due to the cooler temperatures. So, now the body has been removed from the water, degeneration will be accelerated. So, chop-chop we need to get this gentleman to the lab.'

Those present had seen a drowned man who had been the receiver of a bullet to the head. Many wondered why the forensic man had been required.

Everyone's concentration was broken by unkempt looking man hobbling towards them, 'His name was Tim. Tim was his name.'

Officers swiftly stood in front of the man. He had a distinct aroma surrounding him that attacked their nasal cavities. He reeked of urine, stale alcohol and body odour. A heady brew.

An officer strode through the cauldron and studied the man, 'You claim to know him, sir.'

'I served with Tim in the Falklands. Brave as a lion. The man who shot him is a no-good cunt. Looked like a weasel, thin, but dressed nice. Strange thing. Half his index finger was missing.'

Those in attendance could not believe what they were being told. This unhoused stinking tramp was a war hero, as was the dead man.

The barrage from the tramp continued.

'The weasel looking man kept saying Tim was a traitor. That's something he isn't. Man was a hero, bloody hero. Decorated by the Queen. Strange thing though. It appears he was a queer.'

Jack Philips studied the man and felt a sense of sadness envelop him. He removed his brown leather wallet from his pocket and thrust twenty pounds into the man's left hand and shook his right, 'Get yourself something to eat, sir. May I ask your name?

The tramp looked at the man. No-one had asked him that for years, 'Lieutenant Samuel Brown.' It was the first time he had felt a sense of pride in many moons.

Philips was going to speak to someone about this man and see if anything could be done to help him, 'Sir, thank you for your help, and you sir, are a hero.'

< >

Philips, Drake and Jones sat in the Little Chef along the A127 savouring their Olympic Breakfast. There was a sense of calm anchored in the well- earned meal. All three sat quietly. The only sound coming from the slapping of their lips and the chink of cutlery. Jack Philips broke the silence.

'Gents, Joseph Grimes. What are we going to do? His accomplice, Tiny, has been found dead in Carpenters Road Lock.'

The heads of Drake and Jones shot up with a look of astonishment.

Drake began to speak quietly, 'How?'

Jack considered his words, but decided to be abrupt, 'Shot through the top of his head, although he was tied to the penultimate rung of the ladder so he would have drowned as the water was flowing through. Another fact has emerged. Tiny, also known as Tim, was a war hero. He fought in the Falklands war. Bloke was decorated for bravery. He received the Victoria Cross from the Queen. Secondly, the man who shot him had one half of his index finger missing. A final piece of information, which may put you off your breakfast, but an autopsy on Julie Brown showed she had half a finger in her stomach.'

Jones considered the information, 'The word hero is used too often, but in this case, it is fully deserved.' He then grabbed his mug of tea and proposed a toast, 'Tiny, the unknown hero.'

All three lifted their mugs.

Drake swiftly returned to business mode, 'Shot through the top of the head you said? So, we can assume the shooter lost control of the situation and fired in rage. Interestingly, the drowning aspect takes a specific mindset, usually a psychopath. A person with psychopathy often shows a lack of empathy, guilt, conscience, remorse, lacks feeling or emotion, impulsivity, a weak ability to defer gratification and control behaviour. Does this remind you of anyone gents?'

Jones looked squarely at Drake, 'How the hell did you know that? You are referring to Grimes. He fits the profile on all of those.'

Drake laughed, 'Profile… check you out Juliet Bravo.'

Jack Philips considered everything. He knew the answer was Grimes, but he had now gone missing, 'We need to find Grimes. He's on the missing list. Probably holed up in one of his properties. Which one, we have no idea.'

Jones spoke up, 'I heard Tiny visited the surgeon in Green Lane to have a wound on his head sealed. Members of the underworld go there to have minor operations done. I spoke to the surgeon, who said he was in and out in fifteen minutes.'

'So, Grimes is our focus, totally. We must shake a few trees to see what hits the ground. Any ideas? The finger thing, intrigued me. If we find Grimes, then we'll find a man nursing a missing digit.' Philips looked at Jones, 'I had to say it, Jones. Info' has to flow freely amongst us.'

Gary Jones understood the information had to be shared, 'To be honest with you. I am incredibly proud of Julie. To think she was dying and she had the strength and nous to give us a massive clue. That is amazing.'

Drake excitedly jumped, 'Perkins, Perkins. It's Perkins.'

Philips and Jones looked towards Drake. Both were surprised by the outburst. They had never seen the man show any emotion. He was usually an icicle.

Drake continued, 'The tape. The fucking tape. The tape in Grimes office. It had the name Perkins on it. It meant nothing to me at the time. But it's obvious now. Grimes had something on Perkins and it was on the tape. Perkins has been playing both sides.'

Philips lifted the mug and took a long savouring swig of his sweet tea. He pondered the information, 'You sure about the tape, Drakey?' He realised his colleague was correct, but he had to ask, 'If, and I say if you are correct. Then Perkins cannot be trusted. We have to treat what he tells us with a pinch of salt, or we get hold of him and force him to tell us everything he knows. Either way, it's a game of chance, for all parties.'

# Chapter 17

Perkins strolled casually from Century House situated in Westminster Bridge Road and hailed a black cab.

The driver eyed the man calling. He had obviously come from the spy headquarters. They all looked the same. Navy blue or grey suits, white shirts, black shoes, and ties that did not stand out, 'Yes, gov?'

'Morpeth Arms, please.'

A secret service man visiting a bar frequented by men of the same ilk. How typical was he, 'No problem, take us 10 minutes to get to Millbank. Traffic's a bit slow at the moment.'

Perkins considered the news, '10 minutes is perfectly acceptable, thank you.' During the journey he watched the industrious people of London being busy. Each one holding a secret no-one else knew. It was their private place. He enjoyed looking at illicit touching of hands, knowing smiles, admiring glances… anything. Each told a story of happiness, need, greed or loathing. The journey lasted 9 minutes.

'Alright, gov. Here's your port of call. That'll be £4.'

Perkins removed himself from the vehicle and extricated £5 from his tattered - yet secure wallet, and passed it to the driver, 'Thank you, and keep the change, have a splendid day.'

He watched the black cab leave the area before hailing another.

Perkins jumped sprightly into the back, 'Hoop and Grapes, Farringdon Street, please.'

The driver assessed the man in his rear-view mirror. He looked a civil servant. An Executive Officer in one of the branches. He was well-mannered and nicely spoken. He decided to divulge some information, 'Did you know it's been a pub since 1721. It was well-known for illegitimate Fleet weddings.'

Perkins sat quietly in the back digesting the information. He was neither interested nor bothered by the information conveyed. He wondered why black cab drivers always wished to talk and pass on snippets of useless information. As if he would wish to know when the public house had been erected or who had frequented the premises.

Eventually, the driver stopped rambling, understanding his fare did not wish to talk.

The journey took 17 minutes before the cab stopped outside the tired looking pub.

Perkins retrieved £10 from his wallet and handed it to the driver, who returned £4 change.

Standing on the street, Perkins surveyed the area. The vicinity was pub heavy. The White Swan was directly opposite, and the King Lud stood proud on the corner of Ludgate Circus. Fleet Street was one hundred metres away. An area famed for its drinking culture due to the newspapers printed there in a previous life. He turned and surveyed the pub he was about to enter. It resembled an antique. The outside was a little drab and tired. The black paintwork was covered in microscopic dust and needed a good clean. The stain glass windows were inspiring. Ageing had created a thing of beauty, almost mystical.

Perkins entered the pub and observed Grimes sitting towards the rear of the pub in the corner. He was obviously witnessing those entering, waiting for his lunchtime date to arrive. Grimes resembled any self-respecting gentleman employed within the city. His attire was incredibly smart and beautifully cut. His navy-blue suit had been made for him in one of London's finest tailors and his crisp white shirt spoke of wealth. He looked every inch a respectable businessman. A wolf in sheep's clothing.

'Grimes.' The introduction lacked feeling.

'Perkins. How nice to see you? Pull up a pew. I've got you a Guinness in, and ordered you a sarnie. I've eaten mine. I was famished. It was genuinely nice as well, you'll enjoy it.' Grimes studied the man's face. He looked worried, concerned almost pathetic. 'What's wrong, Perkins? You look like you've dropped a tenner and found a pound. I'd also like to thank you for the final snippet of information you passed me.'

Perkins understood that Grimes was playing a game of cat and mouse with him. The man must have thought he had the upper-hand, which he did have until the video was retrieved, 'Let's be honest, Grimes. I want the tape, badly, and you have possession of it. I have jumped through hoops for you, and passed you information you would receive from no other. So, do I want the tape. Yes.'

Grimes was enjoying the scenario being played out. He felt like a wasp continuously buzzing around someone watching them become annoyed, 'You have played your part, Perkins, thank you. Your debt has been paid.' Grimes laughed falsely, showing his gleaming white teeth, 'You are free. Smile man, aren't you pleased?'

Perkins considered the question. Lifting his head, he spoke quietly, but with authority, 'The tape, you do have the tape?'

Perkins let out a raucous laugh and slowly placed a hand into his jacket pocket producing a package, 'There you are. A deal is a deal.' He passed a VHS video cassette to Perkins, 'Let it never be said that Joseph Grimes reneges on a deal.'

Perkins hands greedily snapped hold of it, 'Thank you. You swear on your brother's soul there are no other copies?'

Grimes considered the response, 'On my life, and Luke's. There are no other copies. I'd like to say though. You certainly did service those two school girls. You randy 'ole bugger. Anyway, enjoy the sarnie. It was pretty decent. I have other people I need to see. Have a good life.' He removed himself from his seat and strode away mingling with the overworked lunchtime commuters along Farringdon Street.

A bead of sweat fought its way down the side of Perkins cheek nestling just above his collar line. He was free, but knew he was tainted with dishonesty and betrayal. Betrayal would eat away at his soul until it consumed him unless he dealt with its hunger. He leant back in his chair and admired the books on the shelves, obviously for show as they were all covered with a layer of dust. His wandering eye was attracted to *The Count of Monte Cristo*. The novel's themes were hope, justice, vengeance, mercy, and forgiveness. All of these linked to his current situation with Grimes. The man was a pariah, and one that needed removing from life. Leaning forward he took a satisfying bite from his cheese and ham sandwich, followed swiftly with a slurp of Guinness. The dark liquid had a caramelized flavour that brought resolve to his soul. Replacing the pint on the table he leant back and placed his hands across his torso considering his options.

I. Resign.
II. Coerce fully with Philips and Drake.
III. Bring the whole sorry affair to its knees.

He immediately knew his next move.

Grimes made his way home to Chigwell listening to the soulful sounds of George Michael, unsure of Perkins and his loyalty. What concerned him was Perkins and his length of service in security. It aligned itself to someone who was respected, honourable and dedicated. He hoped and prayed Perkins would not become a Judas, yet doubt was eating away at him. He knew the man, if faced with a choice he would side with the greater good. Grimes could lose everything for nothing, and that would not be acceptable. It was a shame because he had a sense of respect towards Perkins. There was only one option. Perkins had to go missing forever.

<　　　　　　　>

Gary Jones left Fleetway House, having had a productive meeting with his Barclays Bank advisor. He turned right and began to stride out towards Farringdon Station, yet something brought him to slow standstill. His brain was telling him to stop. He slowly turned to his left and noted Joseph Grimes getting into his car. Jones, eyes locked on the man, his breath even yet deep. It was as if his brain was suffering a massive-short circuit and was struggling to compute the reasons for Grimes being in the vicinity. He noted the public house Grimes had just vacated. It was not his usual fare. He had obviously had a meeting. He decided it could be productive waiting a while to see who would emerge.

Jones, changed direction and made his way to the White Swan public house. Striding to the bar he kept glancing at the building housed on the opposing side. He ordered half a pint of Castlemaine and a sausage baguette with onions, before finding a stool and table housed by the window which gave him a vantage point of everything.

Jones, wrapped his hands around his meal and was mid bite when he froze. Out of habit, he moved closer to the window hoping his eyes were not playing tricks.

Perkins, left the Hoop and Grapes. His usual swagger fled faster than a losing gambler from his bookmaker. He swallowed. He lifted the tape and kissed it like a man would his long-lost lover.

Jones, replaced the baguette and watched Perkins. The man had kissed a video tape. Drake had said something about a tape in Grimes office. Drake had been correct. There was only one thing to do.

Perkins, decided to walk a little. His emotional state was jubilation mixed with relief. He bounced along

Shoe Lane before face planting the pavement and being the receiver of a short sharp kick to the bollocks.

'You fucking slime ball. You've played us all.'

Perkins was fighting for his lungs to work. The desire for much needed oxygen made him feel like he was drowning in the middle of a busy London Street. Spittle was running from his chin onto the grey cold slabs that had seen millions of people trapse over them, Slowly, in time his internal breathing apparatus began to resume back to its normal operation. He turned his head allowing him to see his attacker. His dry mouth mustered one word, 'You?' His head then rested on the floor before he could raise another one syllable question, 'Why?' He felt like his eyeballs were burning.

Jones looked at the pathetic specimen on the floor. Anger mixed with curiosity was unusual feeling he was experiencing. Perkins was meant to be an ally, yet here he was dancing with the enemy. Perkins began to rise to his knees, allowing Jones the chance to begin his interrogation, 'Grimes, you were with that slag in the pub, and what's on the tape? Do not lie or fuck me about, or I will peel your skin off with my bare hands.' Jones let the information sink into before going forward with the hammer blow, 'Tiny is dead and I have a feeling you snaked him. Julie Brown is dead, and whoever killed her I will finish personally. That person will have fuel poured down their neck and be set alight inside out.'

Perkins rose unsteadily to a standing position. He studied his attacker. Jones was taller than he remembered and immaculately dressed. The man had a presence about him, although he guessed inner-demons would consume

Jones due to his truculent and aggressive lifestyle. Perkins considered his options, and decided there was only one avenue to walk down... the truth, 'Grimes played me like a fool. A bloody fool.' He hoped Jones found him convincing as he realised this man was a controlled psychopath. He was the epitome of danger.

Jones stared deep into the man's blue eyes. They had a pitiful, almost lost look in them. External damage may have healed, yet damage to the man's mind would last forever, 'I got where I am by being tough, but the real prize was staying honest to myself, knowing my strengths and weaknesses. You have not stayed true to yourself, Perkins.'

Perkins could not believe he was being given words of wisdom by a man who walked both sides of law. He knew all the nonsense being spouted. The wise support with wisdom and the foolish man becomes a king. Did that make him the Macbeth character?

Jones wanted to pity the man, but he was passed pity. He was out for revenge, 'Tell me something that'll interest me, Perkins? We are seriously passed the time of bullshit.'

Perkins swiftly racked his brain for something that would inform the man opposite him he was telling the truth, 'Something that may interest you is his fingerprints.'

Jones's eyes bored into the man, 'Are you really trying to fuck me off.'

Perkins understood once the information he was going to pass to the neanderthal facing him there was no going back, 'Fingerprints, there are none for Grimes on any police or security file anywhere. He sliced them off in his teens. He would have placed them on a sand grinder removing all traces. The pain must have been unbearable. Once done, he would have dipped them into salt water and TCP mixture, before bandaging the tops for six weeks. After this period of time his fingertips would have a fine indelible finish, untraceable. Does that satisfy your thirst for knowledge?'

Jones took a deep breath and exhaled noisily. He considered the implications. Grimes was almost untouchable. The man was the bedrock of all the problems, yet no-one could lay a finger on him. He turned away from Perkins and began to pace, 'Perkins, if you're playing me, us, I'll fucking end your life. I don't know what's on the tape, but people are curious.' He turned to find the position held by Perkins's empty. If anything, the man was fleet-footed and light on his feet.

The soles of Perkins shoes were moving swiftly upon the solid ground towards the safety of Fleet Street. Blending in with the crowds were an encore for the heart of Perkins. He felt immense relief that his testicles still remained attached to his body, and relief he was still able to live another hour. Grimes and Jones were a formidable double act. Both believing they were acting for the greater good. He needed to remedy the situation, yet it would need to be resolved swiftly, correctly and decisively.

# Chapter 18

Joseph Grimes had been the receiver of interesting news. The man investigating him was retiring to live out his days with his wife, Catherine. He pondered the information in the security and sanctity of his safe house.

Going to ground had been easy for Grimes. The population of East London was approximately 2,500,000 people. This meant removing himself from the oncoming explosive situation was easy – if you understood how. He had stocked up with a few weeks of provisions to aid his disappearance. He knew this would concern those seeking him as they would be wishing to speak to him about events that had taken place.

The mid-terraced Plaistow home had been erected in the 1930s and was solid made with real bricks, not like the cardboard houses erected now-a-days. Grimes had also purchased the terraced houses either side and the one behind.

His brother, Luke, had thought it a ridiculous idea, purchasing three houses next to each other in Plaistow. Joseph had not informed him about his reasons behind it. He had also added extra security measures. Knocking a hole through the wall linking to house number 13, and another sharing number 17 gave him an extra feeling of invincibility. Sturdy wardrobes on small coasters had been placed in front of the holes, and cardboard had been positioned across the holes to hide them. Whether it was paranoia or sharp-thinking he did not care, it was security.

He sat in his chair, which faced the window listening to LBC, and their thoughts on the Prince's Trust concert taking place at Wembley. The idea seemed plausible and worthwhile, but would it help? He did not care.

The name Perkins sprung to his mind. Since that man had come into the family's life everything had gone tits-up. Luke had been murdered, Tiny had turned traitor, Julie Brown had suffered a magnificent ending on the cross and it all linked back to fucking Perkins. On top of that the filth were all over him. The family was being investigated thoroughly, due to that secret service slag. Perkins, had proven to be a reliable and dependable source for information, although he had only done it due to the £250,000.00 casino debt, and the under-age sex tape. Yet, his time on earth was ending. Grimes, stood and walked slowly towards the window and looked down the desolate and quiet street. He made his decision. Perkins was a dead man.

Perkins had stopped attending all gambling institutions, yet was a man of routine. He dined in the same places; Oslo Court based in St. Johns Wood being his favourite. He visited the establishment every Sunday at 1pm, and ventured to the Morpeth Arms most Friday's from 5pm until 7pm. This could mean his removal would not be difficult. Yet, he kept returning to Oslo Court. Grimes had dined at the restaurant and vaguely remembered it had five or six floors.

A smile formed. From the Cheshire grin came a glorious sense of hope. Certain ideas made him deliriously happy. Somehow, this one brought him to life inside. His heart was pumping, he felt the incredible pulse racing through his fingertips. He was going to enjoy this… really enjoy this. Fuck, he felt alive, like he had been during the early days.

Oslo Court had been built in 1937 and contained one-hundred and twenty-five one-bedroom flats, many with balconies. The flats were owned by business people using them Monday to Thursday, or people using them for illicit affairs. A high majority were empty over the weekend.

Gaining entry would be easy. Looking and acting confident were necessary tools for deception and blending in essential. He knew he would have to insert two points of the bobby pin into the lock and press the pin forward into the lock. Depending on the door, simple forward pressure would be enough to open the door successfully.

He would have to use bait to get Perkins into the flat. Using a young girl would be no good. The man would be too wily to fall for such a trick. This leant itself to a woman in her thirties being required. She would have to be one who oozed class and sophistication. Someone privately schooled and someone who understood restaurant etiquette.

Grimes deliberated over those he knew and suddenly realised there was only one lady for the job. Sexy Suzy. She had been privately educated at Roedean, born to a wealthy family, a friend of people with influence and a lady who had starred magnificently in two adult rated films. She had won an award for her roles in the extremely successful 'ET – The Extra Testicle' and 'The Empire Fucks Back.' She had been the recipient of countless cocks during the film and loved every moment. Yet, she had principles and a working brain. Everyone had to pay with cash and pay straightaway. Those that did not pay were usually striped across the face from her hidden switchblade.

He mulled over the idea. Suzy would fit the bill perfectly. Everyone liked Suzi, a little too much. Yet, Suzi enjoyed being used in a physical manner. It was one of the reasons Roedean had informed her parents to remove Suzanne from their institution. She had been caught with her head immersed between the legs of their head of P.E.

The female-teacher had her contract annulled, and it was swiftly swept aside as the school did not wish to have any adverse publicity.

Suzi, or Suzanne as her parents preferred to address her, were aghast when they had also been informed their daughter had been caught pleasuring two other pupils orally from her school as well. Suzi's father, a prominent member of parliament sat bewildered when informed. All he could say was, 'This had better not get out.'

Joseph Grimes, reached for the olive-green telephone and dialled the number.

Immediately, a succulent silky voice answered, 'Hello, to what do I owe this pleasure?'

'It's Joseph Grimes.' The statement was said without feeling.

Suzi considered the words. Joseph Grimes, why had he removed himself from his pit of filth? A man with a small cock, small mind, mountains of cash and well-known humongous temper, 'Joseph, a silver tongue is a blessing if you use it to help, heal or spread love. Yet, I am sure you do not fall under the three categories; therefore, I am not interested.'

Joseph Grimes could not believe how he was being dismissed like a naughty school-boy, yet he knew Suzi had a weakness, 'Does twenty-five bags moisten one of the categories?'

Suzi licked her lips and considered the offer. She understood it would be murky, yet murky intrigued her, 'Speak Joseph, you have Suzi's attention for one whole minute. £25,000 has grabbed my attention… briefly.'

Grimes smiled. Money had always been Suzi's downfall. Since her father passed away, and her mother had remarried she had become the family pariah.

Her father's will had bequeathed her the family flat in South Kensington and the estate in Devon. Suzi had wealth and assets, but she was a lover of cash… lots of it, 'Suzi, your talents are needed to ensnare a member from your background.'

'Background?'

Grimes replied swiftly, 'Someone who speaks nicely and was privately educated.'

Suzi let out a deep-rooted laugh, 'You want me to arrange a sting. Soften someone up so you can do whatever you wish to do to them. Please don't think of me as naïve. Only a fool would think that, Joseph.'

Grimes laughed gently. Suzi was a game girl. She understood the rules of day-to-day life. For the next thirty minutes he explained what was required from his new employee. The only thing demanded by Suzi was the cash be delivered to her during a luncheon at Oslo Court the following day.

< >

Suzi entered Oslo Court looking her premium best. Everyone's eyes glanced her way. The men lusted after her, and the women secretly wished to be her. She had a sense of power dressing, yet maintained a feminine charm. The maître d' checked Suzi's name on his list. He then raised an eye at Suzi and studied here surreptitiously, 'Do you have any identification, madam?' Suzi leant forward so her pert breasts could be noted. This ensured her assets were given full attention. Suzi opened her Yves Saint Laurent black handbag and dug in to it producing her black passport, 'Is this sufficient? May I ask why you require this documentation?' Suzi understood the reason, yet wished to play the innocent victim. She watched the man look at the picture displayed in the passport, he then studied her.

The maitre d' took a couple of seconds to respond. He had been immersed in the ladies beautiful and fuckable breasts. He returned Suzi her passport and looked apologetic, 'I am sorry, madam. We had a package delivered to the restaurant addressed to you and I had to be sure I passed it to the rightful owner. I am sure you understand.'

Suzi noted the apologetic look in the man's eyes. He was obviously a person who avoided confrontation, yet someone who was very professional and honest. Suzi thought he would make someone a good husband, assuming he was not gay and by the way he had studied her cleavage he was not. Suzi accepted her passport, 'Thank you, your professionalism shines through, and the restaurant is fortunate to have someone like you at the helm of their business.' She watched the man, and he was trying not to smile at the compliment. He had also gained an erection she noted.

Suzi was shown to her table, and the waiter materialised as if he had risen from the ground. She ordered a crisp white zinfandel and was shown the menu. Having perused the menu, she settled for griddled pink grapefruit segments and a beautiful Dover Sole.

Dining at the restaurant allowed Suzi to survey the surroundings and those employed by the establishment. It also permitted her the chance to seek the emergency exits, should they be required. Nothing could be left for chance. Just in case Grimes slipped up on his quest for ultimate power.

Ninety-minutes later Suzi left the restaurant, comfortable with the knowledge gained. She had ensured those employed remembered her. Leaving a sizeable tip and kissing the maitre d,' leaving a red outline of her lips on the gentleman's cheek.

Suzi left the restaurant and hailed a black cab. The cab driver was a chatty person. She could not help but think that passengers were his release system and that he was enjoying the audience in the rear of his cab, whether they listened or not made no difference.

Upon entering her flat, Suzi made a cafetière of strong coffee and considered the afternoons events. Having mulled the information, she telephoned Joseph Grimes.

'Yes.'

'Joseph. You must improve your inter-personal skills. You are a little aggressive and abrasive when answering the telephone.' Suzi was met with a couple of seconds of no-noise.

'I'm not selling double-glazing am I, Suzi? Did you get your wedge?'

'Everything was in order, Joseph. Thank you. Now, down to the finer details of your operation. When do you want it to happen?' The immediacy and ferocity in the reply, shocked Suzi.

'Straightaway. I want that cunt, and I want that cunt, now!'

<     >

Perkins left the underground station and strolled along St Johns Wood Terrace admiring the homes. The terraced homes were immaculate, like freshly pressed garments and the people he strode past spoke using formal language, not the estuarine dialect the younger generation chose to use now-a-days. They were unable to string two words together without using a form of profanity, or the informal word *like* at the end of a sentence.

He entered Oslo Court to be met with a warm smile, and immediately the maitre d' held out his hand and greeted Perkins with a firm handshake.

'Good afternoon, Mr. Perkins. Your table is ready, although we have had to place you with another guest, a beautiful lady.'

Perkins listened with interest. The beautiful lady section grabbed his attention. One man's beauty was another man's poison he thought.

The maitre d' extended his arm to follow.

Perkins was instantly drawn towards a lady in a fitted electric blue dress with structured shoulder pads. She had a look of sophistication and class. Her devil red lipstick left a coating on the lip of her glass. The maitre d' had been correct… she was beautiful.

'Mademoiselle.' The maitre d' moved the chair allowing Perkins to place his frame on the opposing side of Suzi.

Perkins decided he needed to take control of the conversation, 'Thank you for allowing me to share this table with you. Do you come here often?'

Suzi understood the man was attempting to show his dominance, but she decided to play along with the game.

Over the forthcoming two hours Suzi decided Perkins was a good man. He listened to her conversation as if she were the most interesting person he had met. Occasionally, he was thinking deeply, considering how the conversation will change in two moves. His conversation was attentive and offered kindness. She believed this the most attractive feature she had ever found in a man. Suzi had to keep reminding herself that this man, Perkins, was going to die soon. For the first time in her life, she felt an instant pang of guilt. This was wrong. She had to right it somehow.

Perkins had an odd feeling in the pit of his stomach. He knew this lady was going to play an integral part of his life. The thought excited him. He decided to vary on the conversation, 'Every discussion I ever have revolves around fear, terrorism, money, politics - no-one ever focuses on the real puzzles of our age or love. I want to talk to someone who understands our intellectual prowess. I want to converse with someone who understands the cages of the mind are there to be broken down.'

Suzi was melting with the intellectual barrage coming her way. This man was her equal. He wanted everything she wanted. He was the opposite end of Joseph Grimes. She felt a sudden loathing of Grimes. The man was a cesspit full of malodorous waste. She felt the man dining with her held specific secrets, but he was a hemisphere in class away from Grimes. Suddenly, she blurted out, 'I like you; cannot stay here. Someone wishes to cause you harm, and I do not wish that to happen.'

Perkins lifted his short, stemmed brandy glass and took a sip of its contents before looking at Suzi.

Suzi felt emotional, and when Perkins was staring at her she felt he was analysing her soul.

Perkins then began to talk, 'Suzanne Belchambers, father deceased, lives out of South Kensington, owner of an estate in South Devon, not married, no children, removed from Roedean. How am I doing?' He knew he had trumped anything the lady in front of him had gained. Her mouth had dropped open, 'Close your mouth, my dear. People will believe you are a Jenny doll.'

Suzi's mouth had run dry of her fluids. All she could mutter was, 'How?'

'My dear. When I dine here, I make it my business to know those dining that day. That is all I shall reveal. Finally, Joseph Grimes. You know him I take it, and let me guess, this is a honeytrap?'

Suzi could only nod. Yet found the energy to make a statement, 'Yes, it was, but having met you I began to really like you. I do not know why, but for the first time in my life someone was my equal. I cannot explain it.'

Perkins raised his eyebrow. He knew the lady facing him was not lying. When she had tried to sway the conversation in another direction, she flicked her hair behind her left ear. He had a deep-seated feeling that she honestly did like him. What worried him was he liked her.

During the next thirty minutes both discussed what was due to happen. It was decided they would need to follow through with the plan devised by the two of them.

<  >

Grimes had been sitting in the flat waiting for Suzi and her pray. He had remained at the window watching every move to and from the restaurant.

He ran his hand over the silky paintwork and felt his insides squirm in a way they had not done since the crucifixion. His mind felt like it was on the ocean waiting for the incoming storm. He felt calm on the surface, yet underneath the deep currents were swirling ready to sink anything that stood in its way, and the good ship Perkins was ready to be sunk.

Patience was a virtual he had gained through experience. The person waiting had to follow a specific itinerary. Empty bladder, go without food and drink, suffer aching muscles, stay alert and not become bored. Grimes knew he had to be professional, but also understood he was wound up and would want to punch Perkins when he entered the plush apartment.

Although patience was a virtue, he was beginning to wonder why Suzi was taking so long. She only had to butter Perkins up, flirt with him a little and entice him upstairs to bed. His concentration was momentarily broken. Suzi was leaving alone. Curiosity was eating away at him. He understood it was how a person learnt, but Suzi was diverting away from the plan and where the fuck was Perkins?

Suddenly, there a short sharp rap on the door. Grimes stood swiftly and bound quietly to the door. He soundlessly looked through the spy hole and saw the cleaning lady standing there in her blue trousers, pale blue top, and pinafore - that stopped just below her waist. She was alone. This unexpected nuisance had to be removed. He mulled over the calculations and decided to answer the door.

Grimes was met with a lady in her sixties wearing her blue uniform. Her grey curly hair was perfectly set and she was wearing blue slippers. Grimes had to smile at the woman's endeavour. She was obviously a resident who cleaned the flats as a part-time means to earning a little more cash.

'Hello, do you want your flat cleaned. I usually do it for Mr. Smith and his young wife when they are present during the week.'

Grimes noted a little smile when the lady mentioned wife. Whoever Mr. Smith was, he had a young fuck buddy, 'No thank you love. I'm only here for one night, so I am not expecting to leave too much grime.' Grimes laughed falsely. He hoped the lady would fuck off.

'Ok. If you want anything I'm on the third floor, number 6.' She turned and left the area.

Grimes shut the with a pinch of annoyance. He began to remove himself from the hallway when the there was another rap at the door, 'Fuck me, won't the woman go.'

The door opened slowly, and immediately Grimes knew it was a mistake. At the last second, he noted two fingers heading towards his eyes, and a short sharp jab was administered. He felt a sharp burning sensation in his socket and dropped to the ground struggling for vision. Tears were cascading from his eyes effecting his vision, yet he could make out the blurred outline of Perkins. The man stood behind him and lifted him as if he were no weight. Perkins planted two of his fingers into the nose holes of Grimes and dragged him effortlessly like an underfed pig.

'Hello, old chap. Now, do not fight it. I am going to apply a little pressure to the Stomach 9, which is located in the neck, adjacent to your Adam's apple. The Vagus nerve measures the blood pressure of the arteries to the neck. This means your brain will receive a high blood pressure sign and will endeavour to lower your body's blood pressure. Since blood pressure is actually not high for real, lowering the blood pressure will result in you going into a short sleep. Now, doesn't that sound jolly? Remember 'ole chap. Never try to take on a member of her Majesty's service. We are elitist.'

Grimes tried to speak, but his mouth had no fluid, and his legs were like jelly. He tried to stand but immediately dropped to the floor.

Perkins wasted no time in taping Grimes. He ensured the yellow cleaning gloves had no marks. He then hoisted Grimes towards the bath and lowered him into the tub. He handcuffed the hands of Grimes to the bath handles using cable ties. The final act performed by Perkins was replacing the plug and turning the hot-tap anti-clockwise. Water began to rush from the tap filling the bath.

The hot water attacked the skin of Grimes who awoke. He wanted to shout, but he could not move. His mouth had been taped securely around his head. He saw Perkins smiling.

'You look like a boil in the bag dinner. Anyway, I am going now. Enjoy the last moments of your life. When I drop this appliance in the bath you will suffocate when your diaphragm is restricted through paralysis. He then lifted a two-bar heater and dropped it in the bath.' Perkins stood watching as the body of Grimes thrashed about in the bath as if he were dancing.

Grimes was staring at Perkins. He was a man of resilience, and one he should have been more careful around. He looked at Perkins harder and saw his father standing next to him. He was mocking him. What was his father doing there? He tried to speak, but breathing was taking maximum effort. He again stared into his father's eyes and roared with everything he had left, 'You always were a cunt, dad.'

Perkins stood watching Grimes out of interest. He thought he had heard him say something about his dad, although he was unsure. Anyway, Grimes was now past tense.

# Chapter 19

Water began to cascade into the apartment below through cracks in the ceiling. They resembled silent tears slowly creeping down the walls.

The occupant raced upstairs and banged on the door. She received no response and was about to leave when she noted a trickle of water trying to escape from under the entrance. She returned to the door and rapped harder, again without reply. She hastily returned to her apartment and contacted the management company whose operative arrived within thirty minutes.

The maintenance engineer showed no urgency when entering the premises. Contempt showed on his face. Sunday afternoon, and here he was in St. Johns Wood sorting out an idiot's plumbing problem that could have been stopped had they taken due care. Finally, he reached the flat and noted the water running from under the door. He imagined opening the door to be met with a tidal wave of foam similar to Inspector Clouseau, it made him smile. He opened the door and became more concerned with the water suffocating the carpet. The water was moving constantly from the bathroom.

A terrible shriek could be heard by everyone within the vicinity. The sort of noise that would haunt the listener forever.

The bath in the apartment was overflowing like an angry waterfall. The maintenance engineer could not remove his eyes from the artwork in front of him. In the bath was a man, fully dressed, who's skin and flesh looked cooked, and the room had a sickening aroma of boiled pork.

The engineer violently spun towards the toilet and removed his wife's roast beef Sunday meal.

Sirens were heard in the distance, informing those present the emergency services were imminent.

Upon entering the scene one of the police constables repeated the maintenance engineer actions. No-one had ever witnessed a death so severe or brutal.

The hot tap was turned clockwise halting the flow of scolding hot water, although the plug was left untouched so no forensic evidence was washed away. The plug from the two-bar heater had already been switched to off, ensuring no current was swimming in the water.

The forensic pathologist arrived within the hour. Having introduced himself, he immediately studied the body. The body was gently lifted from the bath tub, although segments of boiled flesh remained in the tub, and the two-bar heater had descended to the bottom of the tub like a sunken submarine.

The pathologist walked around the body that lay on a piece of water proof sheeting. He stood looking at the corpse that had once shown life. Turning to the officers he cleared his throat, 'He's well boiled. It can be assumed that the individuals' stomach, liver, heart, kidneys, and intestines have been cooked slowly in their own juices. Makes it sound like a Fray Bentos pie.' He let out a slight guffaw at his gallows humour. 'What makes it even worse is he would have been conscience as he was being-boiled. The change of colour indicates this, turning bright red before blistering and swelling. This happens because the body senses things are wrong. It sends more blood to the surface of your skin to combat the burning and pain. It also triggers a histamine response, which causes redness and swelling all over, making you bloat. In other words, when boiled alive, we are not so different from lobsters being dropped into a scolding pan of water. Our fingers have more nerve endings than many other areas. So, he would have felt indelible and intense pain. The physical effects of boiling to death prove this to be pretty frightening experience to go through, even up to his last breath. Death can be minutes or hours of long lingering torture. In this case, the electric current would have killed him swiftly, although he was boiled for a while before the current was added. The electrical current sent into the water would have entered his body before electrocuting him.'

Jack Philips turned to towards the Home-Office pathologist assessing the man. He had met several of these body obsessed people and they were all cut from the same cloth. They spoke in a jocular language and were obsessed with consuming ham rolls, 'Anything else?'

'Well, the cadaver is now a piece of meat. Yet, we will treat it with the upmost respect. This needs to be done as a range of clothing will adhere to the skin, and if we remove the clothing harshly, then the skin and flesh could fall away like petals from a rose. Funny thing really.'

Jack Philips replied swiftly expecting another piece of relevant information, 'What's that?'

'I have boiled bacon for dinner. How ironic.'

Philips studied the body one final time. It had a ghostly look with the skin looking pinched. He felt cheated. Grimes was a villain who deserved to spend a lifetime behind bars, yet he felt a sense of pity towards the man. Being electrocuted in the bath was bad enough, but being boiled before electrocution offered a grim perspective of human life. Whoever performed this heinous crime had done the world a justice, yet the person needed to be apprehended and arrested.

Drake and Philips visited the restaurant below and explained the situation. They asked to view the list of those dining for the day.

Both officers were shown into the restaurants small, but quaint office. Paperwork and menus were strewn across the manager's desk, along with invoices from suppliers. The brown leather booklet was placed on the desk for them to peruse. Slowly, and carefully their fingers slid down the list until they both stopped. Each man turned to the other open mouthed.

Drake spoke first, 'Perkins. Perkins was here.'

Jack Philips was more interested in the name alongside, 'Suzanne Belchambers, I know that name. Where do I know it?'

Drake's internal computer was whizzing at high speed, 'Father was an M.P. She was engaged in a sex scandal, can't remember what it was. But it was seriously salacious, that I do remember.'

'What would a man like Perkins be doing with a woman like that? Something iffy is going-on.' Jack looked at his cohort. 'We need to meet our favourite villain from Dagenham. He always fleshes out a form of dodginess, along with a touch of suspected brutality.'

Gary Jones was enjoying his full English breakfast at Westlands Café. The home-made bubble and squeak were a thing of beauty. He dipped his buttered slice of crusty bread in to his egg yolk and was about his plant it in to the caverns of his mouth when he noted two shadows looming across his table, 'Pull up a chair. The breakfasts are lovely. Today's special is liver and onions.'

Jack Philips and Drake sat in the chairs. The metal noise scraping on the floor like a distressed mouse.

Both men waved at the young waitress, 'I'll have what he's having, and a mug of tea, please.'

'So, gentlemen, you have found my quiet hideaway. I thought no-one knew of this place. When you two are both on patrol that means trouble is brewing and my day is about to go tits-up.'

'Grimes is dead.' Drake watched for any reaction from Jones, but there was no movement, 'You didn't do it. I know.'

'Fuck me, Drakey. You're not doing that weird studying shit you do? I'm having my brekkie and you're analysing me. Take time out and enjoy the occasion. Occasion, as in your breakfast.'

Jack Philips decided to join the jousting party, 'He was electrocuted in the bath and his body boiled. Pretty nasty. His flesh looked like a boiled ham.'

Jones stopped mid-flow, spinning his fork in his hand, 'So he looked like this piece of bacon?' The speared bacon was then engulfed like a hungry lion.

Two huge full English breakfasts were deposited on the table. Both officers spread copious amounts of butter over the toast and sprinkled pepper over their meal as if it were decoration. A loud splat of Daddies brown sauce could be heard being flopped on the side of their plates.

Jones studied both men. They were machines. They ate as if they had not eaten for years, 'Slow down fellas, you'll get heartburn eating at that speed.'

Jack Philips took a bite from his toast and replied, 'Catherine has shoved me on a diet. It's driving me mad. Everything is boiled or surrounded by a forestry of salad. She won't give me chips.'

Jones laughed, 'A diet? You're proper married now old son.' No-one in the café noticed. The place was full of builders enjoying their mid-morning breakfast, regaling tails of their building exploits and jobs they had quoted.

The meals were devoured in record time. Philips rubbed his belly, 'That was just what the doctor ordered. Anyway, Grimes, boiled in the bath having been electrocuted. What are your thoughts, Jones?'

'Where did it happen?'

'Place called Oslo Court.'

Jones immediately looked up, 'Oslo Court. As in St Johns Wood. Place makes amazing trifles. You two would love it. You get well sized portions of food. It's not poncey. The restaurant is at the base of the flats.'

The man amazed Drake with which they were sitting. He could be considered one of London's most-wanted, yet he looked and smelt a million dollars, ate in the finest restaurants, and knew people in important places. The man was certainly a jamboree of personalities, and he now understood why Jones had survived for so long, 'That information is remarkably interesting, but what are your thoughts.'

Jones rubbed his chin in deep thought, 'It's a little out of the way, not cheap, has a specific customer base. I would look for someone who is out of place or someone who is a regular.' Jones watched the two officers look surreptitiously at each other. He had hit the jackpot. Something he had said had caused consternation between the two. 'Spit it out, men.'

'Perkins dined with someone at Oslo Court. A high-class lady who has rubbed shoulders with people in the adult industry, if you know what I mean.' Philips winked at Jones. 'We also believe they were inadvertently placed together, yet got on for an unknown reason. The woman had a parcel delivered to the restaurant which she had to sign for.'

Drake continued the onslaught, 'The high-class lady was Suzanne Belchambers also known as Suzi Belchambers – or Sexi Suzi by those that know her well. Father was Hugh Belchambers, the M.P. Parents divorced, father remarried, Suzanne did not agree completely with her father's new bride. When he died, he left Suzanne an estate in Devon and a flat in Kensington. Interestingly, and surprisingly she starred in adult movies and was removed from Roedean for inexcusable behaviour. There are rumours, but nothing concrete. School swept it under the table.

Perkins dining with a porn star did not feel right. There was something important missing. Why would a man from the security services enjoy the company of someone who was employed for her passion towards horizontal refreshment? They must have something in common.

Jones interrupted everyone's private thoughts, 'Let's go to Oslo Court this afternoon. Unless I am mistaken, they open 12-4pm. I can book us a table for 2pm. My treat. Just don't tell Catherine about your excursion, Jack.'

Philips offered a wry smile, knowing his wife would be annoyed should she find out about this magnificent breakfast and his lunchtime dinner date, both would be huge in calorific content.

Jack pondered his life. Marrying had been an absolute blessing. Particularly to a lady who was as near to a princess as he would ever come. He was not in the flushes of early youth and he realised he could not go on much longer. Marriage had turned him into an incredibly happy softy. He was struggling to remove himself from bed each day and was happy to sit in bed and read biographies he had borrowed from the local library. Catherine would sit next to him reading novels by Jeffrey Archer. The teas maid would ring at 7am each morning, informing Jack to wake up and start the day with his favourite beverage. He wanted to smile. He wanted to go home. He made a decision. 'Gents, we don't really need to go to Oslo Court. We've been there already. It's just like raking over old ground, somewhere we've already trod.'

Drake did not say a word. He understood the real meaning behind the statement. His governor wanted to go home. In fact, his governor's vocation in policing was ending, and soon. Drake understood the struggles Philips would encounter. Initially, he would feel euphoric with a sense of freedom. Yet after the primary sense of escape his emotional state would change. He would struggle with adjustment due to the fact he had become institutionalised having served thirty years with the force. The man's life was now heading in a different direction, a well-deserved one as well.

Drake contemplated his own life. It had been from institution to institution; school, army and policing. If there was a man who could suffer mental anxieties at the end of his working life it was him. He only knew orders. During his army days a psychologist had informed him the key to restoring mental wellness was to understand where it had broken down, he understood the mind needed rebooting like a computer. Talking problems through allowed individuals to unburden their needs meaning no medications were required. Popping pills was easier, but in the long term it was only a treatment, not a cure. His time was still a long way off, consequently, it would be put on the back burner until it needed re-evaluating.

# Chapter 20

Both men sat pondering their next move. Grimes had paid them handsomely to end another's life, which was not a problem, but this death did not feel right. The person in question had done nothing wrong. In fact, they had never even received a parking ticket. This murder was simply wrong. Grimes was acting out of extreme devilment and when people went down this route problems arrived from all areas for all concerned. Yet, they had been commissioned to do a job and they had been paid handsomely. They had fifty thousand reasons to complete the task.

Initially, Grimes wanted the subject snatched and butchered, yet that style was something they would not entertain. It was messy, difficult, and left too many loose ends. Whereas a bullet to the head or heart was clean, decisive and life-ending.

They considered themselves chameleons, blending in to all situations. Analysing their targets whilst maintaining cover and identity. Their past exploits in warfare had left them scarred, unable to form attachments. The only friendship they had was with the other. Yet, their brotherhood was built on life - ending it. Joy was not a story which entered their pitiful lives. They were stuck on a never-ending journey of death, with no end in sight. The money they grossed had murky and criminal origins from birth, and spread like a pandemic, responsible for unimaginable sums of misery and death. Yet it was their vocation.

To become an instrument of corruption empathy was considered a disadvantage and mental weakness. Love was a feeling God wanted everyone to develop, yet the operatives had sold their soul and silenced it for financial gain. No-one knew their identities. It was a secret. Employees knew them as M1 and M2.

The M stood for mercenary.

The operatives devoured their scrambled eggs in silence, both lost in their own private thoughts. The clink from the fork touching the plate brought both back to reality.

'We need to talk about this next assignment. I've a bad feeling about it. Grimes, is a slippery cunt and one not to be trusted. The target has absolutely no reason to die, and when we started down this path, we said we'd never end the life of someone who didn't deserve it. It's simply wrong.'

His friend raised his mug to his lips and slurped a mouthful of sweet, strong tea.

'You ain't wrong, but Grimes has given us fifty-grand in cash to sort it. I've been thinking about it as well. Yet, I keep coming back to same thing. It's our job and we're in the business of death.' He knew his friend was calculating the information like he always did. It's what made him deadly, nothing was left to chance.

'You're right, but this one is wrong.'

'Ok. I take you point, but we need to decide how to end this. After this, we'll go missing for a while. Let everything calm down.

A holiday, something neither had experienced. When they had served in their regiment, they had been recalled so many times from a break it had become a standing joke with the men.

Their skillset was retrieval of information. They had a one-hundred percent record of relieving information from those holding it. Water boarding had been their speciality. It left no marks on the body, yet almost drowned the person until they could take no more. They had been employed by various governments endlessly for wet work, and the same message was relayed constantly, 'If you are caught, we will deny all knowledge of what you are doing. You are on your own.'

The poofs from Whitehall and Eton endlessly left them out to dry, whilst they continued their lives hidden in their offices. Hiding like diseased rats.

Upon returning from an 'unregistered' assignment no-one ever thanked them, and the faceless men of Whitehall remained hidden in their cages, back slapping each other on an assignment well-done.

'A holiday will be good. I want to swim in a warm sea, drink fruity cocktails and eat fabulous meals of an evening without constantly living on my nerves and looking over my shoulder.'

'Done. Right, let's get this plan sorted and go on holiday… for a long time.'

<   >

'Suzi, do you think they will ever find out about our coupling? It is fair to assume they now know we dined together, but whether they can join the dots is another thing.'

Suzi turned towards Perkins. Her silky slender naked form arousing Perkins again. This pleased her. He was everything she was not attracted to, but for some unknown reason every time he spoke or looked at her, she melted inside. Could she be in love? She had never felt like this, yet she loved the feeling, 'Perky, and you're looking a little perky again.' She raised a knowing eyebrow, 'I do not care. I really do not care.' She slowly slid down the bed and swallowed the entire length of her Perkins, until he had filled her mouth with love.

Perkins lay watching her sleeping form. He could not believe a lady of Suzi's looks and wealth would even consider an old duffer like him. A life together was certainly promising, and not without hope. In fact, it had every chance of happening. Yet standing in their way were the loyal police officers and their underworld operative.

Philips, Drake and Jones were a formidable force and one to tread carefully around. Yet, he had the resources to puncture their investigation. He just needed a little misdirection. A gentle nudge to the authorities where skeletons may be residing. The obvious one being Van Der Leer. Evidence would be minimal, yet it would worry Gary Jones. Enough for him to lose his edge a little. A simple telephone call was the only thing needed to set the wheels in motion.

Perkins removed himself silently from the now well-used and bedraggled bed, trying not to disturb Suzanne.

Suzi raised an eye and murmured, 'Where are you going?'

Perkins lifted his head, 'Thought I would nip out and buy us a nice crisp Italian white.'

'Make sure it is cold to lift the delicate aromas and acidity.' She then drifted off to sleep, again.

Perkins stared at her in amazement. How could anyone do that? Speak fluently and diligently about chilled wine, before drifting off into a deep sleep. It was a talent.

He dressed in his pale-blue and yellow striped Adidas shell suit and trainers. He studied himself in the mirror. The tracksuit made him appear a little portly.

Perkins opened the door and left the flat making his way to Brompton Road. The telephone boxes based near Harrods store were perfect for communication purposes. So many people used them, meaning tracking would be virtually impossible.

Perkins lifted the solid black receiver and punched the number. He was immediately met with a reply.

'Emergency services. Which service do you require?'

Perkins had been practicing his reply, 'Police, and the message is. Go to Tobacco Dock. There is a body buried in cement. Look for a circle which looks out of place in context with the rest of the flooring.'

He disconnected, knowing the message would be relayed immediately.

<   >

Jack Philips gave the speaker full attention. Listening as if the words were spiritual. His internal being in quandary. The information being imparted was concerning, yet he had no idea why. His sixth sense told him it had something to do with his present case.

Drake watched his superior officer, understanding he was thinking deeply, trying to negotiate a situation that could place him several moves ahead of the caller. This attentiveness was part of his professionalism. Yet, he looked a little concerned. His brow was furrowed, and he was rubbing his days old growth of stubble that resembled a dark shadow crossing his face. The man looked tired, as though he were counting the days until his reign was over. This case, although his last, was beginning to drain him. There were too many players, and each player was a high-roller. Each variable in the case leant itself to another variable, and the monstrous death count, along with their ferocity was taxing even the stronger minds.

Philips replaced the receiver gently, and studied it. The police had received a tip-off about a body buried in Tobacco Dock. This needed careful and critical thinking. Being open-minded and willing to see all perspectives was required here. Jack Philips considered himself a wise person, yet this now had to be proven. He looked up and studied his brood of law enforcers. Each busying themselves trying to locate information that would develop the case on which they were working. The case was getting bigger and bigger, and more complex at every turn. Grimes, Perkins, Brown, Van der Leer and Jones were incredibly complicated and strong characters, yet something had to give somewhere. The murders of both Grimes brothers had offered no clues as to who had performed the dreadful slayings, and Tiny's death had offered no information. It was like a ghost was ridding

London of the those deemed unworthy. Someone, somewhere knew something and that something held the key to unlocking the door to this merry go round of death and misery.

< >

The mercenaries laid down a picture of their next victim. Both looked at the person, studying their features. This ensured their photographic memory remembered the finer details.

M1 broke the silence, 'We need to understand the person's movements, routines, lifestyle, places they visit... basically their life.'

M2 stood motionless, 'The usual then. If we want to make a statement, then this requires a statement ending. Something big. We can then sail into the sunset and enjoy the money we've earned, and a vast amount it is.'

His colleague looked and smiled, 'This will be our last job then. To be honest. I am ready to bring it all to an end. Twenty years for serving our nation, and ten for serving master's that pay for ending life.' He screwed up his face and turned away from his one and only faithful friend. 'Personally, I would like to slice the neck of all those in Whitehall who pay us for doing their fucking dogshit work. Sitting in their ivory towers, and...'

His speech was interrupted by his friend who understood that anger was beginning boil and take control, 'Forget about it, that's the past. Let's just get this last job done and fuck off into the sunset. No more bureaucrats, arse holes or well-spoken knob jockeys.'

His colleague laughed. He knew when his friend was placing a dressing over an open wound. He also understood that his temper could erupt like a steaming kettle, 'You're right. Get this one done and fuck off in to the sunset. In fact, fuck off in to retirement.'

<  >

Exhumation of the site had delivered a male body at a depth of seven feet. The lime and alkali characteristics in the concrete had drawn all moisture from the body, mummifying it. The mouth was open. Giving it the impression, it was singing, yet the gap was filled with a solid mass. The opened cavity had a raw intensity to it that screamed urgency, and spasms of desperation could be imagined until the inevitable shut down of the body's response.

Those looking at the exhumed body stood trying to imagine the horrific last moments and feelings this human had endured. A majority were overalled by its chalky colour. It resembled a dead body from Pompeii. There was no such thing as a beautiful body when death had occurred so dramatically. The flesh rotted, hair matted into the soil and a look of anguish from the victim. No-one could believe someone had ended this person's life so coldly.

The pathologist noted the thin skin on the eyelids had dried out, while fatty areas of the body had turned into a soap-like substance called grave wax. He turned towards the lead police officer, 'He's dead.' He smiled at his dark sense of humour, 'Without having a look inside, I'd say he's been there for a few weeks. Body has dried out, due to the chemicals based in the concrete. He's been trussed up beautifully. I would guess he was placed on the wet concrete and allowed to sink, slowly.'

The pathologist played out the scenario slowly, as if he were a world respected Oscar winning actor. Those in attendance were hanging on to every word he said.

'If you look at his mouth, it is full of concrete. As he we sinking, he probably gasped for a final breath of air, but miss timed the gulp and instead fed himself the gritty substance. How misfortunate. No need to take the body temperature. It would read 98.6 degrees Fahrenheit when alive. During death it reduces by 1-2 degrees every hour. So, he is now jolly cold due to his sabbatical in the earth.' Again, he guffawed at his dark sense of humour. 'When I get him back to my room, I'll evaluate the stomach and digestive system. They often hold many clues that will help determine when the person passed away. By examining these bodily systems, one can determine when a person ate his last meal, based on how far the meal's contents travelled through the digestive system, and what it was.'

Jack Philips arrived and noted the pathologist. It was the same one who had examined Joseph Grimes. He looked over at the corpse. The skin was ashen, and he looked as lifeless as the unused warehouse where he had been found. Having heard the pathologists lack of compassion Philips felt the overwhelming need to say something, 'Don't think I am being rude, but a lack of compassion can be as vulgar as an excess of tears.'

Those in the vicinity turned towards Philips. No-one had ever heard him chastise any person in public.

The pathologist turned towards Philips, understanding the rebuke had been aimed towards him. He realised why the comment had been made, and understood that an apology would smooth things over, although it was not necessary, 'Superintendent, I am sorry if you are offended, but humour is part of deflecting the ghastly scenes those in my profession come across.' He stared into the eyes of Philips. They looked tired, no exhausted. The dark circles under his eyes showed tiredness, and aging. The man looked like retirement should be his next case, but he knew that serving police officers struggled to give up their vocation. He decided to tackle the Philips about the tip off, 'How did you find out about this burial?'

Jack Philips decided to inform the pathologist, although it was none of his business, 'We received an anonymous telephone a call. Strange really. Anyway, when you complete your report, I would grateful if you could send it to me swiftly. Thank you for your help.' Philips held out his hand and shook the pathologist's hand warmly like he was an old friend. He turned and made his way to the waiting vehicle.

When in the car Philips considered the anonymous telephone message. He felt the person who had called may be trying to create havoc. He also had a nagging feeling they may have been present during the execution. Yet, it came back to the same old question, 'Why would they do that?'

# Chapter 21

Perkins sat in the Victorian easy chair. He was not fully sure, but he felt it was by Cornelius V Smith. One thing the Belchambers had was taste. Suzanne's flat was impeccable. The centre of the living room was covered with an antique Persian rug that had the beautiful worn appearance each should have, and a majestic Rosewood coffee table was positioned centrally on it. The wall was littered with paintings of London. Each detailed a specific area of the great city. They varied from watercolour and oil, and each was surrounded in a gold frame that offered age.

The pictures were a time machine. One fleeting look and Perkins was back in his early years within the security services, based in the capital, his life stretched before him. He considered some choices he had made throughout his life, good and bad, but always with an end goal. Yet, here he was now in this magnificent apartment, having spent the night with the more beautiful lady he had ever met, who he had fallen in love with. However, he felt he had made an error of judgement. Informing the police about the body at Tobacco Dock may prove to be an unwise move. He had considered his reasons, and each time he kept coming back to Gary Jones and his penchant for extreme commodities of violence to those who had wronged him.

His mental meanderings were disturbed by Suzi entering the room. She slid in smoothly and silently. He studied her impeccable form and knew she was wearing no undergarments, only the long red silk dressing gown covered her modesty, 'Morning, my love. How are you feeling?'

Suzi offered her Perkins a warm smile. She glided over to him and kissed the top of his head, 'I'm fine, my little stud. I have to say, Perky, but you're beginning to wear your Suzi out.'

Perkins smiled, 'I'm sorry. I've never felt like this before. This is a new feeling to me.' He suddenly felt a sense of guilt towards Gary Jones. Guilt had been his master, yet now he understood his freedom could be removed if things did not roll the way he hoped. Everybody confesses something, their deepest crimes, and fears in everyday life, yet acknowledging this could be damaging to his one shot of love. He stared at Suzanne, 'Would you like a nice cup of tea, my love?'

She returned his smiled and winked at him, 'Perky, Suzi would love a morning brew.' She let out a joyous and loving laugh, and danced around the room.

Perkins strode in to the kitchen and filled the kettle, before shovelling two large heaps of PG Tips tea-leaves in to the tea-pot. He flicked the wireless on to be met with the morning sounds of Ken Bruce, who was about to play 'Love of the Common People' by Paul Young. Perkins smiled, how apt that a renowned DJ was about to play a song that could link to Gary Jones.

Allowing the tea leaves to dance in the pot he considered his hastiness about informing the authorities of Van der Leer. Lust had broken his will. He had fallen for his own employee's betrayal technique; Money, Ideology, Coercion, Ego – MICE. His ego and ideology had interrupted his straight forward and logical thinking. This had never happened before. He had no idea how to rectify the situation. The game was in play. Suzi broke his thoughts.

'Perky, tea, where is my tea, big boy? I need it, bad.'

<  >

Jones sat in his home. He had heard about the body being exhumed in Tobacco Dock. Pensively, he considered all players in this ever-increasing game. Each character had an important part to play. Yet, one of these players was dirty. They had amended the rules for their own benefit. Closing his eyes, he considered every situation and scenario. His eyelids jumped open. Only one person had something to gain and knew where the body was buried, Perkins, but why had he informed the police about its whereabouts. A meeting with Perkins was urgently required, and if it meant the man had to go on the permanent missing list, then so be it. Perkins, a traitor. There was an irony to the situation. Mr. Big Shot M.I.5 man.

Sitting in his favoured chair he considered reasons why Perkins would turn informer. He was an honourable man, his vocation proved that. He did not appear to have any vices, apart from his penchant for fine dining and the occasional visit to the casino. He was a single man; he was beholden to no-one. The only fly in the ointment was Suzanne Belchambers. She had come from no-where and had a significant part to play in this saga, yet Jones could not put his finger on it. There had to be a link and Perkins was the man who could chain everything together.

Drugs had been the predominate source of drama, but that area had been eradicated. Something had to be driving Perkins to act in this extraordinary manner. He had become too confident, too self-assured. Nothing had changed in his life.

Jones took a swig of from his mug, savouring the sweet, strong tea. Leaning back in his chair he decided to forget about the problem and have a short snooze. Jones considered a nap his time to relax and consider his world in the language of thought and dreams. He believed the brain needed downtime to replenish its stores of attention and motivation, encouraging productivity and creativity. He also believed it was essential to achieve the highest levels of performance and form secure memories of everyday life. When he had told Philips and Drake about his theories, both had looked at him in a quizzical manner, although Drake had been the one who understood the benefits.

Drake had spoken about grabbing short bursts of sleep when in Ireland on patrol with his unit of four men. They had been in situ for six weeks once analysing the movements of players within the I.R.A. He had mentioned he could go to sleep within one minute and this allowed him a few of hours of rest each day, enough to fight off exhaustion.

Jones looked at his ceiling and thought it needed painting. It had a noticeably light creamy colour to it. The thought of decorating bored him. He felt his eyes closing like shutters on a shop front. He began to drift off, but was awoken by the answer. It was Suzanne. She was the change in Perkins. He was infatuated with her. They came from similar backgrounds, and mixed within the same circles. They must have met previously, and Perkins must have known her father. Perkins had tried to sacrifice him for a woman. The deceitful cunt. Perkins had received one slap already. Now, there were a plethora of them heading his sorry arsed way.

Philips and Drake would need to be informed. Jones thought it would not hurt if the three of them met with the ex-commissioner. The man had a wealth of knowledge, and knew all the major players in society. He was the sort of man who would know valuable information on the Belchamber's family.

<   >

Charles Johns had been pleased to hear from Gary Jones, and this had been heightened when he had been asked to arrange a meeting somewhere quiet where he, Philips, Drake and Jones could meet to discuss a situation.

Charles felt the inner stirrings of his inquisitive nature. When he felt these movements, it was like a tap that could only be turned off by figuring out the conundrum. The meeting had to be somewhere public, yet known only to a few. He sat pondering and realised The Reform club in Pall Mall was perfect. Members spoke in hushed tones, and conversations were much more than words. It was the smiles, gentle shrugs and knowing looks in members eyes. Every member had wealth, and every member had integrity. It was the perfect place to meet where knowing eyes would not be welcome.

Gary sat quietly in his chair; his peace shattered by the electronic sound emanating from his newly installed Trimphone. The noise was irritating, it did not have the traditional bell-ringing sound. He picked up the cream receiver and placed it to his ear, 'Hello?'

'Good afternoon, Gary. Charles here. I've sourced a venue for our clandestine meeting, The Reform Club in Pall Mall.'

Gary listened to Charles Johns. The man seduced those listening with his effortless array of vocabulary. It flowed smoothly, 'That sounds excellent, Charles. I will inform our crime fighting friends. I have never been to the Reform. I assume it is formal dress; jacket, collar and tie?'

Charles smiled. One of the reasons Gary Jones survived in all levels of society was because he left nothing to chance, and blended in where ever he went. Asking about dress code summed him up, 'That is correct, Gary. Formal dress to the max. Ensure Philips and Drake are aware. Occasionally, they look a little dishevelled.' He let out a little laugh.

Jones smiled himself, 'I'll ensure they take a trip to Burtons or Top Man to sharpen themselves up.'

'Excellent news. I'll meet you in there. I've booked us somewhere private. The room is reserved for Friday 1pm, and lunch will be on me. I have one question; can you give me a hint in which direction the conversation is heading?'

Gary studied those walking past his Living room window. Each busying themselves, each wrapped up with their own problems. His concentration returned to the moment, 'The Belchambers family and those associated with them, specifically the daughter.' Gary thought he had heard the name Suzanne mentioned by Charles, but decided not to pursue it, believing it was slip of the tongue.

Charles John knew of the Belchambers family. There were a number of skeletons in that family's history. Charles regained his poise and replied dutifully, 'Thank you, see you Friday, Gary.'

< >

Jones, Philips and Darke departed Fenchurch Street station. The tube ride had taken them twenty-five minutes along the District Line. Both officers mentioned continuing their journey by the underground taxi. They had complained about their new suits not feeling particularly comfortable.

Jones studied both men. They looked smart, yet together they looked like they had walked from a Burtons shop window. Jones realised his Crockett and Jones shoes cost more than everything they were wearing. Casually, he informed them, 'I'll get us a black cab. Charles, has done us a favour getting us admitted into the Reform. So, we'll turn up look like city gents, not like a concoction of East London barrow boys.'

Drake immediately replied, 'Fuck you, Jones. You are an East London barrow boy.' The comment had gnawed him. To think Jones felt superior to them, annoyed him. Philips had completed thirty years' service, and he had served in his majesty's most exclusive regiment. Yet,

East London's most dangerous, and least known villain had the arse hole to feel superior.

Jones stopped in his tracks and turned towards Drake, 'If you had listened, I included myself. Yes, I do come from Dagenham and frequent East London, but I look and smell the opposite of what I am. Whereas, you are not from my parts, but often look like you do come from the said area. So, the inclusive we, makes sense.'

The annoyance in Drake was bubbling. He knew it was bubbling because he realised Jones was correct, and that fucked him off even more, 'All right, we'll get a cab, but you're paying.'

Philips listened to the exchange, knowing Jones was correct, yet he could not go against his serving officer, 'Ok ladies, it's a draw. Shall we go an enjoy this gaff, and listen to our old commissioner. I still can't get used to being friends with someone like him.'

The journey took nineteen minutes and cost Jones fifteen pounds. It stopped outside an old grey looking building, which looked solid and magnificent. The three men immerged from the cab, unaware of the opulence and grandeur they were about to witness.

They climbed the ten stairs and entered the pantheon.

Immediately Drake was startled, 'Fuck me, who'd have thought this lay behind those doors.'

The atrium smelt of history and the balcony's overlooked it like guarding soldiers. A number of marble busts noted those entering the highly esteemed establishment. It was like they were watching you, deciding whether they should allow you entry.

Charles Johns strode briskly towards the party and beckoned them to follow him, 'I've booked us lunch in the Coffee Room, and then we can adjourn to the Hansard Bar for drinks should you have time.'

The party were shown to their table and each ordered their meal.

Johns noted the officers ordered steak, 'I'll order a nice bottle of red to compliment your meal. I recommend the Aloxe-Corton 1er Cru if that is acceptable to everyone?'

All three nodded with the suggestion.

'Gents, Jones informs me you require information regarding the Belchambers. They are a family with a checkered background. Hugh Belchamber remarried after his wife was killed by the I.R.A in unfortunate circumstances. It was a case of wrong place at the right time. He remarried, and the new wife was American, and a little bit of a drama queen. She and Suzi, did not see eye to eye. There were reports of fights between the two, with Suzi usually being the benefactor of the win. Now Suzi is an interesting character. She was removed from Roedean for having sexual practices with her Head of Physical Education – who was female. There were also rumblings of her becoming involved with a pupil or two. These were only rumours, although I have it on good authority, they were fact.' Johns turned to Jack Philips, 'Close your mouth, Jack, in case an unfortunate fly enters. You look a little shocked. Anyway, where was I? Yes. Suzi leaves school and becomes difficult. Her penchant for sex and drugs became an issue. Her father became estranged from her, sadly. Yet, he left Suzi an incredibly wealthy person when he died. Reports suggest she is worth around fifty million pounds.

Drake was the next to allow his jaw to drop, before mouthing to himself, 'Fuck me, that's dough.'

'There is more gentlemen. Suzi did have a brother. Yet he went missing many years back. Interestingly, he was interviewed for being involved in the drink driving death of an elderly couple, but this is where it gets interesting. The couple had a granddaughter, and that was... Julie Brown.'

It was Gary Jones turn to mouth now, 'Fucking hell, Julie.'

Charles continued, his tone not changing, 'Julie was interviewed for the murder, but there was nothing to arrest or charge her with as there was no evidence. Now Perkins, he's lived a life.' Johns raised his eyebrow and sipped his wine, 'Served in the army, and spent his entire career in the security services. He is considered a man to be relied on. Yet, he has a penchant for casinos. He can be a high roller, and once or twice has sailed close to the wind. It's been suggested he was in debt with Joseph Grimes for a sizeable sum, although this cannot be corroborated. Another interesting piece of material is that Perkins knew Hugh Belchambers. He attended the wedding of the first Mrs Bechambers, Suzi's mother, so, did he know of Suzi beforehand?'

Jones was the first to respond, 'I always thought he was a slippery cunt. There was something not quite right about him. After I slapped him in Farringdon, having seen him with Grimes I knew it. That fucker has played us all.'

Jack Philips joined the conversation having evaluated the information, 'Perkins has been a player from the start and he has helped us, but helped himself I suspect even more. He has to become a person of interest. Significant interest.'

Johns allowed the party to digest all of the information imparted to them. It was the first time he had seen the three men concentrating. Deciding to intervene their thought process, 'Regarding Suzi, she was involved, as I am sure you are already aware, in the adult entertainment industry. Now, word to the wise, it is rumoured that she conceals a knife, and if anyone attempts to trip her up in any way then they are left with an indelible stripe across their cheek. She is a ferocious female. Now, I have no idea what you wish to do, but I wonder if she knows that Perkins attended her mother and father's wedding. She was young - five or six years of age, and her mother and father were married at twenty-two. They had her noticeably young. I believe Perkins may have served with her father. He allowed the momentous piece of information to circulate around the brains of each man. He guessed Philips would break the silence first, and he was proven correct.

'Perkins knew Suzi as a child, and now he's dating her, although he's done nothing wrong. It just feels wrong,'

Johns continued, 'I agree, but does Suzi know?'

# Chapter 22

Upon the umbrella the spirited sounds of dancing droplets floating down from the heavens could be heard, and from its rim came the vision of its adventurous cousins diving towards the floor. The rain became more intense and began to soak the bottom of each pale blue jean leg, deepening the denim to a deep dark ocean blue, bringing the white boots Suzi wore to a glossy mirrored-twinkle. Suzi had always thought the rain offered romance and magic, as if this were an old love story.

Bouncing along, her mind a void of anything negative. She felt alive and genuinely happy for the first time in her life. Perkins, although nineteen years older, was everything she had ever wanted. He was from her social class, held a professional job - all be it secretive, used standard English and most importantly had manners. To think she had agreed to remove this most endearing man from life. Suzi began to laugh.

Her father would have been absolutely delighted to have had Perkins as a son-in-law. Suzi stopped, she realised what she had just thought. If he asked, she would marry the man now, right now. It had only been ten days, but she realised it was meant. Perky was the one.

Her daze was broken by two hurly-burly builders knocking into her. Both were holding a polystyrene cup of tea and a bacon roll, in which oodles of tomato sauce was trying to escape. Suzi had arranged to meet a friend at San Lorenzo for a light-lunch and gossip. She was going to tell her friend about Perkins, and could not wait. A beaming smile shot across her porcelain fresh face again.

Dining out at beautiful places had always been an occasion Suzi had taken pleasure in. Her late father, had always taken her to opulent places to dine, from The Ritz and The Savoy to Simpson's, but always opulent and expensive, and he had been paramount when it came to manners. Something he had learned from his boarding school background. She never thought of her father, but in the last few days she had done so many times. He would be proud of her, for the first time. A small tear began to form like a pearl in the corner of her eye. Suzi swiftly removed it from its existence.

She became aware of footsteps mirroring hers. Suzi decided to stop and browse one of the boutique windows. The footsteps stopped and slowly looked at the window alongside her.

'Ms Belchambers, don't think of removing your hidden blade. My blade is significantly longer and sharper. I also do not wish to intervene in your new love affair… with Perkins.'

Suzi glanced to her left at the mirrored refection. The man was approximately six-feet tall, good-looking, and impeccably dressed. His diction was a little rough, suggesting, he was educated at a London comprehensive school, 'You have my attention, man with no name.'

For some unknown reason, the gentlemen made her feel a little nervous. Suzi knew nerves and anxiety were feelings to protect you; yet they were just a warning mechanism. It was like a protective coat that shrouded the person from harm. Yet, this man had crawled under her skin. He was like an itch that could not be scratched. He had a reason for being there and this concerned her as well.

Gary Jones realised Suzi Belchambers was in turmoil. She had slowly and gently flicked her hair behind her left ear three times. He knew that feeling anxious was difficult for all because it was supposed to be short term. A person adapts to get along, but it normally takes considerable strength, and the lady standing adjacent to him had potency, character and arsehole. He sensed it. She was calculating her odds of survival, escape and victory. Jones sensed she was planning to instigate the next move, 'Suzi, is it ok if I call you by your Christian name? I need to speak to Perkins. It is important. Is he holed up in your Kensington flat?'

Suzi was silent. She had underestimated this man's resources. Her brain faltered for a split second. Every part of her paused whilst she regathered her thought process. This man was obviously connected with people who could aid him. Yet so was she. She decided to try a dangerous game that could be fruitful if played perfectly, 'Perkins has told me about the merry band of men he has become involved with.' The man's silence was all she needed to know. Suzi decided to push the gamble a little further. 'I assume you were the man who marked his face with the unprovoked assault near Holborn viaduct.' Jackpot! The man was shocked. He had not expected this information. His eyes darted towards here.

'He deserved it. Perkins, has too many sides, and a man with too many sides becomes circular, meaning he goes back to where he started.'

Suzi turned to face the man, 'There is always a side we hide and a side we display. There can be more sides in many cases due to a person's natural convolution, defence mechanism, a way to cope.'

Gary Jones admired this lady. She had depth. He guessed she had no idea about the altercation, but it had surprised him she had thrown it in so early. This one did not play the long game, she played only one way… her way. 'Listen, I don't know anything about you apart from what I've heard, so, I don't judge anyone. Your business is your business. But as soon as someone fucks with me… I end it.'

Suzi felt a little intimidated by the man's ferocity. He was calm and never raised his voice. Yet the use of profanity was spoken in a deep menacing threatening growl. He had the look of wealth but the frightening bravado of primate defending its nest, 'Instead of talking on the street. You should offer to buy me a drink. That would be a more civilised way to continue our conversation. Do you not think?'

Gary Jones smiled. She was trying to gain control of the conversation, and removing the discussion to a new venue gave her five minutes thinking time. It was a smart move on her behalf and one to be applauded.

Suzi proceeded with her intentions in gaining control, 'Let's go to The Goat, and on the way, I will tell you about its history.'

Gary turned and studied her. She was certainly good-looking. She oozed class and sophistication. She was approximately five-feet-seven inches, slim and dressed immaculately. She immediately began to stride away with purpose.

Suzi turned towards her suitor, 'Pick your feet up.' She then began to regale the history of the pub. 'The Goat is the oldest remaining pub on Kensington High Street, being constructed in 1695. The area had become a regular east–west route when King William built Kensington Palace. Being so ancient, The Goat is rumoured to have underground tunnels linking it with Kensington Palace. This has never been confirmed, but if we are drinking there and Princess Michael of Kent suddenly pops up from nowhere, you may assume the rumours to be correct.' She laughed at her humour.

Jones enjoyed history, and this lady had heightened his interest.

Suzi allowed a wry smile to form. She could see she was having an impact upon him; all be it only marginal, but she would take that or any advantage at this stage.

They both entered the public house and made their way to a corner located in the deepest darkest recess.

Gary Jones returned with two drinks. He handed Suzi her glass of Cinzano and lemonade and took a hearty gulp from his lager and lime, 'Perkins, he is very slippery. The man always has an angle. Suzi, what is his angle? Help me here.'

Suzi replaced her glass on the table and studied the red lipstick mark left on its lip. Perkins was such a charmer. He was perfect. How could her Perky have a dark side? It was not possible… was it. This was making her reconsider her judgement, was it miss directed? Had she jumped in too fast?

Gary watched the lady battling demons. Her face spoke a thousand words. He decided it was time to take full control of the dialogue, 'Listen love.' He knew the informal approach could rattle her. 'You obviously like, Perkins, and I'm sure he is an upstanding gentleman with you, but he is one slippery cunt. He is dabbling in both sides of the law and people like that need watching.'

Suzi pretended she was not flustered, but the pits of her stomach were bouncing around like a ball. She could not escape the nagging feeling that this man could be giving her correct information.

Jones understood he was nearing the winning line. The woman's silence spoke volumes. Speaking to her harshly had worried her. She had pinched her bottom lip with her teeth three times. Concern was eating away at her. Jones decided to go for the kill, 'I'm going to be blunt with you. If Perkins, fucks with me, or any of my friends. I'll cut his bollocks off and feed them to him whilst you watch.'

The deep- seated ferocity shook Suzi to the bones. This man, although educated, was in another league to those she had met before. He made Joseph Grimes appear a pussycat. He had menace running through his veins. Every word he said was spoken quietly, yet there was malice stamped through every syllable. Worry was enveloping her, 'Please don't hurt me and Perkins. I love him and I want to leave the life I am tangled up in. I know he is not the finished article. He knew my father, and he thinks I do not know. Every person has their secrets. You have yours, I have mine, and Perky has his.'

Jones wanted to roar with laughter. She called him Perky. The man had a nickname like he was a pet, 'Listen, I don't wish to harm you, or anyone else. Just pass the message on to Perkins, and remember, if he, you, or anyone else fucks with us, I'll mutilate them.'

Suzi felt her legs begin shake. She wanted to visit the toilet, but wondered if he would see her legs shaking like a leaf in the wind. Fortunately, the resolution was removed from her grasp.

Jones stood up, 'Suzi, it's been a pleasure meeting you, and for the record. You are proper attractive lady.'

Suzi sat there perplexed. She had been threatened and given a beautiful compliment within fifteen minutes. Life was certainly full of turn-ups. One thing of which, she was sure. Perkins needed to told, but when.

Suzi studied the man slowly walking towards the door. He told an engaging tale, and if true, it certainly painted Perkins in a different light. The love of her life was not the sort of person she suspected he was. She understood his job was secretive, but he had a dark side to him she did not wish to know. She lifted her glass and took a longer lingering luxurious gulp from her Cinzano. The zesty citrus clove flavours cheered her soul, although the nagging feeling of discontent remained. Perkins may be using her for the wealth she held, yet he did not appear to be a man pushed by financial gain. Yet something was eating away at her. She did not know what it was, although she had felt something was wrong. Deep down inside their love, although true, was not due to finish with old age. She knew the power of love brought hope, yet at times love caused pain, and this was the ominous feeling she had. She did not want to experience eternal loneliness like many did. She wanted a family, she wanted to experience motherhood, she wanted a husband… she wanted Perky. She felt her eyes begin to moisten. Her life had always been like a tornado, yet the tornado was beginning to lose its power.

&lt;          &gt;

Perkins had left the flat shortly after Suzi. He had decided to stroll into the office. It was four miles from Suzi's flat to Century House in Westminster Bridge Road, and would take one hour.

Perkins whistled happily bowling along the street. People were moving along the pavement like a busy school of fish. In this movement the bright colours from their clothing resembled a flash of summer flowers. Having been walking for five minutes he noted Suzi on the opposing side of the road. Taking one step towards her he stopped abruptly. Gary Jones was ten paces behind her and mirroring her soft steps. Swiftly, his mind calculated all options available.

He was pleased that Suzi had noticed the antagonist following her. Pretending to peruse a shop window was a smart move. Yet Jones was one step ahead of her. He confidently stood approximately two paces from her and instigated a conversation.

For the first time in his life Perkins was incredibly annoyed. He could feel the fury building within him trying to jump out. He finally realised how a person knew when love had enveloped their soul. He never thought he would be in this predicament. Fucking, Jones. This man was everywhere. Perkins decided to play out the game. He would wait to see how long this unexpected meeting would last. He would contact the two operatives who were employed by the specific government departments to remove any unwanted problems. A smile formed across his face. He knew how to bring the entire deck to its knees. It would finish careers, break friendships, and offer him freedom - with his Suzi, hopefully.

# Chapter 23

The annoyance felt by Perkins was extreme. He could not escape Jones meeting Suzi. He had asked Suzi what she had been up to and how her lunch had ended. She had replied confidently that it had been an absolute riot of laughter and chat. There was no mention of Gary Jones and the unofficial fifteen-minute meeting in The Goat. Why was she withholding information from him? Was it to protect him? Was she being two-faced? Was she getting ready to remove him from her life? The possibilities were endless. His mind had never computed this way. Love was fucking with his heart, and more importantly his mind. Jones was becoming a pariah. He had to remove the man, and he knew the specialists available. Yet initially he had to remove Jones from his mind. He had to redirect his attention to something that would bring him back to the present. A sudden flash of Suzi in her black silk stockings amended his mind set. Suddenly he stopped, and turned. He was returning to Suzi. He needed his cock sucked.

Perkins returned to the office fully refreshed. Suzi had happily engulfed his weapon of love, along with her arse. Now, it was time for work, and arranging contact with the two men who would be the solution to his problem.

An advertisement had been placed in the Evening Standard classified section asking for two gardeners to start work immediately. Interested parties were told to ring a number, although the one had been changed to an I. The removal team would understand this message was coded for them. They had previously been given an alternative number to use when their services were required. Any other interested parties would be met with a disconnected tone as the number advertised did not exist.

The following evening Perkins received a call from one of the gentlemen on the department secure telephone line. He had informed the listener that an urgent meeting was required, and the meeting place was The George Inn near London Bridge at 1pm the following day. Perkins realised the clandestine meeting smacked of dishonesty, yet it served a purpose. Nevertheless, it had to be hidden because the subject matter.

Perkins had to remove Jones. He was the nemesis of the entire operation. He was the only man who could link something to everyone. Jones could bring everyone down. Yet he was a man of secrets himself. This meant he would not wish anything announced he could not control. Surprisingly, he had shown no remorse or worry over the excavation of Van der Leer's remains. In fact, he had continued with his day-to-day life. Perkins, pondered the mental complexities of Jones, could he be psychotic? He held all the characteristics shown. He lacked empathy, was charming, took unnecessary risks, lacked a conscience or guilt, and refused to accept responsibility. Jones was a perfect case for analysis from top specialists.

<   >

London Bridge, although busy, resembled a concrete metropolis. The grey buildings looked sad. They rose from the ground and stood like miserable guards overlooking The Thames.

Perkins entered the old, cobbled alley leading to the public house, noting the operatives were already in situ. Both staring at their pint glasses.

The three men sat at the old wooden table. Each holding their pints glass as if someone were going to remove it from their grasp. The silence was deafening.

Whenever Perkins spoke to the men known as M1 and M2 he felt his blood chill. The coldness emanating from them brought his brain to an icy stand still. Menace ran through their souls, and when their time on earth was over, the good lord would not welcome them.

Perkins decided to initiate the conversation, 'In the envelope there is all the information you require. People to remove.'

Immediately, both men looked up sharply, 'People. It's usually one. How many are there?'

Their brusque reply took Perkins by surprise, although he swiftly regained composure. His voice remained warm, and the masculine well-spoken pitch did not alter. His heart beat bounced steadily even though he believed it had skipped a beat with the swift retort he had received. 'Gentlemen, there is one we would like removed, specifically.' Using 'we' allowed the operatives to believe it was for their government. 'The name is Gary Jones. A distasteful chap. I have heard he enjoys the company of young boys. Ten or eleven-year-olds I believe.'

'A fucking nonce. They are scum of the earth. All paedo's should die. Would you like us to cut his dirty cock off with blunt scissors?'

Perkins knew these men were ferocious, but their ferocity was going into an unchartered stratosphere. He took a swig from his glass and replied calmly and quietly, 'I simple bullet will suffice, gentlemen.'

The quieter mercenary decided to enter the conversation, 'When do you want it done?'

Perkins stared at him coldly, 'As soon as possible.'

A hand swiftly moved the envelope into the confines of the inside pocket. The man looked up and stared deep into the soul of Perkins looking for nerves. There were none, yet there was something about this operation that did not feel correct. He decided to tackle Perkins, 'Do you want to hear something strange? Joseph Grimes wanted a similar set of people removed, permanently. Now, coincidences do happen, but the same people. Something iffy is taking place. I have no idea what it is, but if something is off, and I find you are at the bottom of it. I'll find you Perkins, and gut you like a fish.'

Perkins was surprised by the sudden outburst. Feeling anxious was a normal and natural emotion. It was an alarm system, and one a person should heed. Yet this time he felt a small drop of fluid forming in the corner of his eye. He hoped it would not find its exit and slide down his cheeks. These two men would find weakness in this, and believe he is being untruthful. He mustered an icy composure and stared at the men, 'Never ever doubt me. I am the man who sorts problems, and you are the men who removes problems, so, we are collectively solvers of difficulties.'

The silent assassin decided his time had come to enter the affray, 'You talk too much, and in my lifetime, people who talk too much are either nervous or a two-faced cunt... which are you?'

Perkins was immediately intimidated by this man. Those that spoke silently yet swiftly were the ones to be careful around. A person who is volatile shows the opposition all of their traits, meaning they have no secrets, whereas the silent man may have a plethora of them, and this man obviously had dangerous skills due to his line of employment, 'Come now gentlemen, we are here to sort a problem.' Perkins slid a brown zipped briefcase across the table. He noted both men's eyes zoom in on package. 'My briefcase contains the money you require to complete your mission. It's in cash. I know that is slightly unusual, but it's what we had.'

The mercenary looked at Perkins, again. The man was beginning to agitate him. He was a bullshitter, just a well-spoken one, 'Do we look like a pair of clowns? The government has nothing to do with this job. This is your job, and I reckon we're cleaning up your mess. Do not deny it. If you do. I'll ram this pint glass in your fucking eyeball. You have five-seconds to come clean.'

Perkins was in a quandary. Did he come clean, or brazen out the situation? 'May I ask what your problem is? You have a job. You have your payment, and it is irrelevant whether the job is for me, the government or the barman who served you your drinks. Do not threaten me young man. You may be a man with specific talents, but so am I.'

This turn of events puzzled both men. The man facing them had obviously served in the military, which division perplexed them. Both thought Sandhurst. Yet, where he had gone from there was curious.

Perkins broke the ten-second silence, 'Gentlemen, it has been a pleasure, but now it is time to venture to the world I know. Enjoy your rewards, and good luck with the job. Toodle pip.' Perkins then left the area as if he had never been present.

Both stared longingly into their glasses, lost in their subterranean thoughts. Eventually, the silence was broken.

'Something's not right here, and he's a slippery bag of shit. He pauses too much like he's surprised.

'And I'm not too sure that nonce story is true either. If the bloke was noncing young 'uns, then the filth would be all over him like a rash. Let me have a look at the info'.' Slowly he removed the contacts from the envelope as though he were a bomb disposal expert. He studied the picture and names, 'He's muddled it up or is fucking us over. He got the name wrong. Look at the photo and the one circled. Its even got the name on.'

His friend looked menacingly at the picture, 'Well if that's the one, that's the one. Do it, and we fuck off into the sunset with all our well-earned dosh.'

None of the passing trade took any notice in the sudden clink of glasses such was the regularity of it.

Perkins stood watching the men from the balcony striking their pint glasses together in celebration. They had not noticed him slip into the stairwell. He realised the game was now afoot, and he would have to vanish swiftly should it be revealed he was the one behind the assassination. Hopefully, it would not come to that.

Where he would go was a conundrum, and whether Suzi would join him was a puzzle. One thing he was sure of and that was everything had to go right, otherwise there would be a significant fall-out, specifically for him. Fucking Jones, everything was his fault. If Suzi found out she may decide to leave him, and that would never do. Jones had to be removed from the earth. Hopefully, the specialists would do their job like they usually did and solve the problem. He rubbed his temple. It was pulsating like it was alive. He knew the headache was a sign of something telling him to ease down. Yet, time was against him, in fact everything was against him. His life had been spun around like a washing machine. Getting into debt with Grimes had been the catalyst of everything. He had known what was happening, but the addiction had taken control of him. He had not visited a casino since, and the casino addiction had been short-lived, twelve months. Yet the year had been like a release factor. To date, his life had been totally organised from the moment he had entered the world; nannies, boarding school, Sandhurst and SBS. His life had become one of secrets and silence, yet for the first time he needed a little guidance. He felt like his mind was stuck behind a wall, one he would knock down before, but for the time he was entombed.

<     >

Jack Philips returned home and made a tumultuous decision. It was time to call it a day.
    He had spent the evening discussing it with Catherine, who was incredibly pleased with his choice.

Jack could tell by the beaming smile showing across her face. This woman genuinely loved him, and he absolutely adored her. He realised it was time to stop for the day when he had turned down a free meal at a five-star restaurant. As soon as the words had emerged from his mouth in the cafe, he knew it was time to leave. The thirty years had gone by in a blink. He was going to have a small leaving meal in a restaurant with those who had helped him. Those in attendance would be the people who had helped him the most, and although it was a brief list. It was a list that many would have second thoughts over: an ex-member from the SAS, an East London underworld operative, the ex-commissioner of the metropolitan police and his perfect wife. An unusual collective, but the correct collection.

Catherine had cried. Tears of joy ran down her face like little warm rivers. She had come and sat on his lap, 'Thank you, Jack. Together forever.'

For the first time in his life Jack had a lump in his throat. She had used his term of endearment on him. Jack looked at her, 'Ditto.' He had cuddled her never wanting to let her go. Moments in life were special, and this one was one of those moments.

Unbeknown to Catherine he had already started the ball rolling. Human Resources in Regency Street had received his retirement papers. He was aware his lump sum would be approximately sixty thousand pounds with the additional monthly pension. He also had two weeks holiday due, so, this would be his final week. For the first time in his life Jack felt as free as a bird. He had everything; a magnificent wife, beautiful home, a career he had loved. He was ready for the next chapter, although he felt nervous. There was a nagging feeling that something was not right. Something unfinished.

Catherine broke the comfortable silence, 'We shall have your leaving meal the at the army restaurant where Drake goes. It would be quite fitting to go somewhere with splendour that you have wanted to dine.'

Jack lifted his head and looked at his wife. He was the brains, but she controlled his neck and pointed in which direction they were heading. He knew she was the power behind the throne, 'Sounds like a plan my love. I'll leave you to arrange it, after all, you are good at that. I'm bloody useless at that sort of thing.'

Catherine gave him a knowing look and rolled her eyes. He was correct of course. Her Jack was useless at arranging anything. Yet he was a good man, the best. Catherine thought Jack may have been a victim of the trauma's he had experienced during his policing career, and assumed he had an inability to see his own worth. Catherine knew Jack was wonderful, yet he had no idea how perfect he was to her.

# Chapter 24

The party stood on the steps outside The In-and-Out restaurant. Drake had arranged the soirée to celebrate his mentor's career in the force. The cool wind gently caressed their poppy red cheeks, and their laughter could be heard by those passing.

Those on the steps were Jack, Catherine, Drake, Charles and Gary. Everyone in attendance had marvelled at Jones's amazing piano skills, they began to soften their stance towards him.

Catherine looked at her husband. He was her soulmate. She had loved him from the first minute, and she knew it was reciprocated. Each Sunday Jack would say, 'Catherine, my heart is happy.' She also knew he loved his vocation, but his marriage to the force had to end, and now was the right time. Her husband had left with his head held high, and his 30-year police record perfectly intact.

They had decided to visit New York to celebrate his retirement. It had a been a magnificent adventure. They were tourists and had a river of smiles, each brightly reflective in the chaotic Big Apple sun.

The time away together was a little luxury. Jack would say, 'Aeroplanes are boring, airports are a drag. I'd rather spend money on the house, the garden and the kind of food that makes us feel like royalty. Catherine my love, that's a vacation, and it's the kind that makes the rest of the year all the better for you and I.'

Jack could vacation at home with ease, as he found happiness in simple things - decent food and company. Yet

Catherine wanted him to expand his horizons. He was Mr. Provincial. The break allowed both the time and space required to replenish and relax their brain.

During the retirement dinner Jack had regaled stories of New York and its splendour. Those around the table were similar to Jack, having never left blighty, although Drake had visited Calais for a twice-yearly booze cruise, and countries when serving, which was as good as it got.

The party of five were deciding where to go when...

<  >

The mercenaries had studied their shooting positions and getaway routes. They had dined at the restaurant to understand the layout and routine. Nothing had been left to chance. The weapon had been chosen. They had decided to go with a suppressor. The noise from the gun was not completely silenced, although anyone over fifty metres away would struggle to place it. The weapon of choice was a suppressed semi-automatic Beretta 71. It used a cartridge that suppressed better and provided rapid follow-up shots. It was rumoured that it had been the choice of Mossad. The main instruction given by their latest employer was, 'Do not dare fuck it up.'

They departed their rendezvous at high speed. Both wearing Black bikers gear and a crash helmet. The ruck sack hung over the passenger's shoulders. Each felt the adrenaline flowing through their body like a rushing river. Neither had to work again, however, they both realised they were adrenaline junkies, and murder was the ultimate high for them.

They reached their focal point fifteen minutes before some of the guests began to leave. It took a further forty-nine minutes before the targets came into view.

The passenger jumped from the back of the bike and retrieved the semi-automatic pistol. He unclipped the safety catch, and slowly held the pistol waiting for the kill moment.

Traffic nearby was bumper to bumper, with childish faces staring vacantly out the window wishing they were at home, and people ambling happily in their own world.

The party of five stood outside the restaurant laughing and joking, obviously feeling the effects of an alcohol laden lunch. He thought about the money and considered it the easiest two-hundred thousand pounds he had earned. Slowly, and carefully he lifted the weapon and took aim, the safety catch flipped down. He whispered to himself, 'Boom,' and fired.

At the last moment there was movement in the party and a swapping of positions. It was too late.

The expert shooter was sure he could see the bullet travelling towards the heart. The switching of positions was unfortunate, but that was life.

Under 0.27 seconds later the target hit the floor. Blood pumping from the wound seeking an escape path into the gutter.

The scene was shocking, Jack Philips mind was sent reeling, unable to comprehend or process the image being relayed to his eyes. Jack jumped on the floor next to the love of his life. The final words he heard, 'Jack leave, I love you.' Catherine's eye lids began to flicker.

She saw Jack mouthing, 'Catherine don't go. I need you. I love you. Life is for living, and we need to experience it together. Always together... forever.' She smiled with all her remaining strength and drifted away knowing she had found true love.

Drake swiftly surveyed the area and shouted aggressively, 'Targets acquired.'

Gary Jones and Drake began running towards the motorbike. The West End traffic for once was aiding them. It was like a slow-moving tin growling in the late afternoon. Jones ran towards the driver and Drake the passenger.

In the wing mirror the driver noted Jones and Drake only feet await, He roared, 'Jump and defend.'

Immediately, both ex-military personnel left their bike and faced the on-coming ferocious partnership. They had never been defeated.

Drake was surprised how fast and fit Jones was. He reached the sharpshooters before he did by two seconds.

Jones immediately grabbed the shooter by the neck who was turning and kicked him in the shin with all his force. As the man yelped, he grabbed his arm and fed it towards the wheel that was still spinning at speed. The arm breaking sounded like a million corn flakes being stood on. Fingers flying through the air like discarded sausages.

The scream could be heard for an eternity, such were the decibels.

Drake was met head-on by the motorbike driver who had removed his helmet such was his confidence.

The ferocity of the attack took him by surprise. His head was being continuously pummelled into the floor. The last thing he heard before passing out was, 'Who Dares Wins, cunt.' He understood the police officer was not just a police officer, and realised he had met his match.

Drake felt someone pulling him away from the mess that was once an expert shooter, 'Leave it Drakey. Don't kill him. We'll do that in our own time. This one told me who had arranged it… Perkins. Did you hear me? Perkins, that slippery private schooled slag.'

Jack Philips held Catherine in his arms. In the sorrow of death was the proof of love. No-one needed to see how love had lived in this man. He was broken like a smashed mirror.

Drake noted the outline of the bullet hole, although he fixated on the person around it. He saw the perfect skin, the mouth that had known joy and laughter. He saw Catherine rather than a statistic. Drake also noted the pain and suffering in the one still living. Revenge would be had, and he knew Gary Jones his one-time nemesis, would play an integral part in finishing Mr Secret Service man Perkins, and he would do all he could to aid Jones.

Emergency services were swarming. Before leaving, Jack Philips strode over belligerently to the sharpshooter who was being tended to by the medical officers. Without a moment's thought he stood on the mans withered arm with his left foot. A guttural cry could be heard. Philips turned towards the medical officer, 'Sorry, I didn't see the arm there.' He then turned and stood on it again with his right foot, which repeated the in the cry becoming a shriek, 'Sorry again. How clumsy of me.' He returned to the ambulance that held his departed wife. Slowly, and carefully he walked the steps. Gingerly, he made his way to her side and knelt down, whispering, 'Catherine, there will never be another, wait for me and I will join you in time. I shall avenge your death.' He kissed her gently on the lips before tears cascaded like a waterfall.

The two members of the ambulance personnel left Jack as he said goodbye. The female operator began to gently sob.

< >

Perkins paced about his office like an unfed dog. News was slow arriving. Good news always arrived swiftly, whereas bad news travelled slowly. He had an ominous feeling in the pit of his stomach. It was almost aching. The knock on the door woke him from his despairing thoughts. 'Enter' hollering at the unseen person. He studied the messenger. He looked nervous. He was about to be the bearer of unbelievably unwelcome news. 'Don't just stand there man. What do you want?'

He began to open his mouth that had become dry. When Perkins was the receiver of shocking news, he often became agitated, 'Sir, we have had reports of an incident involving a police officer and his wife. We have also received reports of two men being attacked in an on-street altercation.'

Perkins felt the rage bubbling beneath his skin and knew an explosion was imminent, although he had to maintain control, 'Which men? Or is it a secret you are keeping to yourself?'

'Ours sir. They've suffered life changing injuries. One is in a coma. The other has lost an arm. It's the operatives used for unofficial work.'

'Did you say lost an arm?'

The messenger began to relax, 'Yes sir. Anything else, sir?'

Perkins looked at the young administrative officer, 'No son, you go and toddle off.'

The door was gently closed.

Perkins stood looking at the picture of Suzi. He then glanced at the picture of himself standing alongside her father at Downing Street with Margaret Thatcher. Suzi had not realised his association with her father. Hugh Belchamber had been a brave man, who had visited and spoken to many leaders during some serious hostile situations. He was perfect M.I.5 and M.I.6 material. Both departments had used him. Yet now he had a problem, a profoundly severe problem. Did Jones, Drake and Philips know he had arranged the hit. He suddenly realised he had not been informed whether anyone else had been injured in the altercation.

Perkins glided up to the administrative officer, 'Were there any other casualties during the altercation?'

The young male looked at Perkins and shifted a selection of papers from his desk, 'Here it is, sir. A female was shot, named Catherine Philips, wife of a serving police officer.'

Perkins felt his blood freeze over, 'Did you say Catherine Philips? Is she the wife of Jack Philips the serving police officer?'

'She was the wife, yes.' The young man could not understand why a senior officer would be interested in a case the department were not involved in.

'Thank you.' Perkins walked away knowing his life would never be the same again, and his romance over. Those fucking men had shot the wrong person. Gary Jones was the target, yet they had hit Jack Philips wife, his fucking wife. There was only one thing to do. A long holiday, an exceptionally long holiday. His first in over four years. He decided a visit to human resources was required, urgently.

&lt;          &gt;

Jack sat silently with Drake in Gary's home. Tears fell at their own will. He could not stop them. The three men were half way through their second bottle of Jameson when the silence was broken.

'Jack, we have become friends, and friends help friends. I will promise you one thing. Perkins is a dead man walking. I ask one thing. When I start my revenge, you look the other way totally. Do not get involved, either of you. You are both honest, loyal men, like the old commissioner. I will ensure Perkins harms no-one again.' The statement was made without one word being slurred. 'Now drink the rest of the whisky, and make yourself at home. But remember, the best revenge is massive success, and revenge is an act of passion; vengeance is justice. I will use revenge, passion and justice as my focus.'

Drake slowly lifted his head, 'Jones, I may be able to help you with any tricky situations you may face, and believe me. Perkins being a member of the security services will know clandestine areas to exploit, so be careful, incredibly careful. He will retreat, regroup and re-engage. He will come at you from all angles.'

Jones responded swiftly, 'Me. I think you mean he will come for us.'

Drake slowly replaced his empty glass on the table, refilling it with the honey-coloured liquid, 'You're right. He'll come for us all, but I think he'll come for you first. Too be honest. I reckon you were the target, but their operation changed. Shooting a woman gains attention, but a shit load of problems comes along with it. One thing though. It was a shoot to kill order, Jones.'

Jones finished another Jameson and gritted his teeth. The whisky toned down the desperate thoughts in his mind and brought memories of good times. The alcohol steadied nerves and offered resilience. Yet it could not repair. Jones looked at Jack Philips. The man was truly broken. His policing career was over, and the decision to retire immediately had been the correct decision. Retribution for the man would be found in empty bottles for the foreseeable future, and one day he will wake up and finally regain control, yet those days were some way off. The hunt for Perkins was on, and it was a hunt that would never stop.

# Chapter 25

The airport was a skeleton of steel. The walls elegantly rounded to create an inner space or peace and tranquillity, and the glass windows resembled giant tinted lenses. Perkins arrived at noon. He watched the excited travellers move like frenzied rainbows, so brilliant were the colours of their holiday clothing. They flowed from the check-in desks to the cafes like the ebb and flow of the sea. Every person believing their destination was as good as it gets.

Knowing a team may be hunting him he had done his best to blend in with the minions. His attire consisted of denim trousers, deck shoes and a short sleeve white shirt. His destination of choice was Tenerife. The flight was only four hours, and he would be able to move amongst the neighbouring Canary Islands; Lanzarote, Fuerteventura and Gran Canaria should he be recognised. He would have to stay away from the hot spots of tourist activity, yet that did not bother him. Perkins considered the brits abroad. They would dine on Paella or steak most evenings, before washing it down with as much alcohol as their bodies could suffer in fourteen days. He smiled. An army could not march on an empty stomach, whereas the brits only required alcohol…lots of it.

He made his way to the check-in desk showing his passport and ticket. It had been easy gaining a different passport with a new name. He looked at the name, Robin Banks. Why the forger had given him that name mystified him. Yet the name did appeal to his sense of amusement. Perkins realised his passport was a national membership. It comes with all the benefits required to survive in life. That is what passport membership brings, and it makes everyone part of a national community. Perkins considered what he would be leaving behind. Yet the one thing he realised was going hurt him deeply was the loss of Suzi. Perkins felt his palms began to sweat. What was it with the name, Suzi? As soon as he thought of her, he either got horny or sweaty. Bloody woman.

Heartache is a whole-body response; it encompasses the heart and brain function. Everyone is born to make a loving bond, and to suffer when a relationship finishes. It is life's way of teaching us to stay loyal and remain in love. Loving someone could be brutal, yet a necessity, and Perkins knew his life was in a quandary.

A booming voice came over the commercial airport system asking travellers to proceed to the departure gate and board the aircraft. Perkins stood, taking two steps towards the area that would change his life forever. Yet a profound feeling deep within stopped him. His heart told him to stay, yet his brain ordered him to go. Fuck it, what was wrong with him? He legs had turned to jelly and his mind frozen. The booming voice came over the airport system again informing passengers to make their way to the boarding area. Perkins made his decision.

<　　　　　　　　>

Suzi opened her front door, but before she could voice her concern, she felt a force she had never experienced before. She was flying through the air viewing her ceiling. There had a crack in her cheek bone like that from the branch of a tree being broken in half. Tears were cascading down her face, yet no sounds were prominent. Her eyes were blurred, and she can only just make out two shadows looming over her. One of the shadows she recognised, it was the man from The Goat pub, 'Why?'

Jones looked at Sexy Suzi, 'Shut up, you slag. If you tell me where that absolute cunt, Perkins is. I may let you live. If not, I'm gonna destroy you piece by piece.'

Confusion was jumping in her mind, 'I don't know. What has he done?'

Drake decided to intervene in a low-pitched growl, 'He arranged for my boss's wife to be shot at his fucking retirement meal. So, if you have any sense of surviving this visit, tell the man, otherwise he will end your fucking existence on this planet.'

Situations were spinning around Suzi's mind. What had Perkins got involved in? These two men were not going to let her survive. She had two options. She could play the innocent victim, or fight her way out. Before she knew what to do, she was unceremoniously picked up and taken to her butlers' sink situated in the kitchen. She heard the tap being turned and the sink filled.

Jones looked at her deciding to play the softer tole 'Listen love. I don't want to kill you, but Perkins has played a seriously bad hand. He's got everyone after him, and to arrange the murder of a senior police officer's wife was bad, fucking bad. What makes it worse for you is I like the police officer and his late wife. They were good people.'

Drake listened with intent. He realised for the first since knowing Jones the man was showing a sense of emotion. Drake also knew Jones would hunt Perkins until his dying day. Perkins had upset a Jackal, one he would have to meet sometime, and there would only be one winner. Jones was showing empathy towards Philips.

Suzi felt herself being lifted to a standing position and forcibly marched towards her kitchen. She was spun around and her legs parted. She had shot a scene like this for a film she had starred in, yet that had ended with her getting fucked by three men. This was going to end with her death. Why? She had done nothing wrong. Suzi summoned her strength and wailed, 'Perky, what have you done.'

She could hear the sink being filled with water before she could finish her head was ducked callously into the icy liquid. During her younger years she had been an expert swimmer and could hold her breath for sixty-seven seconds. Now was the time it was required. She relaxed when in the water and waited until her head was yanked out before taking many short breaths.

'Suzi, end this now, and we'll fuck off. Where is Perkins?'

Suzi had no idea, but decided to say something. Yet she was breathless, her lungs needed oxygen and she felt as if she were drowning in stale air, 'He went out yesterday in a foul mood. He said nothing else. He didn't even want sex!' She saw her face heading towards the water. She heard a short conversation, 'She knows nothing.' Her head was removed from the sink and smashed on the white porcelain kitchen top. Suzi tried to take one step before crumbling like a puppet whose strings have been cut. The last vision Suzi had was of the dark red tiles on her kitchen floor before she blacked out.

Drake turned and looked at Jones knowing he had gone over the top with the unplanned interrogation. He had broken the girls jaw, nearly drowned her and possibly fractured her skull. There was no getting away with it. Jones was seeking retribution for Philips, yet his rage was beginning to take control. He had to calm the man down, 'Jonesy, we need to locate Perkins. He's the one who's caused this mess, and the quicker we find him, the quicker everything goes back to normal.'

Jones looked at Suzi Belchambers on the floor. He had no idea whether she was dead or alive, but he did not care. He felt no sympathy or concern for her. He only felt rage.

<   >

Perkins stood on the opposing side of the road perusing shop windows, whilst checking movement in the reflection of the glass. He was biding his time. The late afternoon traffic and busy street allowed him to blend into the environment like a chameleon. As soon as Jones and Drake left, he would enter the flat and see what Suzi had said. He assumed both men would be forceful, and aggressive with their questions.

Finally, they left the building. He gave it five minutes before venturing towards the flats entrance. Slowly, yet carefully he made his way towards the doorway, knowing his feet were moving faster the nearer he got to the target area. He carefully placed the key in the door and gently turned the handle like cream, no noise emanated from his movement.

Entering the flat his eyes darted about like they were the windows of life. Perkins was alerted by an anomaly on the kitchen floor which had a puddle of blood surrounding it. He knew it was Suzi. Immediately, he removed his soft white handkerchief and picked up the telephone, contacting the emergency services. He then replaced the telephone on the cradle before turning one final time towards Suzi, 'I love you Suzi, you are the love of my life.' He then left the area.

Suzi lay on the floor. She could not move, yet her mind informed her Perky had just said he loved her. Her mind went into blackness again.

Perkins walked along the high street knowing he was being hunted. He also realised he had been involved in the demise of his chances of love. Suzi would never forgive him. She had been an innocent bystander in this horror show. Suzi had no idea that he was going to take flight and start a new life without her, fortunately he had returned to save her, yet she would never see it like that. Gambling and love had been his downfall. If only he could rewind the clock eighteen months. Now, he was most wanted by one sadistic member of the underworld, and a policeman who had been a member of the King's ultimate fighting regiment.

Perkins stopped mid-step. He now understood what love was, and what it could cause. Suddenly, he knew he had to get to the two shooters. It would mean finishing them, it would aid not solve a problem, although it would remove his link with them. Both would have armed guard, and he would have to be swift of foot to go from one to the other. Ending their lives would be the easy part. Perkins considered the idea and decided pancuronium bromide would be drug of choice. Perkins smiled; experience had told him both men will be paralyzed by the drug causing suffocation when they are unable to breathe.

Pancuronium bromide, commonly known by its brand name Pavulon, was a neuromuscular blocking agent that paralyzes all of a bodies-controlled muscles, including the lungs and diaphragm. Given enough time to act, Pavulon will cause death by asphyxiation. It did not affect consciousness. Nor did it affect experience of pain. Without proper anaesthesia, anyone given Pavulon will find themselves suffocating, but, because the pancuronium bromide inhibits any movement or speech, they will be unable to reveal they are in distress.

Perkins knew Pfizer Medical made the drug at their Sandwich headquarters. Again, his security credentials would gain him entry, and hopefully allow him to source a quantity of the substance. The security personnel would prove easy to manoeuvre into place. The only inconvenience would be using the same employee again whose credentials were high enough. He had trained at Sandhurst with the man employed by Pfizer, and had used him in the past due to his significant gambling problem. The irony of the situation made Perkins laugh.

Perkins knew both men had been taken to the Royal London Hospital based in Whitechapel. Again, his security credentials would gain him entry to their rooms comfortably. Administering the drug into their drips would take seconds, yet going into both rooms inside thirty seconds could prove the sticking point. Perkins deliberated the idea. He needed to gain greater perspective, to take a step back and see the wide-angle version. This would ensure no mistakes were made and success would be had.

<  >

Gary Jones met Charles Johns at Rules restaurant. Both men had visited the establishment so many times that booking a table had been easy.

Jones needed advice from someone he could trust. Perkins was becoming a mental wasp that would not buzz off, and Johns was a man of integrity who offered wise words. He was the only person Jones knew he would listen to.

Both parties ordered their meals and offered small talk before the meetings angle took place.

Johns realised crunch time was nearing as Jones had finally placed the fork on the table, having twiddled with it for five minutes.

'Charles, I need some advice, and it's about Perkins.'

Johns lifted his glass and took a satisfying sip of his vodka and tonic. The lemon peppered his tastebuds with a zingy freshness that brought him back to the moment, 'How may I help?'

Gary lifted his drink and took a long lingering gulp of his Guinness. 'I need to off, Perkins, and swiftly. The bloke is an absolute slag. What he did to Jack was bang out of order. To have the man's wife killed was about as low as it gets. You saw the man after the shooting. He is fucking broken.'

Johns noted a few glancing looks from neighbouring tables. Gary Jones was pent up with anger, it was evident for all to see. His language was a little ripe. Johns waved his hand in the air and was immediately met with a member of the restaurants staff. He whispered in the gentleman's ear, and as if by magic both Johns and Jones were shown upstairs where no-one was dining.

Having had a table laid and their drinks and cutlery delicately placed on the table, both men continued the conversation.

Charles Johns instigated the direction of the conversation, and decided to go full throttle with it, 'Gary, there is one obvious place Perkins will go. The hospital. He will want to ensure the expert shooters do not open their mouths… again.'

Jones stared at his dining partner, but all he could think of was, 'Fuck me.'

Charles let out a small chuckle, 'We are friends, Gary, but that is as far as it goes.'

Jones laughed at the retort, but also knew the man had offered the correct information, 'You are correct. He'll want to ensure no secrets are spilled. How will he do it?'

'Drugs, he'll use drugs. It will be a safe and clean. Guns are too noisy and knives leave too much mess. Plus, he will see it as a fitting end to the game. Drugs have been the downfall for everyone in this sorry saga. So, his ego will take control, and that is where you will snare him, Gary.'

Jones placed a magnificent piece of the steak and kidney pudding in his mouth. His saliva swiftly became a thick coating of decadent meat juice that was magnificence in the mouth. He eyed Johns, who was one person who never backed away from his stare, 'You are one clever fucker, Charles.'

Johns smiled, 'Gary, thank you. I am.'

Both men laughed at the gallows humours considering the conversation they had been engaged in.

Gary broke the laughter, 'Now get stuck into your nosebag. It's fucking handsome.'

<                    >

Perkins felt a sense of jubilation. The drugs had been incredibly easy to source. His old comrade at Sandhurst needed an urgent cash injection, and when offered the opportunity of fast cash he had almost snapped his hand off. It had cost him twenty-thousand pounds, but Perkins thought that chicken feed considering the eventual outcome.

Meeting in The Red Cow had been easy for each party. The old traditional pub had a few lunch time diners, and together they slotted in comfortably. Conversation was loose, it revolved around topics both understood - fear, terrorism, ex-servicemen, war – but not drugs. Perkins felt his ex-partner in arms wanted to experience a deeper conversation, but was distracted. An invigorated conversation would have been dead in the water. Yet each man wanted to do the deal and remove themselves from the arena. Neither man wished to deal in small talk about football, work or family holidays.

Each perused the menu, and selected scampi and chips, which they washed down with one-pint of local bitter. Perkins passed the brown leather zip-up briefcase to his ex-comrade in arms, whose octopus like arms swallowed the case as if it had not been on the table. In turn, the vile was passed to Perkins in a brown self-seal envelope. Perkins smiled, no-one in the vicinity could understand that the humblest of royal envelopes could carry a menace so horrific. It was almost poetic.

The man had not asked Perkins why he required the formula, although he assumed it was for the government as he thought Perkins was employed by a section of Her Majesty's secretive administration, and twenty-thousand pounds would put his final child through university. He had left Perkins nursing the final remnants of his pint, uninterested who the recipient of the deadly concoction in the vile was for.

Perkins left the meeting and travelled the seventy-five-mile journey back to London. Turning the radio on he was met with 'Lucy in the Sky with Diamonds.' It made Perkins smile. It was suggested the songs message was drug based. The irony was not lost on Perkins. The ninety minutes' drive allowed Perkins thinking time. He decided the following evening would be the night he would pay a kindly visit to M1 and M2. It would give him enough time to assess the security arrangements surrounding both patients. He would drive direct to the Royal London hospital, parking ten minutes' walk from the venue in Morpeth Street. This would allow him the opportunity to stroll unnoticed into the building like any other concerned visitor. The irony was not lost upon him.

# Chapter 26

Jack Philips had spent the week of his widower life permanently pissed. He woke up with a vodka and orange, and put himself to bed with a large Jameson and coffee. Weight was falling from the man. Some lose weight gracefully; others enter into the eating disorder regime. The rest lose weight due to love. Philips was heartbroken. He understood that heartbreak offered great pain, yet he could not believe it hurt this amount. It was a feeling so strong that it could not be measured. Seeking solace in the bottle was his only escape. He could remove himself from this perpetual feeling of despair.

His sorrow was broken by a sudden rap at the door. The bang from the knocker sent shockwaves through his entire body. His head shook like a tornado rampaging through a desolate town.

Upon opening the door, the sunlight struck his face like a knockout blow. He could feel his mouth open due to the shock. He could note a man standing in front of him, yet his vision took a few seconds to understand it was a friendly face.

Charles Johns stood looking at the dishevelled wreck standing before him. The smell of alcohol and body odour attacked his nose. The drink reminded him of police officers that enjoyed the subsidised bars at New Scotland Yard and Drummond Gate. Yet, Jack Philips looked like a beaten man. He needed something to eat, something to drink - containing no alcohol and a shoulder to cry on.

Jack allowed his eyes to regain focus on the person standing before him. His blurred vision focused on his ex-commissioner, Charles Johns, 'What are you doing here?'

Johns was slightly taken aback by the diffident welcoming, 'Good to see you, Jack. I have provisions.' He held the Sainsbury's bag up which contained everything required for a full English breakfast. He strode past Jack and made his way towards the kitchen.

Jack stood holding the door, 'Come in, Charles, make yourself at home.' He turned and appraised the man who had just entered his home without being asked to come in. Shaking his head, he closed the front door. Philips walked towards the kitchen, 'Don't think I'm being rude, sir, but what the fuck are you doing here?'

Johns continued removing pans from cupboards, 'Two things, Jack. Stop calling me sir. It's Charles, and have a bloody shower. You smell like something the cat has dragged in. Breakfast will be in fifteen minutes.'

Philips turned and slowly ventured upstairs to the bathroom. He had not showered in seven days. The hot water jumped from his skin such was the build-up of grime and sweat on his skin. He stood with his palms on wall thinking of Catherine. Tears fell from his face. He knew the feeling of loss would never leave him, yet he understood he had to try and move on, and it would take forever. Loss would ensure he would travel through oceans of grief, hoping if blessed, there was a map to navigate him throughout the world of sadness. Loss showed love and he knew it would be his saviour. His thoughts of Catherine were broken by the smell of bacon wafting in the air and for the first time in one week he felt ravenous.

Philips entered the kitchen to be met with a sumptuous breakfast. Nothing had been left from the menu, 'Fuck me, Charles, that looks the business.'

Johns looked at Philips and immediately felt intense sympathy for the once great officer, 'You have scrambled eggs, four rashers of bacon, mushrooms, plum tomatoes, beans, four Lincolnshire sausages and a frightful slice of fried bread. Something I find not to my liking, but I know you are partial to this fatted slice of bread.'

Philips raised a smile, 'Fatted bread, you're certainly not from my manor, Charles.' Picking up the brown sauce he splurged it all over the breakfast like a cold savoury gravy and demolished the meal like a lion with its kill.

Charles watched Philips and noted a fresh look about the man in twenty minutes. He had a look that offered glimpses of hope. He also had an ulterior motive, and one he knew Jack would jump at the chance to be involved, 'Jack, I have a reason for being here, and the reason will be something I would like you involved in. In fact, I think you will demand to be involved.'

Jack swallowed a mouthful of his sweet, strong tea assessing the patterns of green swirls on the recently purchased mug. Without looking at his ex-commissioner he murmured, 'You have my attention.' The intrigue was bubbling up inside trying to escape.

'Drake, Jones and I are aware the operatives who murdered your Catherine are still in the Royal London Hospital under police protection. We all believe, Perkins, will attempt to silence them, and soon. How he does it, we have no idea. Yet, I believe it will need to be silent so as not to cause a massive disturbance. This leads me to believe it will be done using a concoction of drugs. A knife is too messy, gun too noisy and a beating too long. Where he sources the chemicals is another problem, yet being a member of the secret service will offer him help.'

Philips listened intently to every word. It was like a switch had been activated in his mind. He felt alive for the first time since that fateful day. Revenge was all he could think of, 'Whatever it is. I'm in.'

Johns knew this would be the answer from Philips, but he needed to be sure the man was not acting reckless, 'Remember, Jack, fire in the belly – cool in the head. I know you want to avenge Catherine, but if you are hasty or careless, we will fail.'

Philips felt rage swimming through his body, 'Charles, that cunt killed my wife. I'll do anything, and I mean anything to end that slags existence on this earth.'

Johns pondered the swift and harsh reaction from Philips. It was honest, and true, and that worried Johns. It smacked of all out revenge. The man was consumed with rage, and that would lead to mistakes, 'Jack, you will need to be calm. Please remember, you and I are no longer serving police officers. We need to follow the same rules as the everyone else. Drake will ensure rules are followed, and if anything, untoward needs to be done then that speciality falls to your other ally, Jones.'

Jack knew the man was correct in all areas, yet the thought of revenge would not leave his soul, 'What is the plan then?'

Johns quietly and basically explained what needed to be done. Once finished he looked at Philips.

Jack could not believe how basic it was, 'So we take turns in two's and wait for, Perkins. Taking him when he shows. Is that it?'

Johns knew the response from Philips would be amazement, 'Basic and simple, and that is why it may work. Remember Jack, our target is Perkins, not the shooters. They are going to go away for life. We want the mastermind of the operation, and that is Perkins.'

< >

The shrill from the telephone woke Suzi from her slumber. She leant over and lifted the receiver to her warm read ear, 'Hello?'

'Suzi, my love. Are you ok?'

Immediately Suzi was fully awake, 'Perky, where are you? What have you been up to? When can I see you?'

The worry and concern in Suzi's voice was obvious. It also proved to Perkins that she still cared for him, 'Suzi, my love. I need to sort a few things, and then the two of us can go away on a much-needed holiday. How do you fancy Kerala and its coconut-lined sandy beaches and tranquillity? We both deserve a break to somewhere offering peace.'

Suzi was tempted by Kerala, but one word jumped out from Perky's description – 'peace.' This meant hidden. A place where no-one would consider looking. They would be on the run. She loved the man, but going on the run was another thing all together. She decided to play along with the ruse, 'That sounds lovely, Perky. When will you book it?'

Perkins felt reassured by Suzi's need to be with him, 'I will sort something tomorrow for us. Don't think I'm being rude, but I need to nip off to work, but I will call you later my love.'

Suzi heard the telephone disconnect. She gently replaced her receiver on its cradle and sat up, now fully awake. Suzi knew she was sharp and clever. She also realised Perkins was lying to her and he was in deep shit. He had obviously upset a number of people, and was trying to rectify the situation, yet an inner feeling inside felt this was one battle he may not experience victory. Since the man on the street had doorstepped her, everything had gone wrong. Was he the problem?

Perkins stepped from the telephone box feeling a sense of relief. The dark clouds looming above mirrored his mood, yet hearing the soft sexy tones from Suzi's voice had put him at ease a little. It had also made him more positive to finish this problem once and for all. He knew Drake and Jones would be hunting him like hungry wolves, and Jones would be using his infinite list of high society contacts to aid the pursuit. Elements of luck and experience would be needed to complete the mission.

<  >

Perkins pulled up in Morpeth Street and departed his car. Hastily, he walked to his destination via Cephas Street. His soles were moving upon the solid ground. The shoes being the walkers that marched him to his battle. He made no sound and the dark night aided his deception. He felt like he was back in the Special Boat Services on a silent and secretive mission.

The Royal London Hospital had a long history having admitted patients for the first time during 1757. One of its more well-known patients being Joseph Merrick in 1890. It now resembled a tired museum with the brickwork covered with over two-hundred years' worth of filth from the congested Whitechapel Road. The most attractive section being the clock stationed at the top of the building, which very few locals lifted their head to use.

Perkins slowly, but surely made his way along the Whitechapel Road, avoiding the street lights and dancing in and out of the shadows. The hospital loomed like a monster, rearing its head like it would touch the stars.

Perkins stood watching those milling about outside the building. He knew that patience was a virtue, but there comes a moment when a person must stop being patient and confront the problem head-on, and if fights back; fine.

Fifteen minutes passed before Perkins felt confident there were no unexpected surprises. Swiftly, he walked to the entrance and located where both men were recuperating under police guard.

His palms felt wet, yet warm, and he felt the need to dig into his jacket pocket to ensure the potion was still present. The sign ahead read 'Gents.'

Perkins opened the white door. The hospital washroom was immaculate and clean, white basins housed silver taps and the air had an essence of bleach. Perkins noted all of the toilet doors were open, and headed towards the end cubicle. Shutting the door, Perkins slid the bolt across. Removing the syringe, he pushed the needle into the vial, allowing the poison to be sucked into its container. Instantly, he placed a cork on the needle to ensure no mishaps would occur.

Perkins, blew out his cheeks and considered the implications of what he was going to do. It was life changing. Closing his eyes, he wished he could turn back time and not have entered the casino owned by Joseph Grimes. His life had imploded since that one mistake.

Standing, he unbolted the door and made his way to the basins to wash his hands. Stopping, he laughed. Why need he do it? He adjusted his motion and walked towards the exit door.

Entering the corridor, he looked for the rooms where his two victims were based. It only took a matter of seconds before he noted a police officer stationed outside each room.

Confidently, he walked towards the first officer who looked in his twenties. Perkins showed his government security credentials, which were scrutinized in depth.

'We're not supposed to let anyone near the victims, sir.'

Perkins knew he was too wily for the two inexperienced constables, 'Look closely at my credentials, and note my department. If you have a problem, please telephone them. I wish to see each victim for two minutes. It's for our internal reports. I see your FIN number on your collar.' Perkins removed his notebook and was about to write something down when the constable had an immediate change of mind. An uneasy nod allowed him entry to the room.

The room, although clean, smelt of someone who needed their teeth brushed and the stale smell attacked Perkins's nose. The patient monitor was alive maintaining control of the subject and the five hundred millilitre bag of saline hung like Jesus of the cross. The patient was motionless.

Perkins removed the needle and plunged it into the soft tissue of the assassins left big toe. He pushed the plunger ensuring the entire quantity of Pavulon from needle one entered the man's body.

Removing the needle, he replaced the cork and walked towards the door. Opening the door, the young police constable eyed him suspiciously. Perkins decided to ignite a truly short conversation, 'Has he moved or made any contact?'

The young constable felt important that a member of MI6 would wish to speak to him, 'No sir. Man's out cold, like a vegetable.'

'Thank you, keep up the good work.' Perkins strode to the next room and was allowed entry straight away. He repeated the same operation as the previous room, although this time when he plunged the needle in the man's eyes opened and looked at him.

The poison was quick acting and he could see the man's body change instantly. It was like he was drowning in dry air and an interesting thing to witness. Perkins decided the monitor would start beeping all too soon and left the room. This time nodding at both officers.

As the lift door closed, he noted medical staff heading towards the area he had come from.

Emerging from the lift he walked head down like many other visitors. Ensuring he made eye contact with no-one, and no-one made eye contact with him.

He was free, but it would be without his Suzi. He clenched his fists together making them go red with his rage. Drake and Jones would pay, but not yet. He would let them think the game was over, but the game was still in play. Perkins smiled; it was time to vanish for some time. He would then return, and finish the game.

<　　　　　　　>

Jones and Johns arrived at the hospital to be met with a plethora of police vehicle's parked unceremoniously. Both men knew why there was a hive of activity, but neither wished to say it.

Finally, Johns broke the silence, 'I do not feel I have to say anything. We both know what has happened.'

Jones gripped hold of the steering wheel like he was trying to remove moisture from it, 'He's done them both, and fucked off. He's got away with it. He's fucking got away with it.' Jones was full of anger, rage and disappointment.

Johns nodded slowly and whispered quietly, 'But the man has one weak spot, Suzi. He's gone, but he will all ways want to return for her. We know where she is as Jack and Drakey are outside her flat. This game of seek and destroy has many scenarios to play out. We just need to plan diligently, before we capture our prey. This game has only just started and has many twists and turns.

The final part of the trilogy, Underworld Climax will be out in November 2024.

The following pages show the opening from Underworld Climax.

# Chapter 1

Three long years had passed and the sun was starting to become a little tiresome. Perkins had enjoyed the delights of island hopping throughout the Canary Islands; Tenerife, Fuerteventura, Gran Canaria and Lanzarote. Each island had its benefits, yet he missed the seasons. There was something about laying in bed listening to the rain attack the bedroom windows, whereas the only thing that attacked his life now was the never-ending sunshine.

He also missed the English diet. Fish and paella were magnificent meals, yet there was only so much olive oil a man could drizzle over his dinner, although the extra virgin olive oil did have a unique and magnificent nutty taste with fresh herbs, yet he missed feasting in British institutions like Rules restaurant, wearing a suit and dining with a nice bottle of claret. It was traditional. He could not understand how holiday makers enjoyed their evening meal wearing chinos and espadrille's whilst consuming steak and chips smothered in pepper sauce, washed down with local lager. They made full use of the intense Canarian sunshine. After seven days many resembled red cricket balls such was their desire to gain a colour, yet they ploughed on, and after fourteen days they returned home positively glowing. Perkins smiled, one thing the British had was resilience.

He maintained contact with his homeland by reading every English daily newspaper. They provided information that allowed him to understand the daily issues. The current affairs also kept him abreast of all political angles along with any mentions of his name and those of his previous employer. Another avenue was eavesdropping on people's conversations.

During an eavesdropping session in one of the bars located two miles from the centre of Las Americas he heard the name Jones mentioned and it piqued his interest. Perkins ordered a small beer and made himself comfortable at his table.

He surveyed the bar. The tables and chairs created an oasis of peace and relaxation. They also offered comfort to the all-day and evening crowd. It was the sort of setting where people his age would arrive for a pre-dinner drink and enjoy a coffee and toasted sandwich during the day, whereas the younger generation may find it a little quiet for the extravagant needs. The bars overall decoration was aiming at the more affluent consumer.

He opened his newspaper pretending to read the financial section. The conversation was most enlightening.

'Jones and the police bloke are still looking for the government fella who was involved in offing the other officers ole woman. They reckon he's gone on the trot in India.'

Perkins picked up his small lager and took a swig from the half pint dimple mug. The delicate lively bubbles mixed with the slight sweetness and spice left the palate with a refreshed smooth coating. His ears never left the conversation taking place.

'India. Fucking hell. I'd never go to India. Don't like all that spicy food. If it were me, I'd go to Scandinavia. Sweden would be my choice. There are over two-hundred thousand islands and if you can't go missing there where can you go?'

'Two-hundred thousand. That's a lot of islands. Anyway, if the bloke don't want to be found then he won't be found. He was a man from the government. Bet he was one of those secretive slippery fuckers from MI5 or the other one, MI6. They're all wrong 'uns. Killing a bloke's wife was plain wrong. He deserves to be done. I heard there's a bounty on his head. I'd love to have some of that. Anyway, another sherbet?'

Perkins folded his newspaper and picked up his beer swallowing the remnants. He bade farewell to barman and left the establishment knowing a return to his homeland was imminent. He scanned the horizon. He was finally fed up with the sun and he wanted to see Suzi. He had missed her like he could not believe. He hoped, no prayed she felt the same. She was his lifey, his plus one.

He had read some time back he was wanted in connection with the murder of Catherine Philips and the two men linked to the crime. Nothing could be proven, as there were no cameras in the hospital, and the confession of the two assassins would be their word against his. An established and trustworthy operative employed by the English government, against two dead hitmen. They had little chance.

Returning to his apartment Perkins began to consider his plan. To return he would need to use one of the smaller airports in England. Gatwick and Heathrow would have higher security details, therefore, chances of being noticed were higher. The smaller airports would have security but these would be inexperienced and not as sharp as the London based protection.

He would have to use Lanzarote airport to go to Bournemouth as the English airline shuttled between the two airports twice each week. Blending in with the seasoned and exhausted holidaymakers would offer him sanctuary and safety in numbers.

The bounty information was disconcerting. This meant anyone linked to the underworld would be aware, therefore, he would have to be careful upon his return. Visiting London would leave him wide open for retribution so he would have to use all his security skills to ensure safe passage.

In the three years since leaving his old life he had seen no-one, or been recognised. The opportunistic chance of being recognised was always in the back of his mind. A chance meeting was the worst thing that could happen to him, therefore bouncing between each of the sun lavished volcanic looking islands had been a necessary inconvenience and changing his destination left him little time to become friendly with the locals, however the owners of the flats he rented loved him. They knew he would return every eighteen weeks and pay cash for his stay. They never questioned his story of being a sun worshipper, yet they noted he did not appear to sun bath choosing instead to read English newspapers on his balcony. The fact each stay lasted twelve weeks was the security they appreciated - as was the seven hundred and fifty thousand pesetas.

Perkins contemplated his return. He eyed the four passports and selected one named Jack Smith. Over 500,000 UK nationals used the surname Smith, therefore, it made him Mr. Average. The name Smith started as an occupational name for someone who worked with metal, such as a Blacksmith and lent itself to the blue-collar workforce, again it made him average. He held the black passport and studied it. The passport was the equivalent of membership to a nationwide club.

He admired the view from the terrace. The sun was resting for the day and the crepuscular way of life was awaking for its fun filled activities. Sounds from crickets chirping were short. Pure-toned sounds composed of one or more syllables and separated by brief periods of silence. The landscape was sand coloured and the air dry. It was picture perfect, yet the yearning to return home was growing by the minute. It was like a form of homesickness had enveloped his body.

<               >

Jack Philips spent every day of his retirement seeking clues about the whereabouts of Perkins. No stone had been left unturned. He had used every possible source for information. Yet the man had just vanished. Charles Johns, Gary Jones and Drake had spoken to everyone and anyone to help his cause, yet again without success. What perplexed Philips was how Perkins had been able to slip away unnoticed without anyone knowing. He assumed the man had identities hidden away for this purpose. He also knew that one day Perkins would return to his natural habitat. He was a creature of habit with fair skin who would resemble a cooked lobster if he spent too much time in the sun, yet three years was a long time to be on the missing list. What interested Philips more was Perkins had not been spotted once, there had not been a single glimpse of the man, therefore, he was holed up somewhere he could hide amongst the masses in plain site without being noticed, but where?

Printed in Great Britain
by Amazon